Heartstrings of the Khyber
the Khyber
A Collection of Pashto Folktales

Heartstrings of the Khyber
the Khyber
A Collection of Pashto Folktales

Shaherzaad Laila
& Komal Salman

Chicago, Illinois

Paperback ISBN: 978-1-964537-47-4
Library of Congress Control Number on file.

Published by:
Crossed Crow Books, LLC
518 Davis St, Suite 205
Evanston, IL 60201
www.crossedcrowbooks.com

Printed in the United States of America.
IBI

About the Authors

Komal is the founder of Folkloristan, which she founded in November of 2021 with the aim of documenting and digitising Pakistani folklore. Whilst she has documented, translated, and retold several stories for Folkloristan, *Heartstrings of the Khyber* is her debut publication.

Folkloristan is currently partnering with the Pitt Rivers Museum at the University of Oxford to reconnect objects in their collection to local folklore in the series "The Folklore of Resistance." In 2023, Folkloristan displayed Pakistani folklore in one-hundred artworks at the Centre of Folklore, Myth and Magic in the UK. In April 2024, Folkloristan took over the Lahore Heritage Club for a week. The itinerary included "Hazaaron Saal Pehle," a four-day art exhibition, two days of Dastaangoi, and two art workshops.

Particularly interested in leveraging emerging tech for heritage conservation, Komal worked as the Policy Advocacy Lead for Web 3.0 at the Islamabad Policy Research Institute. Her illustrations of folktales were also selected to be displayed at NFT Karachi. Furthermore, she also spoke on "Cultural Identity and Representation in the NFT Space" at a panel at the Islamabad Binance Community Meet in 2022.

Komal has also discussed folktales and the future of storytelling at several events, including the Digital Festival of Islamic Arts and Culture, +92 Disrupt Islamabad, the Asian Study Group, and Romancing the Gothic. In addition to this, she is also the co-founder of the Ethnology and Folklore Guild South Asia, a digital platform intended to bring together people and scholars interested in the intangible cultural heritage of the region.

Komal and her family live in Islamabad. She received her bachelor's degree from the National University of Science and Technology, after which she has worked as a creative professional across several industries.

THE INFLUENCE OF A NAME IS OFTEN PROFOUND, shaping one's very identity. In Shaherzaad Laila's case, her father, a remarkable translator and writer, carefully chose a name for her that reflects both beauty and potential. Named after Shaherzaad, the iconic storyteller, and Laila, a name steeped in folklore, she feels an innate connection to the world of tales and literature. This connection to her name has ignited a deep passion for storytelling, a passion that continues to guide her on an extraordinary journey. She was destined from birth to embrace the enchanting world of storytelling, effortlessly weaving narratives while harmonizing with the traditions of her cultural heritage.

Born and raised in Pakistan, a land of cultural diversity and artistic heritage, Shaherzaad Laila is a rising connoisseur of Urdu literature. Her passion for literature, music, and the arts shapes her creative pursuits. Her journey into the world of arts began in the hallways of her school. From penning scripts for school plays to stepping onto illuminated stages, storytelling has captivated her from an early age. These early experiences planted the roots of her passion for the arts, paving the way for a journey that would take her from school performances to prominent national platforms.

She academically pursued media and communication studies, which enabled her to merge her passion for storytelling with the broader media landscape. Theoretical studies laid a foundation, but hands-on experiences shaped her understanding. Her creative work has transitioned between writing and cinematography. Beyond artistic expression, her love of the written word has been a lifelong companion, fostered by her father, a literary scholar. She devoted herself to her craft, working in a literary and art school where she contributed significantly.

Shaherzaad has achieved distinction in the fields of video production through her noteworthy contributions to prestigious institutions such as the WWF and National Radio and Television. She then launched Zauqverse, a production company dedicated solely to the arts and literature, establishing a platform for creative expression. *Heartstrings of the Khyber* is her debut as a published translator, marking a significant milestone in her literary journey.

CONTENTS

Acknowledgements

WE EXTEND OUR HEARTFELT gratitude to everyone who has been involved with this book. First and foremost, to the team at Crossed Crow Books, for embracing our idea with such enthusiasm and providing technical support throughout the process, and to Mark Norman, for connecting us with them.

We are also deeply thankful to everyone who has been a part of the documentation process, from the narrators to translators, for their assistance. We also owe a special mention to Dr. Zalka Csenge, Ceri Houlbrook, and Muhammad Usama Khan for their feedback, which was extremely helpful.

To our families, thank you for your patience and understanding as we devoted several hours to this project. Particularly to Shaherzaad's father, Mr. Sanaullah Shahid, and Komal's grandmother, Mrs. Shaheen Tassaduq, both of whom are linguists by practice and education, for guiding us with the help we required related to Urdu.

To our friends, Ammar, Angelina, and Javairiyah, who always had words of encouragement to offer. And to Komal's little sister, Rania, who made a point to make good-humoured fun of the illustrations 'til she found them perfect.

Your collective support has been instrumental in bringing this project to fruition.

Note from
the Authors

THE GENESIS OF THIS project was rather unanticipated, sparked by a casual conversation. A chance encounter with a book ignited our interest in mulling over a translation project. As fate would have it, even before we could finish the manuscript, we stumbled upon a call for folklore nonfiction by a fellow folklorist, Mark Norman. We reached out instantly, and he put us through to the team at Crossed Crow Books, who were very happy to embrace the project.

Whilst reading these stories, it is important to keep in mind the fact that they are set in the backdrop of medieval Pakhtun society. They do include certain ideas or events which are frowned on today, such as blood feuds, casteism, honour killings, or the enforcement of the will of the parents on their children. To have excluded them would essentially be tantamount to cultural erasure. The purpose to include them is not to further the stereotypes of "incivility" which exist around several Asian and African ethnic groups. Whilst it is not to say that some of these problems do not exist today, the understanding and contextualisation of the broader cultural context is crucial—it is important to keep in mind that medieval Germany, England, or France, for example, also witnessed analogous circumstances.

When we began to work together, we soon figured that our strengths complimented one another particularly well. With Shaherzaad's strong suit being interpreting Urdu and Komal's writing in English, the translations were truly a collaborative effort. As Shaherzaad proceeded to then proofread and edit our initial drafts, Komal worked her way through the book, adding the annotations and the notes.

A word of caution: romances, particularly those outside one's own tribe, do not always end well! We have tried our best to arrange the tales in a way that they follow an alternating pattern of beautiful, but rather tragic, tales and cute, but delusional, happily-ever-afters. However, if some of the stories contained within break your heart, as they did ours, we are truly sorry.

The aim of this book is twofold: to create a text that makes for a good read for everyone, and to provide valuable insight into Pakhtun culture and society for those who study folklore as an academic discipline.

—Komal Salman & Shaherzaad Laila

Note from
the Illustrators

It has been a delight to illustrate this collection of folktales. With each artwork, we have tried our best to bring to life local fashion, may it be attire or jewellery. Inspired by culture and rooted in tradition, we have tried to incorporate local landscapes, traditions, and language into our work to capture the essence of each one of these romances. We hope that our visual interpretations will not only enhance your reading experience but also open up a window of your imagination and help you appreciate the richness of Pakhtun culture.

—Dayyaan Abdullah & Komal Salman

PREFACE

NARRATIVES IN FOLKLORE TAKE shape from the culture, history, values, and imagination of a society. This book is a humble yet heartfelt attempt to compile a small collection of Pashto folktales. It is worth noting that the common thread tying all these tales together, besides Pakhtun culture itself, is romance. Passed down through generations for hundreds of years, these tales have served not only as a form of entertainment, but also as a way of education.

The tales put together in this book include stories which are a part of Pakhtun folklore and have been previously recorded in writing, tales that the authors have documented and collected firsthand, as well as those which have absorbed into Pashto oral tradition from other cultures. It is important to note that not all of these tales have been transcribed and translated word-for-word. Rather, they are translations of translations, primarily using Urdu versions for this book.

Throughout this process, we have strived to maintain the cultural context and authenticity of the stories. This has been made possible through constant communication with Pashto speakers and the invaluable guidance of Komal's grandmother, a Pakhtun and an MA in Urdu literature. It is also for the sake of cultural authenticity that, due to the vast difference of vocabulary between English and Pashto, we decided to retain words which do not have English translations.

It is also important to understand that not all characters in these tales follow the arcs that English-speaking readers might expect. Some characters, who seem crucial in a Western narrative context, may be irrelevant to those familiar with Pakhtun culture itself or neighbouring cultures with similar socio-cultural norms, such as Persian, Baloch, or Punjabi.

All the tales in this book were translated from various public domain sources freely available on the internet as digital scans. Each source comes with its own folktale informants and editorial voices, resulting in a collection that showcases a wide range of narrative styles. These styles often diverge significantly from modern storytelling expectations, such as clear and satisfying endings. We have attempted to translate these stories as faithfully to the originals as possible, respecting their unique structures and the cultural significance they hold.

1

SHIREEN FARHAD

ONCE UPON A TIME, there lived a great king. The towering minarets of his palace were adorned with intricate tilework and delicate filigree. Beneath the azure skies, the facade of the palace was a beautiful colour of sand, lined with cobalt blue and white mosaic tile. The air of the palace gardens was heady with the scent of jasmine and roses. In the centre of the marble courtyard stood an alabaster fountain, in which sparkling water never ceased to flow.

However, the king, unfortunately, was childless, causing him great heartache. He had a council of five viziers, who managed all affairs of the state for him. The most trusted amongst them was Iqbal. It was only in him that the king confided about his sorrow.

Offering his king solace, Iqbal replied, "It is solely by the grace of Allah that one is blessed with offspring."

The days passed by. One day, something rather peculiar happened. A *faqir* walked around in the city streets,[1] calling out, "May Allah's blessings be upon you. I wish for *khair*."[2] He continued, "In the name of Allah, I beseech you, pray for *khair*."

---

1   *Faqir:* A wandering Muslim ascetic who lives solely on alms.
2   *Khair:* A state of well-being; all being well.

A *kaneez*, observing this, hastened to inform the king of a wandering *faqir*, who sought *khair* from the people.[3] She wondered what possibly could bring *khair* to a *faqir*.

The monarch, stirred by curiosity, instructed her to give away some *ashrafian* to the *faqir*.[4] However, when she went to the palace gates, the *faqir* turned down the alms. "I desire *khair*, not the trappings of riches and gold," he declared.

Perplexed, she asked him, "Then what brings you here?"

The *faqir* smiled at her and said kindly, "I wish to see the king."

She relayed the request to the king, who agreed to fulfil the *faqir's* request. Whilst he was surprised, he thought to himself, "It is not befitting of a king to turn down a *faqir*." He was about to ask his courtiers to present the *faqir* to him, but then he thought, "It will not be proper to ask a *dervish* at my door to present himself. I should go to him,"[5] and decided to meet the *faqir* at the gates.

When the king came to meet the *faqir*, the latter asked him, "Why do you neglect your royal duties?"

The king began lamenting, "What do you understand of what afflicts my heart? I find no solace in anything. Worldly matters do not interest me in the least anymore."

"Of that, I am aware, your majesty. But why is it so?" the *faqir* pressed the king for an answer once again.

The king took a deep cold breath, and his throat went dry as he began to bare his soul. "I possess all: the finest of steeds in my stables, a formidable army, a kingdom, a peaceful reign, subjects who love me, and a treasury teeming with gold, silver, and precious jewels. Yet, I do not have the one thing my heart desires most: children."

As the monarch mourned, the *faqir* made him a promise. "I shall pray to Allah to bestow upon you the blessing of a child. But I want you to

---

3   *Kaneez:* A member of the harem who is not a family member or a wife. Whilst these girls were taken as slaves, their status was more like ladies-in-waiting and not that of imperial concubines. In Islam, the son of a kaneez is an equally legitimate heir to the throne.

4   *Ashrafian* (plural); *ashrafi* (singular): Gold coins used as currency at the time.

5   *Dervish:* Alternate title for a faqir (a wandering Muslim ascetic who lives solely on alms).

remember that it shall be a daughter, and you must name her Shireen."
And so, after many moons, the king was blessed with a daughter, whom
they duly named Shireen. As years passed by, Shireen blossomed into
a fine young woman.

During this time, a father and son rose to fame for their mastery of
masonry. The king summoned them to his court. Whilst the mason fretted
at the unexpected summon, he went to the palace with his son in tow, his
heart fraught with foreboding. Shireen had heard of them, too, and had
told her father, "They are famed craftsmen; bid them to fashion a palace
for me." So, when they arrived, the king tasked them with erecting a
pavilion within the palace for the princess. Winning a commission from
none other than the king himself was indeed an honour for the mason
and his son, so they happily agreed to take up the work.

Some two, or perhaps, two-and-a-half years passed by, and the edifice
was near completion, that one day, Shireen, peering from the *jharoka* of
the *Haram Saraye*,[6] espied Farhad, the mason's son.[7] Their eyes met one
another's, and, after that, Farhad found himself consumed by thoughts
of Shireen and her beautiful face. He struggled to concentrate on his
craft for the rest of the day.

Initially, Farhad's father thought he might have been exhausted.
However, a few days passed by, and Farhad could still not focus on his
work. He cut the stones all wrong. That night, despairing at his son's
distraction, Farhad's father told him off sternly and gave the boy a good
whipping. His father cautioned him, "This palace is entrusted to us by
the king; any misstep could result in dire consequences. We have been
charged to fashion a palace unlike any other in this world. The king wants
something for which neither he, nor anyone else, can find an example.
Do you understand the consequences should we fail to deliver? We
could be thrown into the dungeons for the rest of our lives. He might
even chop off our hands, or worse, our heads!"

---

6   *Jharoka:* A kind of window found in local architecture. The jharokha is a
    stone window projecting from the wall face of a building, in an upper story,
    overlooking a street, market, court or any other open space. The net, made
    of stone, has smaller holes inside, and larger holes outside—you can see
    outside, but you can't see inside properly.

7   *Harem Saraye:* The women's quarters in the palace.

However, his warnings fell on deaf ears. Farhad was entirely consumed by Shireen. He stopped eating, drinking, and even sleeping. Every time someone saw him, he was lost in thought. He was truly teetering on the edge, nearly losing his sanity. When his family would bring him food, they would tell him, "Here. Shireen sent this for you. She made you a *roti* herself!"[8] Only then would he eat.

A few more weeks passed by. Farhad, consumed by his longing for Shireen, relinquished the world and took the guise of a *faqir*. He wandered the city streets, until he reached the gates of the palace, and called out for alms. It was Shireen who heard him. "Mother, I think there is a *faqir* at the gate, I heard someone call for alms," she said, busy embroidering a handkerchief.

"Yes, my dear, I heard it too. Why don't you take a small bag full of gold coins for him?" her mother said. Shireen nodded and went to the palace gates, as her mother had asked. However, upon finding Farhad at the gates instead of a *faqir*, she was shocked. "I seek not alms," Farhad declared, "but rather, I have come here only to speak to you. Since the day I have laid eyes upon your rosy face, I have been ensnared in madness."

Shireen signed. "I, too, have lost my heart to you, Farhad, since the day my eyes met yours. I have been lost in your eyes since then. I have waited for you, every day since, but you never came." Revealing her reciprocal affection, she continued talking. "Happy as I am to see you, what have you done to yourself?"

"I cannot eat, nor sleep. All I do is think of you, my love." Farhad said.

"Yes…yes, my dear…but you need to look after yourself, for me. Your eyes have sunken into your head. You're all but skin and bones. Please. Be careful," she said.

The two decided that Farhad would come to meet Shireen every day in the guise of a *faqir*. For a while, this worked well. But eventually, word got out. When the whispers of the princess and her little tryst reached the king's ears, he was furious. He summoned Farhad to the palace instantly and rebuked him. "I give you respect by awarding you with a commission of a palace, no less, and in return, you taint my honour. How dare you?"

Ignoring the king's admonitions, Farhad adamantly professed his love for Shireen. The king had Farhad thrown into the dungeons. Every day, he was

---

8 *Roti:* unleavened flatbread, a staple in Pakistani cuisine.

asked to renounce his love in exchange for his freedom, and every day, he turned the offer down. Some days, he was even beaten up by the palace guards.

As Farhad endured the torment in the dungeons, the king spent his days and nights thinking about what to do. He was a good man at heart and believed in both justice and mercy. Whilst many of his ministers had suggested executing Farhad, he flat-out refused. "I do not wish to take his life for falling in love. I merely want to frighten him enough to let go of his wish to marry my daughter!" said the king.

One day, the wisest of his ministers approached with a proposition. "Your Majesty," the minister began, "I believe I have a solution to your problem."

Hope flickering in his eyes, the king leaned forward. "Pray tell, what is on your mind?"

With a knowing smile, the minister said, "Why don't you offer Farhad the chance to wed the princess, should he prove himself? He is a mason at the end of the day, is he not? He can prove his skills—if he is a mason fine enough to unearth water from one of the mountains encircling the palace."

A spark of intrigue ignited within the king. He contemplated the plan's potential. He praised his minister for such tactful thinking. Subsequently, Farhad was summoned, and the king told him, "Farhad, since you insist on not forsaking your love, I have a condition for you, which you must fulfil if you wish to marry Shireen. If you can dig deep enough to find water in the mountain yonder, I shall give you my daughter's hand in marriage. As a king, I give you my word."

Farhad happily accepted the condition. He went home, picked his tools, and made his way to the peak the king had pointed to. Now, the mountain was both tall and hostile. Besides the city, the landscape was rather desolate. Farhad wielded his tools amidst the jagged rocks and parched earth, chiselling away at the stone. Each strike of his hammer echoed in the silence. For thirteen years, he toiled, with the heat of the sun beating down upon him relentlessly during the day, and the brutal, chilling winds biting at his bones during the night.

One day, exhaustion got the best of him, and he sank to the floor, on his knees, falling into *sajda*.[9] Overcome with weariness, tears streamed

---

9   *Sajda:* Prostration; the action of touching the forehead, nose, palms, and knees to the ground. Muslims do it in prayer.

down his cheeks, as he prayed, "*Ya Khuda*...it is only by Your will, and Yours alone, that I cherish Shireen.[10] I have spent thirteen years on this mountain, and not a drop of water has come forth. It is You who has put her love in my heart, and it is only You who can make water gush forth from this mountain. Please, I beg of you, please let me find some water, in this harsh terrain, in the shadow of this unforgiving land."

They say Allah is closer to you than your jugular vein. He is, indeed. No prayer you make with a pure heart goes unanswered. Farhad's prayers, too, were heard, and a torrent of fresh, sparkling-clean water burst forth from the earth. As the water filled up the tunnel, Farhad's heart was filled with joy. With new zeal, he began to carve a pathway around the mountain for the newfound spring to cascade downstream, for the entire city to see.

News of the miracle spread swiftly, and it soon reached the ears of the king. Caught up in yet another quandary, the king summoned his minister immediately. "What should we do now?" the king sighed, caught in a quandary. "I am a Pakhtun, and a king, no less. I simply cannot go back on my word. Nor can I wed Shireen to a suitor who isn't of royal blood."

As the king and his minister mused over the situation, the minister reassured him, "My king. Please do not worry. An old lady servant of mine has been studying the art of *makkari* for years.[11] She is educated in the *ilm* and has been serving my family for decades.[12] I am sure she will help us."

The king nodded in approval, and the minister went home and sought the counsel of the old woman. He explained the whole situation to her, and said, "*Amma*, you must help us. The king has given his word; it is no small thing."[13]

The cunning old hag thought in silence for a few moments and then spoke to the minister. "This should not be too much of a problem.

---

10 *Ya:* "Oh"; *Khuda:* The pre-Islamic term of "God" now used to refer to Allah in various ethnic languages in Pakistan, including Pashto; originally a Persian word (*Ya Khuda:* "Oh Allah!").

11 *Makkari:* The art of deception.

12 *Ilm:* The subject and the knowledge, also: knowing about something.

13 *Amma:* mother; used as a term of respect to address older women.

Go fetch me the clothes Shireen wore when she went to meet Farhad. Leave the rest to me."

The minister relayed the news to the king, who asked Shireen's mother to provide the minister with what he needed. He went back home and gave the clothes to his servant. "Here, I brought you what you asked for."

The cunning old woman, donning the princess's white *jorra*, set off to trek up the mountain Farhad was working on.[14] She met him halfway up the peak, where he was busy carving a waterway to the foot of the mountain.

Approaching Farhad, she feigned concern, and asked him, "Farhad. You have spent thirteen years on this mountain. Your family brings you food up here, you live here...you have not once asked for news of what goes on below. Did you not hear? Shireen passed away two years ago. Why are you still digging?"

Farhad froze in his tracks and kept digging up earth. "I don't believe you."

"Don't you recognise these clothes, Farhad?" she questioned him once again. He glanced up at her and recognised the *jorra* in an instant.

"What...what are you doing wearing this?" he stammered.

"The king gave away all of Shireen's belongings in charity. I received this when they gave away the alms. Now do you believe me?" the cunning old woman threw Farhad the bait.

Farhad could nearly picture Shireen, with her rosy cheeks, smiling at him, in that *jorra*. He could feel her scent on the *dupatta*. "No...no... no..." he cried and fell to the ground. Laying on the ground with his tears falling softly on the earth, dampening it, whimpering and writhing in pain, he mustered the strength to pick his tool one last time. He lifted it and smashed it into his forehead.

The cunning old woman, bearing the welcome news for the king, had Farhad's bloodied tool and corpse brought to the palace. Shireen had happened to hear of the news before her father and rushed to see it for herself. Seeing Farhad, the love of her life, lying lifeless, her blood felt as if it was drying up. She picked up his bloodied tool and, with all the force

---

14 *Jorra:* The word used to refer to the whole outfit: including a *shalwar* (lowers), *kameez* (shirt), and *dupatta* (headgear).

شیریں فرہاد

her dainty little arms could manage, she, too, hit herself in the head with it, collapsing cold right next to Farhad.

The king and his ministers reached the scene amid the wails of Shireen's mother and servant girls in the palace. The king suddenly found his feet too heavy to lift off the ground. Sobbing, he sat on the cold floor next to the cold corpse of his daughter. "Had I known they loved one another so much, I would have given them my blessing for marriage," he lamented in remorse.

The king announced that the cunning old hag was to be sentenced to death. He executed her with his own hand. As she met her fate at the king's blade, her form transmuted into stone. "You shall be cursed by all till the Day of Judgement," the king muttered as he joined his daughter's funeral procession.

2

SAIF AL MALOOK

ONCE UPON A TIME, there lived a prince named Saif. He was the son of the King of Egypt. One fateful night, Saif found himself dreaming of a land far, far away. It was unlike anything he had ever seen before. Set between mountains kissing the skies was a beautiful lake as blue as liquid sapphire. It was not nature alone that seized his gaze, for there stood the beautiful queen of *Peris:* Badri Jamala.[15] As Saif watched her, he lost his heart to her.

Desperate to find the lake and the *peri* of dreams, he narrated the incident to his father and asked him for his permission to travel.

"My son, you shall find your *peri,* but only if you pray, for the *peris* are a race pure to the core."

Saif left the palace and kept praying and searching for the lake. In the bustling streets of Egypt, he sought clues and whispers of the lake's whereabouts, yet each lead proved to be nothing more than a fleeting hope. After a long year of wandering, one day, he happened to cross paths with a *Wali.*[16]

---

15 *Peri:* A winged creature, exclusively feminine, known for being gentle, kind, and beautiful.

16 *Wali:* A wali is most used by Muslims to indicate a saint, literal "friend of God."

Seeing the prince, whose journey had worn him out so much that he now resembled more a *faqir* than a royal,[17] the *Allahwala* took pity and gifted Saif with a mystical *Sulemani Cap*.[18] This enchanted headpiece, whispered to have been woven with threads of magic, held within it the power to command two *Jinns* of great might.[19]

With a gesture and a word, Saif found himself whisked away from the busy bazaars of Egypt to the serene tranquillity of Naran, where the majestic peak of *Malika-e-Parbat* soared above a glistening lake.[20]

As the *Jinns* helped him land upon a small hill named Dheri, Saif's heart leapt with joy as he recognised the lake. "Yes," he exclaimed, "this is the very spot from my dream!"

After that, in the shade of a large boulder near the lake, the prince decided to go into seclusion. He prayed for forty days and forty nights in *Chilla*.[21] When Saif came out of *Chilla*, it was the fourteenth and the full moon cast its luminous glow upon the lake. The prince watched as a horde of *peris* descended from *Koh-e-Kaaf*.[22] The *peris* set aside their wings and crowns and went off to swim. Amongst them was Badri Jamala.

He then beckoned to the *Jinns* standing at his command. "Fetch me the crown and wings of this *peri*," he pointed. "They lie at the top of the pile." The *Jinns* fetched *peri* finery for the prince and, for the first time in a long time, he was content and thanked Allah.

---

17 *Faqir:* A wandering Muslim ascetic who lives solely on arms.

18 *Allahwala:* A man of God; a Sufi Saint; *Sulemani Cap:* A cap believed to have been owned by Hazrat Suleman (A)—the Prophet Solomon. In Islamic tradition, he is believed to have also ruled over the Jinns, besides humankind and the animal kingdom.

19 *Jinn:* A supernatural creature from Muslim belief.

20 *Malika-e-Parbat:* The mountain, Nanga Parbat, is one of Pakistan's highest peaks. It is colloquially referred to as Malika-e-Parbat, "Queen of the Mountains."

21 *Chilla:* A spiritual practice of penance and solitude for forty days in the wilderness. Its origins lie in Persian sufi tradition.

22 *Koh-e-Kaaf:* The mythical abode of the peris, Jinns, deozaat, and other supernatural beings in Muslim folklore, particularly in the Persianate world, South Asia, and Arab lore. It is believed to be in Russia.

سيف الملوك

As the *peris* made their way out of the waters, their cheerfulness was disrupted by a sense of alarm. Among them, the Queen of *Peris*, Badri Jamala, appeared stricken with worry as she discovered the absence of her wings and crown. Panic swept through her heart, a fear born from the uncertainty of the unknown. Seven of her closest friends decided to stay back with her, whilst the others returned to *Koh-e-Kaaf.*

As Badri Jamala pleaded for the return of her crown and wings, Saif removed the cap, revealing himself to the Queen of the *Peris* and her loyal companions. At that moment, not only Badri Jamala but also her friends could not help but be surprised to see how handsome the prince was. All of them lost a little piece of their hearts to him. He introduced himself and confessed his love to the queen. Badri Jamala fell in love with him a little more than she had at first sight and told the prince that she would be happy to be with him.

However, Badri Jamala requested Saif for her crown and her wings. She explained that their king, Deo Safed, was a tyrant.[23] He was holding her, as well as her subjects, captive. Should they not return, he shall come to find them and put both Badri Jamala and the prince to the sword. "My Queen, life and death are in Allah's hands and in His hands alone. Come with me. We shall find a way."

With this, Badri Jamala and Saif made their way downwards to Naran and her friends fluttered back to *Koh-e-Kaaf.*

As Badri Jamala's seven friends reached *Koh-e-Kaaf,* they faced the wrath of their king, Deo Safed, who demanded to know of Badri Jamala's whereabouts. Fearful and truthful, they confessed her love for a prince and her departure. Enraged, Deo Safed descended upon Naran in a fury, causing the lake, once vast and serene, to split in two with a single stomp of his foot. It also caused a terrible flood, of which the waters roared downstream to Naran.

At that time, the prince and Badri Jamala were also in Naran. They prayed to Allah for salvation. With a miracle, the earth cracked, splitting into a chasm and carving out a vast cave underground. There, they found

---

23 *Deo* (plural—*Deozaat*)*:* The Persian Div, known as the *Deo* in several languages in Pakistan, is a supernatural being, gigantic in size, and often evil. Deo Safed is believed to be the King of the *Deozaat* in Persian and Pakistani folklore.

refuge. As for Deo Safed, he searched high and low for the Queen of Peris, but he did not find her.

Now, the *Allahwalay Huzur,* who the prince had met earlier, parted from him with a prayer cursing his enemies: "Whoever fights you or comes in your way shall turn to rock and dust."[24] And so, when Deo Safed ended up trekking as far as Skardu, he collided with one of the peaks lining the Deosai Plains and became a part of the mountain for eternity.

---

24 *Huzur:* A title for respect; reserved for saints and prophets (*Allahwalay Huzur:* "The Respected Man of God").

3

DILAWAR O GUL MEENAH

ONCE UPON A TIME, in a village nestled amongst the hills of Mingora, there lived a young shepherd named Dilawar.[25] His days were filled with the simple joys of tending to his flock, the melody of his flute echoing through the valleys as he guided his sheep along the rugged trails.

It was on one such ordinary day that Dilawar's path intertwined with that of Gul Meenah, a fine young maiden crossing a trail through the hills. Their eyes met and, in that fleeting moment, the two fell in love with each other in the very same instant. Love ignited within their souls like a flame dancing on the wind.

Dilawar wove music and melodies with his flute which entranced both the lover and beloved alike. Dilawar used to steer the herds every day, and Gul Meenah went off on a stroll on the trail to meet her beloved. As the days passed, their love blossomed like the wildflowers adorning the mountainside. Silky-black-haired, gazelle-eyed, and rosy-cheeked Gul Meenah often lost herself in the tunes of her lover's flute. Gul Meenah, with her cascading locks and eyes that sparkled, found solace in the tender notes that flowed from her beloved's instrument.

Yet, in a world where whispers carried like the wind and secrets were as fleeting as the morning mist, their love was not destined to bloom in peace. Malice soon poisoned their little world when one day, Gul

---

25 *Mingora:* A town located by the banks of the Swat River in Khyber Pakhtunkhwa, Pakistan.

دلاور وگل مینا

Meenah, resting her head on Dilawar's shoulder as he played his flute, seemed lost in love. It was a rival of Gul Meenah's father who first witnessed this, after which the news of their affair spread like wildfire through the village.

The cacophony of violence soon shattered Dilawar Khan's melodies. They attacked him with sticks and stones one day when they found him perched on a boulder, tending to his sheep and playing his flute. He tried to stand his ground and fought valiantly, but before long, his lifeblood mingled with the earth beneath his feet.

When Gul Meenah learned of her beloved's demise, her heart shattered into a million shards of sorrow. Under the cover of night, she stole away from her home, her footsteps guided by the pull of a love that took her straight to her beloved's grave. It is said that the villagers found her dead next to the grave of her dear beloved, as their love transcended even death.

دلبر و مہ جبین

4

DILBAR O MAHJABEEN

IN THE OLD DAYS, there lived a very handsome young lad in Jani Khel, Dilbar Khan.[26] He was both good-looking and had great strength. Whenever he passed through a village, all the maidens of the village would peek from their windows, and when he was working the fields, girls farming nearby would drop doing everything to stop and stare, whispering of his youth. Many were in love with him and were ready to marry him. The poets wrote of his valour and of how handsome he was, and musicians composed melodies in his honour. Dilbar's mother truly wished to wed her son. She showed him many a young lass, but he did not take a liking to any of them.

Dilbar Khan had a habit of trekking up to a stream just outside his village and enjoying nature whilst he played his *rabab*.[27] Whilst he was lost in making music one fateful day, a beautiful maiden from the village came to the stream to fetch water. Although her *chaddar* veiled half of her face, the sheer enchantment of her eyes had a cold sigh escape from Dilbar Khan's lips.[28]

26　*Jani Khel:* A town and union council in the Bannu District of Khyber Pakhtunkhwa, Pakistan. It borders South Waziristan.

27　*Rabab:* A plucked string instrument. It is a part of Pashto folk music and is also the national musical instrument of Afghanistan. It is also used in traditional music in Balochistan, Sindh and Punjab.

28　*Chaddar:* A large piece of cloth, used to wrap around the body and veil the face by women.

"Oh, you gorgeous young woman! I swear, there is magic in your eyes," he called out. "I have become a slave to your beauty. What is your name, beautiful?"

She removed her *chaddar* from her face and, with a smile and the voice of a nightingale, answered, "My name is Mahjabeen."

Dilbar's yearning gaze shifted from Mahjabeen's innocent smile to the mole on her chin. He asked, "Are you engaged?"

"No. However, my father wishes to give me away to someone I do not like."

Dilbar paused and then said, "We shall meet by the stream at this hour every day, *Haseena*."[29]

After this brief conversation, both of them went their way, all smiles. For months, Dilbar and Mahjabeen kept meeting each other by the stream. As fate would have it, an evil uncle of Mahjabeen—her father's younger brother—found out about her tryst and went straight to her father. He also instigated his brother against Dilbar.

One evening, as Dilbar was playing his *rabab* and Mahjabeen was lying next to him, a few powerful men appeared out of nowhere and attempted to kill Dilbar. He fought bravely; he leapt at them like a lion—it was indeed a tough fight. In the aftermath, among the attackers, someone had a broken bone, another ended up with a cracked nose, a third broke an ankle, and the fourth an arm. It was indeed a sight to see. The enemy fled as fast as they could, not even stopping to look back, and word of Dilbar's bravery and courage reached Mahjabeen's parents. Her father's anger and rivalry towards Dilbar melted away into warmth and kindness after he learned how lion-hearted the young man was.

He invited Dilbar to his *Hujra*, gave him a pat on the back, and said, "Well done!" As the conversation progressed, Mahjabeen's father told him, "It will be an honour for me if you marry my daughter."[30]

Dilbar Khan was extremely happy to accept, as was his mother. And as the story goes, they tied the knot and lived happily ever after.

---

29 *Haseena:* A term of endearment, used for beautiful women.

30 *Hujra:* A traditional all-male space, a designated outhouse, where friends and acquaintances can come visit. Culturally, Pardah is observed in Pakhtun culture, which is why men who are not relatives do not enter the home. It is like the modern-day drawing room, only that it is detached from the main building of the house.

5

LAYLA MAJNUN

ONCE UPON A TIME, there lived a wealthy Arab Bedouin, a *Sayyid* who ruled over Banu Amir.[31] His heart, his *dastarkhwan,* and his purse were always open to the less fortunate.[32] However, he had no children. He and his wife prayed for many years and were finally blessed with a beautiful baby boy, who they named Qays. When Qays turned seven, his father arranged for a learned man who taught the children of many distinguished Arabs to take Qays into his tutelage. Amongst his fellow pupils were both boys and girls. One day, a beautiful girl, Layla, joined his school.

Qays and Layla fell in love with one another at first sight in early childhood. Their eyes became blind and their ears turned deaf for the rest of the world. As they grew up, it was not only their dreams which intoxicated them, they also began to indulge in drinking. One day, they were out for a picnic and suddenly realised that they had been followed. Despite trying to mend the torn veil and hide their naked love from the world, everyone knew. Layla's parents began to keep

---

31 *Sayyid:* An honorific title for the descendants of the Prophet Muhammad (S) through his maternal grandsons, Imam Hassan (R), and Imam Hussain (R).

32 *Dastarkhwan:* A white cloth spread out on the floor upon which food is laid out. Floor settings are the norm in Pakhtun culture, tables and chairs have come into use very recently. The word can be used to refer to both the tablecloth or the entire meal laid out.

her strictly at home, worried for the name of their daughter and the honour of their clan.

Qays began to mourn being separated from Layla. He only paid attention when someone mentioned her name, otherwise, his lips were sealed. Layla wept in silence, but he wore his heartache on his sleeve and began to be known as *Majnun*, "the Madman."[33] As more time passed by, his longing imprisoned him and his poetry became a harp for his pain.

Sometimes, he would make his way to *Najd*, stealing to the tent of his beloved and hurrying back home before dawn.[34] One day, when his strength failed him, he sent a message to Layla, a whisper in the wind, and the wind carried back a whisper from Layla.

A few days later, *Majnun* stole to Layla's tent once more. He felt he would die if he did not see her. Their eyes met and their voices caressed one another. And then, afraid of the guards and the spies, he left, only to find her once more. Layla was a *peri*, beautiful and bewitching, and *Majnun* was her fairy torch—alight from head to toe.[35]

Majnun's sorties did not remain a secret for long. His people began to feel ashamed. They were embarrassed for their *Ameer*. He was the son of their chief, after all. *Majnun*'s father, however, understood.[36] "He has lost his heart to this girl, and he shall remain wounded and confused unless he finds a way to win her."

The *Sayyid* asked the other elders for their opinion, and they agreed. A delegation was sent to Layla's tribe. As there was no feud between them, her people greeted them respectfully. Only when the Ameer asked Layla's father for her hand he said, "A stately man, he would be welcome anywhere, but we know better. Your son is a madman. *Majnun* is no son-in-law for us."

This was a bitter pill for the Ameer to swallow, but what could he do? He returned home with his heart heavy. When *Majnun*'s father failed to win Layla's hand, his friends and family tried to cure him. They praised the beautiful women of their tribe and asked him why must he go after

---

33 *Majnun:* The one who has gone mad.

34 *Najd:* The Central Region of the Kingdom of Saudi Arabia.

35 *Peri:* A winged creature, exclusively feminine, known for being gentle, kind and beautiful.

36 *Ameer:* Title for the leader of a tribe, city or state in Arabic.

a *ghair* woman.[37] Whilst they meant well, what could they possibly know of the fire in *Majnun*'s soul? That night, he left his tribe and ran.

Keeping his eyes on the road, paying no attention to the men around him, he peeked into every tent he saw, "Layla…Layla…" he called out. Exhausted, he fell to his knees. After talking to himself, he collapsed and was carried back to his tent.

The further away his moon, Layla, shone from *Majnun*, his madness and his passion seemed to grow. However, his family and his friends did not give up hope. In the twelfth month of the year, the old *Sayyid* took a small caravan to Makkah to make pilgrimage. In front of the *Kabah*, he asked Qays to pray to Allah to free him from his madness and the evil of his love.[38] *Majnun* laughed and prayed, "Oh Allah! Let my love grow stronger. Let my name always be mentioned with hers."

When they came back, the elders gathered around the *Sayyid*, "Did Allah help? Is he saved?" *Majnun*'s father shook his head. "I asked him to pray to Allah to free him of this madness. Instead, he clung to his own ideas. He blessed Layla and cursed himself."

News of the *Sayyid*'s pilgrimage to Makkah to heal his son, which had gone in vain, soon spread everywhere. Gossip reached Layla's ears, but what could she do? However, her tribesmen went to the Caliph's vizier to complain about *Majnun*. Having listened to them, he unsheathed his sword. By chance, a man from the Banu Amir heard this and reported the incident to the *Sayyid*. "They are now baying for blood. *Majnun* must realise the danger he is in," said the informant.

The *Sayyid*'s wounded heart, now worried, sent out a party to search for his son. However, all the men who went to look for him returned too, dejected. "Who knows? Perhaps his fate has already taken over him. Maybe he has been shredded by a wild animal. Or something even worse has happened."

Whilst *Majnun*'s kinsmen and tribe mourned him as dead, *Majnun* had found a sanctuary in a wilderness. He began to live alone, neither seen nor heard. A Bedouin from the Saad tribe happened to be passing by the area travelling back home. At first, he thought it was a mirage— what

---

37 *Ghair:* A stranger, outsider, or not from amongst you. It can be used for someone outside the family, tribe, or even a foreign country.

38 *Kabah:* The House of Allah, the holiest site for Muslims in Makkah, the Kingdom of Saudi Arabia.

else would accompany him to the middle of nowhere besides his shadow? When he looked carefully, it was a person! He tried to ask *Majnun* who he was and where he had come from, but when *Majnun* did not answer, he went on his way. He narrated the peculiar incident to his family.

When word of this got around to the *Sayyid*, he set off to find his lost son. He found *Majnun* rambling to himself, muttering verses, delirious and wasted to the bone. He tried to stand up but fell at his father's feet. "Crown of my head, forgive me, forgive me. Do not ask me how I am. You can see I am weak. Forgive me."[39]

His father tore his *pagri* from his head and flung it to the ground.[40] The day became dark as he mustered the courage to speak. He spoke of honour and patience. Soon, his voice began to falter as he began to express how much he missed him and begged him to come home.

When his father finished talking, *Majnun* poured out all his hopes and sorrows to his father. "You gave me life, *baba jaan*, may you never lose yours, and may I never lose you. I did not choose to shackle myself.[41] It was *qismet*, and it was written.[42] Your words scorch me, but what can I do?" *Majnun* then interrupted himself and began to narrate a fable to his father about a partridge and an ant. An ant is caught by a partridge in the leg. It tells the partridge, "Only if you could laugh as I do."

When the partridge opens its beak to laugh, the ant falls. Its life is saved, but the lesson remains: if you laugh at the wrong time, you will fare no better than the partridge and regret it with tears that you laughed too soon.

Majnun continued to talk, explaining how he had no reason to laugh. *Majnun's* father began to weep. He took his son home. His family nursed him and cared for him and called on old friends, entrusting the child of sorrow to their care, hoping that something would cure *Majnun*. But to him, they were all strangers. Life at home tormented him, just as it

---

39 *Crown of my head:* An expression used in Arabic to refer to something or someone you deeply respect and love, for example, your parents, or your homeland. In Urdu, Pashto, and other ethnic languages spoken in Pakistan, women also use it to refer to their husbands.

40 *Pagri:* A type of headgear.

41 *Baba Jaan:* "Father dear."

42 *Qismet:* Destiny.

tormented those around him—those who loved him and saw the tears in his eyes.

For three days, he stayed in his tent. When he could hear it no longer, he escaped again to the deserts of *Najd,* wandering the mountains, reciting his *ghazals*.[43] And even as the world called him a madman, no one could find a single fault in his poetry. Many came to hear him at his retreat. Of those who came, some became lovers themselves.

In the meantime, Layla grew prettier by the day. Half an enticing gaze from her could have imprisoned a hundred kings. Anyone who gazed at her flower of a face became thirsty to taste the honey of her lips. However, her eyelashes refused to bow and raise for anyone. She burnt in the fire of longing, like *Majnun,* but no smoke rose from it. Whilst she appeared to blossom, on the inside, there was nothing but ashes.

Sometimes, when the loneliness would get unbearable, Layla would pen verses herself. She entrusted the pieces to the wind, asking it to carry them to *Majnun.* On occasion, someone would find one of these and take them to *Majnun,* who would reply immediately in verse. Within days, his verses would be on the tip of everyone's tongues in the *bazaar*.[44]

She often crept out of her tent; her eyes fixed on the path to her tribe. Who was she waiting for? *Majnun,* of course. He never came, but his poetry found her, which she memorised and responded to.

One day, Layla's friends were sitting in the garden, making merry, whilst Layla sat a little way off by herself. A nightingale fluttered past her. She read a poem of hers to the bird, lamenting her sorrow and destiny, which had not made Qays for Layla and Layla for Qays. She spoke of the bitterness of separation and the secrets she told her shadow.

---

43 *Ghazal:* Originally a form of Arabic poetry, which expressed love and loss. It was absorbed by Persian and Urdu, and later, by other languages in the region. Verses are syntactically and grammatically consistent. Each couplet ends on the same word or phrase (the radif) and is preceded by the couplet's rhyming word (the qafia, which appears twice in the first couplet). The last couplet includes a proper name, often the poet's. In the Persian tradition, each couplet was of the same meter and length, and the subject matter included both erotic longing and religious belief or mysticism.

44 *Bazaar:* Market.

As she daydreamed of her beloved, she heard a melancholic strain. "*Majnun* is torn my grief and suffering, yet Layla's garden blooms as if in spring. How can his love live joyfully at rest, and smile when arrows pierce at him at a jest?"

She recognised the verses and the voice to be *Majnun*'s. She wept and sobbed. Inquisitive, one of the girls had noticed her absence, heard the stranger's song, and followed her.

She told Layla's mother what had happened, who was frightened nearly out of her wits. "My poor daughter. I cannot give her to *Majnun*; he will infect her with his insanity. If I urge her to remain patient, she may collapse entirely, and with her, I too."

Layla did not know that her mother could see through the facade of her smile. She was unaware that her heartache tormented her mother the same, if not more. However, as Layla had not spoken of her heart to her mother, she remained silent too.

On the same day in the garden when so much else had happened, Layla also chanced upon Ibn Salam, a young man from the Asad tribe. A thorough gentleman, his family and his clan were both well respected. He fell in love with Layla the moment he saw her and couldn't forget her on his way back, so he decided to send his parents to ask Layla's parents for her hand in marriage. Whilst they did not wish to refuse such an ideal match, they did not want to agree in a hurry either. So, her parents suggested they wait a while.

Let us go back to *Majnun*. Now, he was living in an area ruled by Prince Nawfal, nicknamed "The Destroyer of Armies" —fierce, courageous, valiant, and kind, the prince was a lion at war, a gazelle in love, and soft as wax to his friends.

One day, Prince Nawfal rode out to hunt and came across some antelopes huddled together at the mouth of a cave, shivering. He dropped his bow and steadied his horse. As he inched closer, he found the antelopes nuzzling a creature he had never seen before.

Naked, wasted, and crouching against a rock was a man—perhaps a savage or even a demon. His arms and legs were scratched with thorns and long, tangled strands of his hair fell over his face and hollowed out cheeks. When he realised that the man was weeping, Nawfal was no longer frightened. He asked his friends, "Does anyone know of him?"

His friends told him that this was *Majnun*, a young man who had lost his sanity after falling in love with a woman and now lived here alone in seclusion from the world. He muttered *ghazal* after *ghazal*, hoping a cloud would carry it to his beloved. Sometimes, people came to visit, some even travelled long distances just to come and meet him. They brought him food, but he would eat and drink very little.

The hunt was forgotten. Nawfal wished to help *Majnun*. He laid out a feast, but *Majnun* did not touch the food. The more the prince talked, the less *Majnun* heard. Then Nawfal brought up Layla. It was as if he had been struck by a magic wand. He lifted his head and he looked at the prince. He spoke, "Layla, nothing but Layla," and smiled.

He then began to sing her praises and took a bite of food. The more he sang of her, the more he ate. Nawfal and his friends listened in admiration and shock. He was no madman. Poetry as fine as his couldn't have been found in all of Arabia! Nawfal made up his mind and spoke to *Majnun*. "I promise you, you shall have your Layla. I will find her and marry her to you. Why do you abandon hope? I will balance the scales of your fate. Even if she transforms into a bird and escapes into the sky, I shall find her."

With these words, *Majnun* threw himself at Nawfal's feet and begged him to leave if he was showing him a mirage. Nawfal swore to *Majnun*, who then consented. After many months, peace returned to his mind. Now in the protection of Prince Nawfal, he was no longer *Majnun* and became Qays once more. He ate to his heart's content, dressed well, began to hunt, and recited his *qasidas* and his *ghazal*s to his friends, rather than to the wind.[45] Nobody was happier to see him regain his strength and his sanity than Nawfal was. The days passed by and turned into months. However, a storm was brewing on the horizon. One day, as *Majnun* and Nawfal sat in the garden, *Majnun* recited to him a couplet:

"My sighs, my bitter tears leave you unmoved! My griefs and sorrows do not harass you;

Not one, not half a promise you did keep; Of many hundreds, I received from you."

Nawfal did not know what to say. He knew he had made a promise, and he knew it needed to be fulfilled. As they were almost age-fellows, he had grown fond of Qays and regarded him as a friend. He sat with

---

45 *Qasida:* A laudatory, elegiac, or satiric poem that is found in Arabic, Persian, and Urdu literature.

his eyes lowered, ashamed, as *Majnun* continued to lament. "Unite me with Layla or I shall throw my life away," said *Majnun*.

When Nawfal heard his friend speak like this, he decided to take action quickly. He went to his chambers and changed into his armour. Readying his men, he rode all the way to Layla's tribe. Once they arrived at their pastures, he threatened them, "Bring me Layla, or I shall bring war to your door." However, her tribesmen refused. "Layla is no sweetmeat for your kind. This will not get you Layla. It is not your decision."

Furious, he sent a second message, threatening them once again, but they responded with abuse. Consumed by fury, Nawfal tore his sword out of his scabbard and charged. A fierce battle ensued. Cries of the warriors rose to heaven and blood flowed into the earth as the wine flowed into cups. *Majnun* alone did not take part in this massacre. He stood aside, his sword sheathed. It was not because he was a coward; it was because he was a poet. He thought not of destroying the enemy and defending himself but felt the pain of both sides.

His head began to spin. Did he hope for Nawfal's victory? Indeed. Was he grateful for friends who would go to war for him just to bring him back to life? Of course he was, it is not a blessing everyone is bestowed with. Did he wish to win Layla? More than life itself. Was he not ready to lay down his life at Layla's feet? Yet, here were her tribespeople dying for her. Killed by whom? Nawfal and his friends—*Majnun's* friends. Were they really his friends?

After night fell and the battle ceased, respite followed. There were no victors, a great number of brave hearts had fallen on both sides. As Nawfal was prepping his diminished troops, he was informed by his scouts that the tribe had been reinforced by other tribes. A hero, but not a fool, Nawfal sent a message wishing to pursue peace and asking for Layla once again. He offered loads of treasure in return. However, whilst Layla's tribe did not agree to hand her over, there was no objection to a truce. The prince and his men returned home.

Gone were the days when Qays enjoyed life with his friends and with Nawfal. The wound of our *Majnun* had been opened again. He drew his sword and spoke. "Is this your grand plan to unite lovers? Is raiding with arms and men your wisdom? I no longer wish to be friends with you. Not the enemy, but you, my friend, have broken the thread of my cause—it is no longer pure. You may be great in your generosity, but you are small when it comes to keeping your promises."

Whilst his words pierced Nawfal's heart like an arrow, he shielded himself. "You must understand. They tricked us. They had greater equestrian might, it is why I pursued peace and did not win Layla. I shall not rest 'til I win her for you."

And the prince meant every word he said. He sent messengers to tribes from Madinah to Baghdad and opened his treasury to them. He assembled an army which rose on the horizon like a sea of iron and went to war once more to win Layla for his friend.

The sound of the kettledrums beat and Nawfal's army appeared on the horizon outside the tents of Layla's tribe. A battle even bloodier than the first one followed. Soon, her tribe was decimated. Too many had either died or were wounded. They accepted defeat and Layla's father came forward, bent double with sorrow. "If you leave me my daughter, I will be eternally grateful. If you do not, kill her now, but I will not give her away to that madman. He is the reason her name is on every tongue in all of Arabia. I shall never give my daughter to a man in marriage who is not fit to marry."

Nawfal, at this daring speech, fell silent. His friends agreed with Layla's father—it was *Majnun's* own doing. After all, had he not sided with the enemy last time? Unable to do much else, Nawfal said, "I will only take Layla if you give her willingly. A woman taken by violence is like a salty-sweet and dry bread."

The prince decided to forgo the price of victory and gave the order to break the camp. They had not gone far before *Majnun* turned his horse towards Nawfal. "Faithless friend," he screamed. Admonishing Nawfal, *Majnun* rode away into the wilderness sobbing. When Nawfal returned to his hunting grounds anxious to comfort him but they did not find him, Nawfal was afraid that he had lost his friend forever.

After he left Nawfal, *Majnun's* horse galloped away at the speed of light. Singing about his friend's unfaithfulness, he suddenly saw three dots moving in the distance. Two gazelles had been caught in snares and a hunter was about to kill them. *Majnun* saved the two gazelles, kissed their eyes, and read them a couplet. The next day, *Majnun* saved yet another stag from a hunter, and whispered his poetry to it, asking it to take it to Layla. "I am yours, however distant you may be! Your sorrow, when you grieve, brings grief to me."

On the third morning, it was a raven from an oasis who he chose as his messenger.

"Help me, oh help me in my loneliness, Lonely, my light fades in the wilderness, "Be not afraid, I am yours" you said, Do not delay—lest you should find me dead. Caught by the wolf, the lamb hears all too late, The shepherd's flute laments its cruel fate."

On the fourth day, *Majnun* could endure separation from his beloved no longer. He made his way to the pastures of her tribe as fast as his horse could carry him. The closer he got, the more Layla's scent intoxicated him, the clearer her face became in his mind, and the more he heard her voice in his ears. All the strength seemed to have left his body when he stopped to take some rest.

While he sat there, two strange figures approached. A woman dragged a man behind her, his hair and beard were dishevelled and his limbs weighed down by fetters and iron chains so heavy that he could barely walk. Shocked, *Majnun* asked the woman to not treat her prisoner so roughly. She explained that he wasn't her prisoner. He was a *dervish*, and she, a widow. They acted like he was a madman, so people took pity and gave alms. They distributed whatever they earned in half. It was a ploy to make some coin so they wouldn't go hungry. *Majnun* asked her to take him prisoner instead and he would give her all they made. She happily agreed. The *Dervish* was freed and *Majnun* went around reading his *ghazal*s from one tribe to another.[46]

One day, they came to an oasis which *Majnun* recognised. It was where Layla's tribe had erected their tents. He began to weep uncontrollably, his tears falling down his face like a cloudburst in the sky. He fell to his knees and cried out to Layla that he had given up his freedom as penance for making her and her people surfer at Nawfal's hand. He called out to her to chastise him.

"As long as I am alive, there is not a single road which will lead me to you. So, spare yourself, save me from myself, and let me rest my head at your feet for eternity," were *Majnun's* last words before he could say no more. He raved and tore his chains apart as if he had been possessed by a demon. Striking himself on his face, he ran away from Layla's tent towards the mountains of *Najd*.

His parents were informed. Many times, his kin and his friends tried to visit him and speak to him, but all memory of the past had been erased

---

46 *Dervish:* Alternate title for a *faqir* (a wandering Muslim ascetic who lives solely on alms).

from his mind apart from Layla's face and her memory. As soon as they talked of anything else, he fell silent or walked away. Eventually, even his father, the *Sayyid*, and his mother abandoned hope of ever getting their son, their little Qays back.

Back at Layla's tent, when she learnt of Nawfal's victory and his father announced that he had successfully kept *Majnun* away from his daughter, Layla's heart shattered with grief. However, she did not share or show it in the presence of her father and other people. She lost sleep and peace and wept in secret away from prying eyes every night. Her parents' home had become her prison.

Meanwhile, suitors from every tribe who had heard of Layla from *Majnun*'s poems approached her father, but her father remained unmoved. He guarded his daughter carefully, like protecting glass from stone. Around him, Layla drank the wine of gaiety, and when she was alone, she ate the bread of grief.

Ibn Salam, too, heard of her countless suitors and began to become impatient. He prepared a caravan worthy of a king and went to Layla's tribe once more to remind her family of their promise. He showered her father with respect and gifts and was a magician with his words. Layla's father caved to his demands and agreed to give her to Ibn Salam. His hands were tied. He had already promised his daughter to him and, even though he would have liked to wait even longer, the enemy had him cornered.

The day of the marriage was fixed. At dawn, the guests gathered. Women around Layla made merry, tossed coins into the air, chatted, and laughed. No one noticed the bride's tears, bitter as rosewater and hot as fire. Regardless of how much people around her praised her beauty, Layla carried death in her soul.

Ibn Salam returned with his caravan and Layla. When they arrived at his tribe, she saw that he had prepared a fine tent for her. "All that is mine is now yours: my possessions and my kingdom," he promised his new bride.

The shadow which clouded Ibn Salam's heart soon began to darken. Layla refused to share a bed with him. Ibn Salam remained patient and hopeful, night after night. One day, he thought to himself, "She is my wife. Why should I not take what is mine?"

His actions followed, but as soon as he reached for the flower in his garden, he felt the thorn instead. The gardener hit him so hard that his vision blurred. "Should you try this ever again, you will regret it, for both your sake and mine. I have sworn an oath to my Creator that I shall not give into you. You can shed my blood, but you cannot take me by force."

Ibn Salam loved her very much, so he gave in to her wish. He told himself, "Even if she does not love me, I can still look at her from time to time. Otherwise, I will lose her for good." Whilst Ibn Salam's eyes searched for Layla's, her's searched for *Majnun's*. She lived on, thinking about him, waiting for a message.

As for *Majnun*, he carried his grief with him wherever he went. A year had passed since Layla's marriage to Ibn Salam and he had not yet heard of it. One day, as he was resting beneath a thorn bush in the desert, a rider came up to him and spoke ill of Layla and her fickleness. Seeing *Majnun* nearly lose what was left of his sanity and feeling sorry, the guilty rider told him that Layla was chaste as ever and, as he apologised, his words brought peace to *Majnun's* agonised heart. He wept and wept with no shoulder to rest his head upon as the stranger continued to speak of how Layla would never forget *Majnun*, not in a year, not in a hundred thousand years.

Majnun continued to mourn Layla and sing to the wind. The *Sayyid*, his old father, succumbed to illness and weakness. His heart ached from being a stranger to his son, so he set out to look for Qays once more.

He found *Majnun*, who recognised his father's voice instantly. Resting his head on his father's lap, he sobbed. After that, his father begged him to return home, for the few days he had left in this world, anyway. *Majnun* obeyed his father's wishes and, for a few days, lived amongst his tribesmen. However, unable to keep up the pretence, he confided in his father his pain and his feelings and that he was lost, not only to his family, but also to himself. "Let the dead not mourn the dead, *baba jaan*," he said, and as he rose to depart, his father bid him farewell one last time.

A few days after *Majnun* left his father's tent, a hunter from the Amir tribe was stalking a deer. His prey wasn't *Majnun*, but his words were as sharp as a blade. He admonished *Majnun* for forgetting his parents for Layla and for abandoning his father whilst he still lived. "Your place is at his grave. Do not refuse this last sign of affection to the dead. Ask for his soul to forgive you for your sins!" were the last words *Majnun* heard before he fainted.

When he regained consciousness, he rode day and night to reach his father's grave. He lamented and begged for forgiveness, sitting by the grave all night. It was only when day broke that he retreated to the caves and ravines of *Najd*, after which the wilderness was the only home he ever knew.

To the people's surprise, the beasts of the wild never threatened *Majnun*. He was a stranger in their world, but people feared him more than animals. Soon, the animals even gathered around him whenever he slept. A lion began to watch over him, guarding him like a dog. Other animals followed: a stag, a desert fox, and a wolf. Even the panther let him stroke its fur. He became a king of his court, like Suleman (A). Even though he was all skin and bones, he slept peacefully in the shade of the wings of the vultures.

Has anyone ever known a shepherd like *Majnun?* People were too surprised for words when they heard the story. It seemed to be a *peri* tale. Some even went to witness the safe for themselves, doubting hearsay. Many pitied him and brought him food. However, he never ate more than a morsel and never drank more than a sip. He gave the rest to the animals.

Majnun prayed to the planets as he prayed to Allah. Yet, the heavens remained silent, for what do the stars care of pain? He begged them to not exclude him from this charity and to keep lighting up his way for him to guide him out of his dark fate. When he ended his prayers and drifted off into sleep, he felt like his head was touching someone's shoulder. The dream *Majnun* saw was strange: a tree sprang up from the earth in front of him and reached all the way to the sky. A bird fluttered through its leaves, carrying something glittery in its beak. Just over *Majnun's* head, the bird let the jewel drop on his forehead. He woke up, and his dream vanished. However, he was filled with happiness he had not known in a long time. His body felt light and he felt as if his soul could fly.

Sometimes, dreams bring us hope, light, and good tidings—precisely that happened to *Majnun*. Whilst he was on one of his retreats on a mountain slope, surrounded by animals, he suddenly noticed a violet-coloured cloud of dust in the distance appearing into sight. As it got closer, it looked like a veil over a woman's face.

The face of the rider was unfamiliar. Perhaps someone was looking for him, but why? Was it an enemy? *Majnun* was reminded of the rider who brought him the ill news of Layla's marriage.

The rider rode closer and *Majnun* saw that it was a dignified old man. The animals became restless, but he raised a hand and they fell silent.

Majnun asked him where he was and where he had come from. "If you have come with bad news, turn back, please," he pleaded.

The rider threw himself at *Majnun's* feet. "I am not the enemy, I am a friend, and I come carrying a message from your beloved. With your permission, I shall speak, or I shall retrace my steps and begone!" said the stranger.

Majnun's heart jumped with joy. Perhaps fate had grown tired of abuse and brought happiness at last. "Speak, speak quickly!" *Majnun* exclaimed.

The messenger from Layla began to recite *ghazals Majnun* had written in praise of Layla. After that, he told her that he found her weeping and had asked her what pains her heart, to which she sobbed her heart out. She confided in him that fear alone made her give in to her father's wish to marry Ibn Salam. "I am no longer Layla, I am *Majnun*, madder than a thousand *Majnun's!*" she cried.

"He is a target for arrows of pain, but he is a man. He is free and need not be afraid. I am a woman, a prisoner with no one to talk to. Shame and dishonour will be my fate should I speak of my suffering," she lamented.

"A woman can conquer a hero and enslave him so he may prostrate at her feet. She may thirst for blood and have the courage of a lioness. But she remains tied to a woman's nature."

"I cannot end my suffering; I had to yield. Yet, I hunger for news of him. How is he? Does he have any companions? Who are they? How does he spend his days? What does he think about?"

"She begged me to ask you, these are her words," the messenger told *Majnun*.

Majnun told the messenger to tell her that he lived alone, wrapped in the memories of his beloved. Suffering had broken him and made his mind sick. He mourned Layla and his late father. He read some more verses about his grief, and the messenger went on his way.

The messenger recounted everything to Layla. She was heartbroken to hear that *Majnun* had lost his father. She changed into a dark blue robe in mourning for the old *Sayyid* and begged the messenger to return the next morning. When he set off, she gave him her robe and, within it, hid a sealed letter. The messenger returned with the gift.

Majnun could not believe his eyes. It was more precious than the entire world to him. He clutched at the robe, smelled it, and began to dance at the mountaintop as if he had been possessed. He spun and spun 'til he fainted from exhaustion. When he opened his eyes, he clutched at the letter. His heart began to calm down as he broke the seal.

Layla penned words of love and loyalty, of pain and grief. *Majnun* wept and wept, and then cried out, "Oh God...oh God...I have neither paper nor pen, but how can I not respond to her?"

The messenger smiled and opened his travel bag. In it was everything a writer may need: paper, ink, and a *qalam*.[47] "Here, help yourself," he spoke.

Majnun painted verse after verse, the paper placed tenderly on his knees. He handed the letter to the old man, who sped away on his horse back to his tribe to deliver Layla's Amanat to her as quickly as he could.[48] *Majnun's* letter was full of love, prayers, and grief, upon reading which Layla's eyes became veiled with tears.

Salim Amiri, *Majnun's* maternal uncle, was very fond of his sister and his nephew. He truly wanted to help *Majnun*. One day, he mounted his fastest camel and rode off to visit the hermit. Salim was astonished to find his nephew in the company of animals instead of being alone. He stopped a little way off and shouted a greeting. "Who are you, and what do you want?" came the answer. It hurt him a little. "I am Salim, from the tribe of Amir. I can see that the sun has changed your complexion to that of an African, but do you not recognise your uncle anymore?" he said loudly.

Only then did *Majnun* recognise his uncle. He calmed his animals and greeted his uncle politely. One by one, he inquired about all his kinsfolk. Salim was surprised to see his nephew being so reasonable. He wondered if Qays deserved the title of *Majnun* and felt ashamed of allowing this to happen. Salim could stand the sight no longer. He begged *Majnun* to dress up, but he was adamant that he did not need clothes. He nibbled on the delicacies Salim had brought him. Despite his uncle insisting he had more, he said he was content. His uncle then narrated to him a fable about a king and a Dervish, and *Majnun* was nearly smiling when his uncle finished the story with, "Free is the man who desires nothing."

---

47 *Qalam:* A type of pen, made from a cut, dried reed, used for calligraphy and writing scripts which follow the Abjad writing system: Arabic, Persian, Urdu, and formerly Ottoman Turkish.

48 *Amanat:* Something which has been entrusted to you.

Majnun liked the story and listened with rapt attention. He almost even laughed. For a while, he remembered his friends and suddenly remembered his mother. "My mother, my bird with broken wings, how is she?" When *Majnun* told his uncle he longed to see her, he promised to bring her along next time and, several days later, he did. When his mother saw him from afar, her heart shrank. How the rose had withered! The animals did not frighten her. All she could see in Qays was unhappiness, and all that she wanted to do was caress her re-found child. She wept bitterly in his embrace, fondling his hair, before she found her voice again. "My robber of a son…" she began. She lamented the loss of her husband, her loneliness, fear of dying alone, and begged *Majnun* to return home.

Qays threw himself at her feet. He sobbed and cried for forgiveness, but did not return with her. There was nothing the old woman could do. Sobbing, she returned home. Longing for her child and without her husband like a mountain on her back, it felt like a prison. Soon, she followed the old *Sayyid* into the afterlife.

Salim visited *Majnun* again and broke the news of his mother's passing. It distressed him deeply and he wailed like a bewitched harp. He ran and ran to his father's grave, where his mother now lay beside him, and his lament rose to the sky. But when has wailing brought the dead back to life? It was only the living who heard him as he sobbed, his face buried in the dust of her grave. They felt sorry for the old *Sayyid*, his wife, and even for *Majnun*. They opened the doors of their homes to him, asking him to stay, but he tore himself from their hands and rushed back into the wilderness.

Majnun's letter did not soothe Layla's poor heart. It pained her even more to see that he was torturing himself as he reproached her, even though he knew that she—her heart, her body, and her soul—were still his. Her husband's house was as much of a prison to her as her father's. Ibn Salam laid siege to her fort with tenderness, jealously guarding the gate he was not allowed to enter.

One night, as black as a moor, Layla crept out of her tent. Her sixth sense told her that it was no ordinary night. She did not know where to go but followed the voice in her heart. It led her to the edge of a palm grove at the same crossroad she had met the kind old man.

She stopped as she saw a shadow in front of her. At once, she recognised him as the messenger. Who was he? Perhaps it was *Khizar*—but

Layla did not ask.[49] Instead, she asked him what news he brought of her beloved.

Neither surprised by Layla or her words, the old man told her of *Majnun's* sorrowful state. She loosened her earrings and handed them to the man. "Take these as a present. Please fetch him for me. I want to meet him in secret, here in this garden," she said. The old man carefully stashed the pearls she had given to him in his sash and rode into the desert. Recognising the old man instantly, *Majnun* greeted him with great respect. "Spring awaits you in the garden. Come with me," the rider told him, handing him Layla's sash and her earrings.

Majnun accompanied him at once. The closer they got to Layla's tribe, the more he trembled with desire. For once, stubborn old fate was on the side of the lovers. The old man left, sending Layla a pre-arranged signal. After waiting for what had felt like an eternity, she rushed into the garden. She stopped ten paces away from the palm tree *Majnun* leaned against, but before she could speak, *Majnun* fainted. She rushed to him and he recited to her a *ghazal* before falling silent and running away into the desert.

By that time, *Majnun's* poems had found their way with caravans all the way to Baghdad. A young man, Salam, who lived by the Tigris, was fond of poetry and spellbound by *Majnun's* words and decided to travel to Arabia to meet *Majnun*. Tying his possessions into a bundle, he mounted his camel and wandered about the deserts of the land of the Bedouins for a long time before he found *Majnun* lying naked in the desert. *Majnun* forbade his animals from attacking him and beckoned to the young man. "Where do you come from?" he asked.

"I have reached the end of my journey," replied Salam. He then introduced himself, that he, too, was a man from Baghdad, crushed by love. He requested *Majnun* to let him stay with him for a few days. *Majnun* smiled at him and warned him, asking him to turn back. "How can I live with you when I cannot even live with myself?" He cautioned that the young man would flee if he did not leave now. Salam pressed *Majnun*, who gave in, and Salam settled down next to him. He tried to

---

49   *Khizar (A):* one of the Prophets Muslims believe in. He is believed to have been a companion of the Prophet Musa (A)—or Moses, as he is known in Biblical tradition. In folklore, he helps those who need him most and guides those who are lost, both in the deserts and at sea.

ليلیٰ مجنوں

comfort *Majnun* enough to make him share his food, but it only made *Majnun* angry. "I have eaten the eater within myself. I am free," he said.

For a few days, they lived as companions. But Salam could not tread on *Majnun*'s path for long—life in the desert without food and sleep and beasts for company was not for him. He preserved the poems he had heard in the casket of his memory and returned to Baghdad, where people marvelled at the *ghazals* he narrated. Who can decipher what fate has written? At first, we cannot read, but then, we learn to endure. Fate and desire often come into conflict, just like Layla, who was a treasure to others, but a burden to herself.

Even her husband, Ibn Salam, knew that, whilst he was the magician who possessed the *peri* and held her captive, it was merely an illusion, which needed to be kept secret. In time, he lost hope and fell ill. His grief poisoned him. He came down with a fever. As soon as he regained his strength, he began to eat and drink what the doctors had warned him against. Young, but weakened by illness and heartache, the fever came back, and this time, it was stronger. After two or three days, his soul fluttered away from his body.

With Ibn Salam dead, Layla, who had never loved him, pitied him. For once, she was free—not free to do as she pleased, but free to cry. Her shell mourned her husband, but in truth, she mourned *Majnun*. In Arabia, custom dictated that a woman was to stay veiled, see no one, and withdraw from the tribe for two years after being widowed. Nothing could have been more welcome news for Layla; now she could give her heart and soul to her beloved without fear.

As autumn came, it turned the leaves orange, making them fall like drops of blood. The sun began to lose its warmth. Like the garden, Layla, too, began to wither. The world's Evil Eye cast its cruel shadow upon her and a cold fever gripped her. Blotches appeared on her fair face. She could hardly leave her bed and began to prepare herself for the afterlife. She let no one near her but her mother, to whom she confessed the secret of her love, for the first and the last time. "When I am dead, dress me as a bride. Use the dust of his path as Kohl for me. Make indigo with his sorrow and sprinkle the rose water of his tears on my head. Veil me in the scent of his grief. I want to be glad in a blood-red garment, for I am a blood-witness like the martyrs. Red is the colour of the feast! Is death not my feast? Then cover me in the veil of the earth, which I shall never lift again."

She continued to sob and told her mother that *Majnun* would come. He would sit at her grave and weep. She begged her mother to remember that he was a true friend to her and to treat him kindly. Tell him, "Layla broke the shackles of this world and went, thinking of you 'til the end. Her eyes, which you can no longer see, await you from beneath the earth." Tears streamed down her cheeks and Layla closed her eyes as she whispered her beloved's name—forever.

It happened as Layla foretold. When *Majnun* learnt of Layla's death, he rushed to her grave like a thundercloud driven by a storm. He wept, wailed, and sobbed. His cries pierced the earth and even frightened those who witnessed it. He read her a *ghazal* one last time and returned to his companions in the wilderness. As he trudged along, the sand of the desert wept with him, the wind howled at him, and the stones of the steppe glowed with the colour of his blood. This time, not even the wilderness offered him refuge. He rushed to her grave every night, showering with tears and kisses. People began to avoid Layla's grave, fearful of encountering *Majnun* and, more than *Majnun*, his friends.

The last chapters of *Majnun's* life were written in darkness. Death approached him fast, but he found it slow. Layla's grave was his Makkah and when, one day, he felt weaker than he had ever felt before, he dragged himself to her tomb. Weeping, he recited some verses—and prayed to Allah to free him. He lay his head down on the earth and embraced the gravestone as tightly as he could. "Oh…my love…" were the last words to escape his lips before his soul left his body.

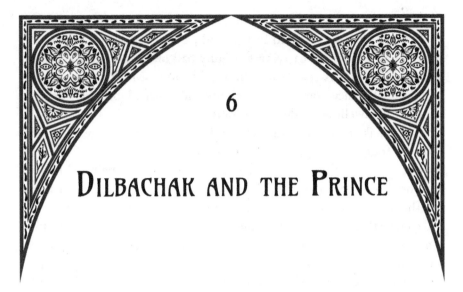

6

DILBACHAK AND THE PRINCE

O NCE UPON A TIME, nestled snugly within the heart of a quaint village resided a charming couple who were blessed with a daughter whom they named Dilbachak. Dilbachak was not only beautiful, charming, and good at her studies, but also possessed a heart as pure as the morning dew and a mind as bright as the noonday sun.

Alas! Fate can be capricious, and one day, her beloved mother fell grievously ill and departed this world, leaving Dilbachak and her father bereft and sorrowful. In time, her father, seeking solace and companionship, took unto himself a new wife. Though she was fair of face, the depths of her heart harboured envy and bitterness like thorns amidst a bed of roses.

From this union, another daughter was born, Saachik, but unlike Dilbachak, she was homely and plain. She smelt horrid and grew up to be an ill-mannered, spoilt child. Poor Dilbachak found herself thrust into a role fraught with toil and hardship. Her days were spent in servitude, tending to the whims of her stepmother and caring for her younger stepsister. Despite her tireless efforts, her stepmother met her with scorn and ingratitude, for the stepmother's heart knew only the bitter taste of envy.

One fine day, as the sun bathed the village in its golden embrace, the stepmother, with a sly glint in her eye, handed Dilbachak a bundle of soft cotton and bid her to prepare it for filling into a pillow, and Dilbachak obediently set about her task.

Just as she was engrossed in her work, a mischievous gust of wind swept through the air, carrying the fluffy ball of cotton far away from her grasp. Dilbachak chased after the errant cotton. Much to her dismay, the fluff ball danced out of her reach until it vanished into the recesses of a nearby dwelling, its door invitingly ajar.

Dilbachak ventured inside, her eyes falling upon the figure of an old woman, frail and ailing, nestled amidst the folds of her bed. Offering a polite "*Salam,*" Dilbachak explained how her cotton ball had flown into her house with the wind.[50] "May I have it back please?" she asked.

The old woman, a sorceress in disguise, often appeared in different villages, testing the mettle of people, leaving them cursed or blessed. This time, she was about to test the true colours of the hearts of Dilbachak and her half-sister. She picked up the cotton and said, "Of course, my child. Can you please help me with some chores first? Then you can have it."

Dilbachak smiled and nodded. "Spread trash in my courtyard," the old woman told her. But Dilbachak, both empathic and understanding, recognised that the house needed to be cleaned, so she took up a broom instead and swept away 'til everything was perfectly clean. The old woman then told her, "My earthen pitchers are useless. All they do is gather dust. Break them, there is no point keeping them."

Dilbachak took the pitchers to the tap, washed them, filled them to the brim, washed their lids, and brought back the pitchers, putting them back in place. The sorceress began to admire her. She gave Dilbachak one final task. "My head is itchy, please bring a stone and hit it on my head, it shall kill any lice I have."

But Dilbachak, with her gentle heart and wise mind, knew better. She tended to the old woman, washing her hair, combing it through, and plaiting it neatly. After that, she asked, "*Khala,* may I have my cotton and leave now?"[51] The old woman smiled and blessed her. "Of course. May gold ingots fall when you walk, may flowers of gold shower from your mouth when you laugh, and may gold pearls roll down your cheeks when you cry."

As Dilbachak made her way homeward, her every step was adorned with the glittering gift of little gold bars. Yet, being but a child, she

---

50 *Salam:* Muslim greeting, "Peace be upon you."
51 *Khala:* Maternal aunt; also used as a title to address older women.

paused after each step, stooping to collect the precious treasures that adorned her path, her *jholi* soon brimming with the weight of the gold.[52]

Upon her return, the stepmother's eyes widened in astonishment at the sight of gold everywhere. However, her surprise quickly turned to suspicion and ire as she demanded an explanation for it. "Where have you been, and what have you done? Why are you going around dropping gold everywhere!" she yelled as she smacked Dilbachak, leaving her cheek smarting.

When she sobbed and beads of gold began to fall from her eyes, her stepmother was even more surprised. Dilbachak recounted her encounter with the mysterious old woman after following her cotton ball. "I did as she asked, and she gave me a prayer when I left," she said.

Now, the stepmother saw an opportunity to claim riches for herself and her own daughter. Thus, the following morning dawned with her sending Saachik off to seek the same fortune.

The cotton ball flew into the house of the sorceress once again. Saachik went after it. Without even saying *Salam*, she spoke with great disdain. "My cotton flew in through your window. Can you give it back to me?" she asked. The old woman told her what she had told Dilbachak. "Can you do a few chores for me? Then you can have your cotton." However, unlike Dilbachak's gentle and wise approach, Saachik did exactly as she was asked.

"Go and fetch some trash. Then spread in my courtyard," the old woman told her. Saachik went into the street, brought along with her a heap full of dry leaves, twigs, and such, and threw it in the courtyard. After that, the old woman told her, "Check the earthen pitchers. Break the ones which are empty. Dry pitchers are of little use to me."

Saachik peeked into the pitchers and found that one or two of them were dry. She picked them up and smashed them into pieces, throwing them on the floor. Besides the trash she brought earlier, it added to the mess in the courtyard.

Finally, the old woman commanded, "Go fetch a stone, and hit it on my head. It will kill the lice and ease my headache." Saachik fetched a rock and hit the old woman in the head as hard as she possibly could.

---

52 *Jholi:* Literally, lap—figuratively, the portion of the kameez which hangs over your thighs from the waist to the knee.

The old woman was drenched in blood. "I did everything you asked me to do. Now can I have my cotton?" Saachik asked.

"I pray to Allah that pits form in the earth beneath your feet when you walk. When you sob, you cry tears of blood. When you laugh, pus flows out of your mouth;" she hands Saachik the cotton ball with a *baddua*.[53]

And so, she returned home, her path marred by bumps. Her foot got caught in one pit after another. When she went home, there were little pits all over her courtyard. Her mother got very worried and slapped her. "What have you done?" she chided. When she began to cry, blood began to flow from her eyes, making her look even more hideous than ever.

As time passed by, Dilbachak found herself with more gold than she could ever imagine. She indulged in the luxury of getting herself a pair of delicately crafted gold shoes. One sun-kissed day, as she wandered by the babbling stream, the golden shoes adorning her feet, fate intervened with a mischievous twist. One of her shoes slipped right off her foot. She tried to chase after it, but the current carried it far, far away.

A little further downstream, a prince was watering his horse. When the shoe interrupted the steed's drink, it picked it up between its teeth, put it aside on the bank, and continued to slurp down water. It caught the eye of the prince. The exquisite craftsmanship had him marvelling at its beauty, his thoughts drifting to the maiden who must surely be its owner. "How pretty must be she who wears this? Only a princess could wear such a shoe! I must find her and marry her!" he thought. With a heart stirred by curiosity and longing, he returned to his palace and shared the tale with his parents, the king and the queen.

The prince's desire to find his destined bride stirred their hearts with joy. Thus, they dispatched *rishtay-walian*, handing them the golden shoe.[54] "Go around the area. Make every maiden try it on. Ask for the girl whose foot it fits perfectly; she shall be our daughter-in-law," they told the women. Across the land, they journeyed, offering the golden shoe to maidens far and wide in search of the one whose foot would fit its golden embrace. Their quest led them to the humble abode of Dilbachak. Her stepmother attempted to dissuade them from making Dilbachak try on the shoe, however, the *rishtay-walian* insisted. "What's the harm? Let both try it on!" they said.

---

53 *Baddua:* A prayer to Allah, for harm to befall someone.
54 *Rishtay-Walian:* Women skilled in the art of matchmaking as a profession.

دلچپک اور شہزادہ

Dilbachak's foot slipped into it effortlessly and it fit her like a glove. She went inside her room and brought the other shoe for the *rishtay-walian* to see. Delighted, they returned to the palace, raving about Dilbachak's beauty, her fine manners, and her grace. And within the palace walls, the prince's heart soared with love for a maiden he had never laid eyes upon, his soul stirred by the promise of a love written in the stars.

As the joyous melodies of their wedding celebrations echoed through the palace halls, Dilbachak and the prince were married amid glorious celebrations. Their days were filled with laughter and warmth. However, their happiness did not last long. Seizing upon an opportunity to sow discord, Dilbachak's stepmother cunningly asked the prince to grant her daughter permission for an invitation to dine with her.

He happily agreed and sent Dilbachak with his guards to spend the day with her mother. She was greeted by her stepmother's seemingly affectionate words, a mask veiling the malice that lurked beneath. With feigned tenderness, she offered to tend to Dilbachak's hair. "Oh, my dear child, come here, let me fix your hair. You still haven't quite learned how to do it properly, have you?" she smiled.

And so, with a deft hand, when Dilbachak sat beside her, she drove a magic nail right through her skull. The enchantment transformed her into a nightingale. As she fluttered away on silent wings, her stepmother sighed in relief. "I finally got rid of her," she huffed.

She then instructed Saachik to don Dilbachak's garments, obscuring her face behind a *ghoongat,* and thus, she set forth to deceive the prince with her ruse when the prince's guards came to pick her in the evening.[55]

As the evening descended upon the palace, the prince awaited the return of his beloved. Yet, when the attendants presented her stepsister in her place, a pall of sorrow enveloped him, for he knew in his heart that this could not be his true love. The maiden before him was a mere imposter. She was ill-mannered and rude and knew nought of gentleness. Heart heavy with grief, the prince retreated to the solace of his garden. His restless heart found calm when a nightingale fluttered by and sang to him in a heart wrenching melody.

---

55 *Ghoongat:* A specific kind of veil worn by brides, which falls over the forehead and veils the face entirely. It has also traditionally been part of attire outside the home for Hindu women. It serves the same purpose as a *chaddar* or burqa. Women in South Asia have observed parda regardless of religion.

This happened night after night. As the days wore on, the prince's anguish only deepened, he could not bear to push a morsel of food down his throat or fall asleep. His mind was consumed by a sorrow akin to that of *Majnun*. Concerned for her son's well-being, the queen decided to search for Dilbachak, who had mysteriously disappeared.

In the quiet of the garden, as the prince lay restless, he awoke to golden beads scattered around him. In that instant, he knew it was his beloved. Moved by an impulse, the prince gently captured the bird in his hands, its fragile form trembling beneath his touch. With tender caresses, he spoke words of longing and sorrow, "You are my Dilbachak, are you not?" he whispered. "What happened? How did you change into a bird?" he asked.

As his fingers brushed against its feathers, they felt a hidden nail protruding from the bird's delicate frame and feathers just on the top of its head. With a gentle tug, he dislodged it and lo! The nightingale's form swirled away as it melted and behold! There stood his beloved Dilbachak right in front of him.

Joy and relief flooded the prince's heart. And so, with the imposter banished from the palace, disgrace trailing in her wake, the prince and Dilbachak were reunited at last, who then lived happily ever after.

7

TORDILAI O SHEHI

THIS IS A TALE from the days when the Mughal Emperor Akbar ruled Hindustan in all his glory. He was the mightiest of kings. The banner of the Mughals flew atop the highest of the Himalayan peaks. Mughal art, power, and military might were the talk of the town for the entire subcontinent.

Around the same time, just west of the Indus, two famous Pashtun tribes—the Yousafzais and the Menandars—were engaged in feudal rivalry. Both were thirsty for one another's blood. On the most trivial of matters, the two would be up in arms against one another.

Two paternal cousins in the Yousafzai clan, Tordilai and Munawwar, were fond of one another just as two blood brothers would have been. Both would have sacrificed their life for one another without a second thought. Their brotherhood had raised the bar for friendship for everyone around them. It had become an example for the tribe, for such love between first cousins was relatively unheard of at the time. For the most part, cousins, the sons of two brothers in particular were known to be adversaries.

However, it did not last too long. Soon, their friendship turned into enmity. It was as if the Evil Eye had snatched away whatever affection they had for each other. After their parents passed away, quarrels over familial land snuffed out the sincerity their hearts harboured for one another and rivalry began to take root in its place instead.

Now, Tordilai was fond of hunting. Most of his time was spent in the forests and the mountains with his friends looking for game. Wanderlust at heart, he used to feel bored in the village. He could never stay put in one place for too long.

One day he was out for a hunt and came across grazing grounds, which he had to cross to reach hunting grounds. The grazing grounds were Menandar property. His friends suggested they return home instead of crossing the grounds. They knew that stepping foot into Menandar territory would be an invitation to war between the clans. However, Tordilai brushed off their concerns of trespassing, and said, "We'll see."

When a Menandar shepherd brought word that the Yousafzais were trespassing on their grounds, everyone's swords came out unsheathed. Every child armed themselves and ran towards the grazing grounds. Women dropped their household chores and flung leather flasks full of water on their shoulders— "The Yousafzais dare to confront the Menandars? They will be taught a lesson of their lifetimes."

Within moments, the grazing ground had turned into a bloodstream. 'Til when were Tordilai and his handful of mates going to fight? The Menandar tribesmen decimated them. Tordilai was severely injured. Thirst had parched his throat. He was thinking to himself, "Who am I going to ask for water surrounded by the enemy who are baying for my blood?"

Just then, a woman passed by him with a leather flask strung over her shoulder. Tordilai whimpered helplessly, "Water." When the woman passed him the flask and his eyes held the gaze of the beautiful maiden, the flask slipped out of Tordilai's hands and fell to the ground. His jaw dropped and he fixed his gaze upon her eyes.

"What happened, stranger…your hands lack the strength to hold a mere flask, how are you going to swing your sword? You're Yousafzai, aren't you?" The taunt flew from the lips of the maiden like an arrow.

"Nothing…nothing as such," Tordilai responded, surprised.

"Here's some water," she said, handing over the flask to him once again. "Having some might do you some good, rather than staring at me. The Menandars cannot bear the sight of their enemies going thirsty."

"I have had water, yet this insatiable thirst within me shall not be quenched by mere water, nor even by the mightiest of rivers," he said.

"Although I passionately hate the Yousafzais, I honour the enemy who has been wounded on his back. I thought you were brave, so I offered you some water, but I can smell cowardice in your words."

"I am a brave heart of the Yousafzais. I will lay down my life for the clan's honour. As for those who hide amongst the trees to ambush us, they should know that my arrows can pierce through the hearts of thousands of Menandars. I pay no need for these jackals. But today…I could not stand my ground. Your darting glances have pierced my heart."

"Come to your senses, young man. This is a battlefield. Swords are swung, couplets aren't sung. If you're in the mood for stringing together some *tappay*,[56] go home and sing in your *Hujra*."

"My love for you is all that flourishes in the pastures of my heart. Throughout history, love and war have gone hand in hand with one another. May I know your name?"

"My name is Shehi. How ignorant are you, young man? I am the only daughter of the Menandar chieftain, Mustajab Khan."

After the battle was over, a *Jirga* was convened.[57] The tribal elders sat down together to discuss amongst themselves to try and figure out the cause of the fight. More importantly, the young men from the clan who had taken part in this feud had to be held accountable. Munawwar made use of his influence to manipulate the elders to a degree which charged Tordilai as the one responsible for the losses to the tribe. To make up for it, the punishment was his exile from the village.

Tordilai was very popular amongst the youngsters of the village. He was someone everyone looked up to. He was the heart and soul of the *Hujra*. When he left the village, many of its young men accompanied him. All of them began to live in the forests and the mountains.

Tordilai was truly and deeply hurt by the unjust decision of the *Jirga*. When he found out that Munawwar had been behind everything and had seized Tordilai's property after his expulsion, the embers of revenge began to seep into every ounce of his existence. He decided that he would no longer live in peace and would spend the rest of his life as a bandit. When the *Jirga* can no longer deliver justice and the elderly have become unjust, why not retaliate?

For a few months, the new life Tordilai had chosen for himself consumed him. He raided people in broad daylight. He robbed and

---

56 *Tappay:* Traditional couplets, created impromptu, and sung—also, a form of folk singing practised at weddings, war, or even mundane daily activities such as grounding flour or washing clothes.

57 *Jirga:* Tribal Council of Elders.

killed. His conscience never called out to him. He knew there was no other way to survive. It was not long before Tordilai became as infamous as he was dreaded. Even the thought of him haunted Munawwar, and he began to fear Tordilai's vengeance.

Then there was Shehi…Tordilai could see no possible way to wed her. It was possible to abduct her, but he knew in his heart that he did not have the strength in his arms to harm his beloved. He also knew he could not go to war with the Menandars.

He decided to pay a visit to Mustajab Khan. Seeing a guest enter his *Hujra,* the chief asked him to sit beside him and asked a servant to serve *lassi* to the guest. "Where have you come from, who are you, and why are you here, dear guest?" Mustajab Khan asked.

"I have only come to pay my regards. I am known as Tordilai," the young man responded.

Upon hearing the name Tordilai, Mustajab Khan's hand instantly reached out for his sword. "Tordilai—the thief—the murderer…" he said, standing up, "with what intention have you come here? If you weren't in my *Hujra,* no power in this world could have saved you from my sword."

"Yes, you know of me. However, I am here not as Tordilai the thief, but I am here with a plea for help," he said calmly.

Mustajab Khan calmed down quickly and sat down again. His sword went back into its scabbard. "Of course we will help those in need, even if it is the enemy. Tell me, what do you want?" he asked.

"Khan baba, you know me well. I am not a thief by profession. It is circumstances which compelled me to become like this…it was Munawwar who manipulated the council and cast me out of the village. He then seized my property. Now I must rob for a living. What else can I do?"

"This is not what I was told. We heard a very different story. If what you say is true, you have been treated cruelly indeed. You have my word; I will do whatever I can to help you," Mustajab Khan reassured him.

"Khan baba, I have no one other than you. Please take me in as your son. I shall be grateful to you for this favour for the rest of my life," Tordilai pleaded.

Mustajab Khan looked shell-shocked for a second. "Come back to your senses, Tordilai. A Menandar and a Yousafzai can never be kin! And if I do something like this, as the head of the clan, I will have to answer to the *Jirga.* What shall I tell them?"

"I only want to stay with you. Please take me under your wing. What is yours will stay with you, in your home."

Upon hearing this, Mustajab Khan began to contemplate. He knew that the odds of finding a son-in-law as courageous as Tordilai for his only daughter, Shehi, were next to none. However, Mustajab Khan feared backlash from the *Jirga*. There was enmity, Pakhtunwali, and the tribe's honour...this made the question of marriage impossible. When the servant reappeared with a bowl of *lassi,* Mustajab Khan sat up straight and became alert once more.[58]

"I have reached a verdict," Mustajab Khan declared, his voice resonating with authority. "From this moment forth, Tordilai is my flesh and blood. He and I are bound by kinship. Anyone who dares to raise a hand against him shall face the wrath of my fury. My only condition is this: Tordilai must forsake his past transgressions, pledging never to steal or harm the innocent again. If he swears this oath, then I give my word: I shall give him the hand of my cherished daughter, Shehi, and he shall henceforth be a member of our family."

Tordilai humbly sank to the floor, grasping Mustajab Khan's knees. He pleaded guilty, asked for forgiveness, and vowed to renounce his former ways. It ignited a blaze of jubilation in Tordilai's heart. All the pains of his past dissolved into insignificance as he saw a future with his beloved—with the cool of her cascading locks sheltering him from the scorching trials of life.

The news spread like wildfire. When Munawwar found out that Tordilai had been taken in by the Menanders, he feared that Tordilai would come for him. With the strength and the wealth of Mustajab Khan behind him, Munawwar would be in deep trouble. "This marriage must be stopped," he thought to himself, "Tordilai must be finished before he becomes a threat."

One day, Munawwar seized his opportunity. Finding Tordilai alone, he swiftly rallied his friends and surrounded him. How could Tordilai fend off so many assailants on his own? Just as Munawwar's sword hovered over Tordilai's throat, Mustajab Khan and his men arrived on the scene. A fierce fight ensued, resulting in Munawwar fleeing the scene defeated and bloodied.

---

58 *Lassi:* A local drink made with yoghurt and water.

Shehi had brought along the *zakhma* of Tordilai's love from the battlefield.[59] Up until now, she had kept it hidden away in her heart like something sacred had been entrusted to her. She loved him a lot. Whenever she looked at him, she got butterflies in her stomach. She felt as if every fibre of her being began to play a beautiful *rabab* melody, pouring her entire essence into the music whenever he was around.[60] However, the love which had begun in a battleground put her at war with herself. Despite all the overwhelming love she felt, an unsettling sensation gnawed at her, whispering that Tordilai was nothing more than a bandit, sending shivers down her spine. Whenever this thought crossed her mind, her little heart shivered and she felt a pang of hate for him. On top of that, he was a Yousafzai, an eternally sworn enemy of their clan. No Menandar ever mentioned a Yousafzai without swearing at them in the same sentence. If she married him, her tribeswomen would ostracise her. Her mind used to go numb overthinking.

One day, gathering all her courage, Shehi went to her mother. "Mama, I will not marry Tordilai," she said. Her mum rushed over and put a hand over Shehi's mouth.

"Shhh, quiet. You insolent girl. Do you not feel ashamed of yourself? What nonsense is this?"

"Mama! He is a thief and a murderer. He is a Yousafzai and an enemy of our clan. We will lose our respect and our honour—how will we face anyone after this?"

Shehi's mother continued, exasperated. "Shut up! Don't you have any shame in tarnishing the name of your fiancé like this? Do you want to disregard your father's word? Do you feel no sense of respect or honour for your family? If Mustajab Khan has said something will happen, it will happen. If your dad hears such talk, he will have your tongue pulled out. And yes, Tordilai is a Yousafzai. But now he is our kin. And he is a very brave young man. Also, there isn't much difference between the Yousafzais and the Menandars—we share the same forefathers. They're distant cousins, that's all. And he is no thief, he comes from a good family. His own family treated him worse than strangers, took away his

---

59   *Zakhma:* The pick of the rabab.

60   *Rabab:* A plucked string instrument. It is a part of Pashto folk music and is also the national musical instrument of Afghanistan. It is also used in traditional music in Balochistan, Sindh, and Punjab.

property, and threw him out of the village; he has been living in the mountains all by himself. Don't you see? He has abandoned all evils and is a good man now."

Tordilai was overhearing this conversation from behind the door. He came inside and addressed her: "Shehi, I am no thief. I had to resort to robbing to stay alive. I left that life of sin behind the day I set foot into your father's house. I have abandoned my family and my clan for you, what else do you wish me to do?" Shehi went red in the face, mortified that he had heard everything. She hid her face between her knees. Mustajab Khan came inside just at that moment and spoke cheerfully. "Congratulations, Tordilai. The enemy has died its own death," he said as he hugged him.

"What do you mean, Khan baba?" Tordilai was surprised; "who are you talking about?"

"Munawwar, who else?" smiled Mustajab Khan.

"Huh? How Khan baba?" asked inquisitively.

"Munawwar has left the village. He has enlisted as a soldier in Emperor Akbar's military," Mustajab Khan told him. "Hashim brought news."

Tordilai sighed. In a resentful tone, he said, "Good. Very good. This wreath will reap the thorns he sowed. He threw me out of my home and cast me out of the beautiful fields of my village. Allah has now pushed him to the hellfire of a foreign land. Now he shall serve others. He shall know the value of the hearth and family when he meets trouble at every step."

"Son, if he has left the village, there will be no delay in your marriage. I will make all the arrangements already," Mustajab Khan said.

The next day, the news of Munawwar being enrolled in the Mughal military was confirmed. The date for Shehi and Tordilai's marriage was announced. It was the wedding of the only daughter of the Mandarrs—there was celebration everywhere. Women sang, kids played, and feasts were held. Vibrant hues, an abundance of flowers, and the enchanting melodies of the *rabab* and *dholak* engulfed every corner.[61] Men clapped their hands as they danced to the tunes of *Attan* in just about every

---

61 *Dholak:* A two-headed hand drum, a folk percussion instrument. The *dholak* is most recognised in countries such as India, Pakistan, Bangladesh, Nepal, and Sri Lanka.

تورد لئی، شهی

street of the village.[62] The whole place was alive with cheer and glee. The wedding celebrations were nothing less than *Eid* celebrations everywhere in Mandarr territory.[63]

Love was playing hide and seek in Shehi's heart. Every time she thought of the fact that she would now be Tordilai's wife, her cheeks flushed. Sweat trickled down her beautiful forehead as she wiped her browns with her henna-stained hands. Whilst she was lost in thought of the man she was going to marry, Tordilai appeared.

"Shehi. What are you thinking?" He called out to her. Shaken out of her daydream and surprised to see Tordilai there, Shehi turned around surprised. She quickly pulled her *dupatta* over her head, which had fallen to her shoulders.

"Nothing." She answered. "I was just sitting. But you look very happy today though. What's the matter?" she laughed.

"My happiness knows no bounds today, Shehi. For one, my cousin admitted his defeat and fled. And today, I am going to be married to the woman who rules my heart, the queen of my dreams, who has enchanted me for years. Shehi, what could you possibly imagine of the tumultuousness in my heart knowing I can finally call you mine? Each passing moment of this wait feels like scaling an insurmountable peak."

"Aha. Well, your happiness is quite palpable, my beloved bandit," Shehi's playful banter began to tease him mercilessly. "But I couldn't help but wonder if that joy on your face is because you've brought the legendary *Sat-Lara Haar* of Akbar's Queen as a gift for me."[64] With a habitual instinct, Shehi couldn't resist throwing in a teasing taunt.

Shehi's words rattled Tordilai to his core. His sense of honour which coursed through his veins by virtue of being a Yousafzai was stirred. His mind whirled in a chaotic tempest. In a vivid vision, he found himself standing amidst the opulent halls of the royal Mughal palace, Akbar's

---

62 *Attan:* A Pakhtun folk dance.

63 *Eid:* The word Eid means "feast" or "festival." Each year, Muslims celebrate both Eid al-Fitr and Eid al-Adha—but the names often get shortened to just *Eid.*

64 *Sat-Lara Haar:* A necklace made from seven individual necklaces, often with gold pendants set at the centre of each. Also known as the *Rani Haar*— "Necklace of the Queens."

Queen seated regally upon her throne before him. He seized the necklace from her neck and fled.

"You seem lost in thought, Tordilai." Shehi's voice broke his vision. "It's okay, we're not in a hurry. You can bring me a *Sat-Lara Haar* some other time." She pinched him and began to laugh.

"The Princess of the Mandarr's truly deserves the *Sat-Lara Haar*. Now, I have decided I will bring for my bride-to-be what she has wished for. If I do not pass this test, forgive me, my Shehi. *Khuda Hafiz*,"[65] Tordilai declared decisively.

Her face looked like someone had shaken her awake from a deep slumber. She began to scream. "No, no, no, come back, Tordilai, my *Sartaj*,[66] my *Janan*, I beg you.[67] I don't want a *Sat-Lara Haar*. I only want you. Please just come back." She started crying, but he was gone.

The delicate string of Shehi's beautiful dreams shattered. In the Mandarr valley, the sound of laughter was choked. The *rabab* melodies abruptly ceased and the cheerful beats of the *dholaks* fell silent. Mustajab Khan's face, which was previously all smiles, was now overwhelmed with sorrow.

"Ah, Shehi, ah! Could you not control your tongue?" her father reprimanded her. "You sent your beloved to his doom! You shattered your father's spirit! What of the tribe's honour? Ah! Ah!" He fell unconscious. When he came back to his senses, he looked as if he had aged way beyond his years. No trace of his former smile remained; only perpetual worry etched upon his face.

The fire of separation began to burn Shehi. She kept to herself, lying upside down. The tears never stopped streaming down her cheeks. She could never rest, not even for a moment. Even when she used to sleep, she used to wake up with nightmares. Some nights, she would see Tordilai surrounded by the enemy's soldiers; other times, she would see him imprisoned. To Shehi, her peace was as precious as gold, yet she felt as though Tordilai had mercilessly plundered it from her grasp. She would be lost in thought, thinking of Tordilai every waking moment.

---

65 *Khuda Hafiz:* Literally "May you be entrusted to Allah." It is a way of saying goodbye.

66 *Sartaj:* Literally "crown of the head"; used as a term of endearment by women for their husbands.

67 *Janan:* A term of endearment in Pashto which means "beloved."

One night, she woke up with a scream. She saw that Tordilai had entered the emperor's fort and had been arrested by King Akbar's soldiers. Her mother caressed her and tried to comfort her, "Don't worry my child, Tordilai is very brave, even the strongest of enemies cannot hurt him. He will be back soon, God Willing."

One night, as darkness swept over Menandar territory, Shehi was lost in the thoughts of her beloved. Suddenly, there was a knock at the door. Her heart raced with anticipation, thinking, "Perhaps my Tordilai has returned."

Mustajab Khan answered the door quickly; it was a friend of his, Bhagwan Daas. "Is everything okay? What are you doing here at this hour?" he asked, concerned.

The two men sat down. "I can tell just by looking at you that there is bad news. Tell me, what is the matter?" Mustajab asked him.

"Don't panic, Khan," Bhagwan began to speak.

"Your eyes tell me otherwise. Speak. What is it which you are keeping from me? My dear friend, speak swiftly! Please don't delay, for Allah's sake. I am ready to hear the worst of the news," Mustajab Khan pressed Bhagwan Daas for an answer.

"Khan, Tordilai has been arrested by the emperor's soldiers." Bhagwan Daas told him, with tears in his eyes and fear in his heart.

Mustajab Khan asked, "Why? What did he do?"

"He was caught trying to steal from the royal palace. The emperor has sentenced him to death."

Shehi was overhearing the conversation from her bedroom. She screamed and fell unconscious. There was a ruckus in the house.

"Whose scream did I just hear?" Bhagwan Daas's concern deepened as he urgently questioned his friend. "Poor Shehi. She's betrothed to Tordilai. She dared to tease him about the *Sat-Lara Haar*, the very one belonging to Akbar's Queen," Mustajab Khan lamented, his voice heavy with sorrow.

"Shehi, my dear niece," Bhagwan Daas got up and ran to Shehi. He affectionately patted her head and reassured her. "Oh, my child, don't you worry now. Bhagwan Daas will even take on a mountain for his daughter." When Shehi opened her eyes, she only mustered the strength to utter, "Bhagwan uncle, take me to Tordilai."

"My daughter, it is not appropriate for you to accompany me. I will rectify this situation. I swear upon everything I hold dear that I will not rest until I bring Tordilai back home and return him to you," Bhagwan Daas declared with a fierce resolve in his voice.

Shehi's parents vehemently tried to dissuade her, emphasizing the impropriety of her pursuit of Tordilai. However, she would have none of it and refused to listen to anyone. Eventually, everyone reluctantly gave in to her wishes. The following morning, Bhagwan Daas, Mustajab Khan, and Shehi were ready to travel to Attock Fort to seek an audience with the king. However, Bhagwan Daas asked Mustajab Khan to stay back and set off alone with Shehi in tow.

Upon reaching the fort, they were met with the gut-wrenching news that Tordilai had been condemned to death. He was to be half-buried in the ground and the emperor's hounds were to be set upon him. When Shehi heard this, she felt dizzy. However, Bhagwan Daas consoled her, "My daughter, you have the heart of a Pakhtun woman, you are Mustajab Khan's daughter, and you are the princess of your tribe. You must face adversity with courage. Pull yourself together. We will need to think of a plan."

Bhagwan Daas urgently sought out the keeper of the hounds, beseeching for aid with a desperate plea. However, the keeper refused, "How can I refuse the emperor, Bhagwan? Come back to your senses." Disappointed, he went home and came back to the keeper with a gift—his daughter-in-law's bangles.

The next day, when the hounds were set on Tordilai, they leapt to attack him, but smelt him and went away. Everyone in the crowd was surprised—this was a first. The emperor, both furious and shocked at the spectacle, ordered Tordilai to be trampled by elephants. Even Bhagwan Daas was frightened. He tried to speak to the elephant keeper, but the keeper was cold. Distressed, he went back home and sat by himself.

His daughter-in-law, Lata, spoke to him. "Baba, we will do everything we can for Shehi. The elephant keeper's daughter is like my sister, we have been best friends since childhood. She will speak to her father and he will find a way to free Tordilai."

The next day, the crowd gathered again. Groups upon groups of people came together in the fort's grounds. "He escaped the dogs, but the elephant is brutal. Nothing can save him today," everyone whispered amongst themselves. Tordilai was put in place and an elephant came trumpeting. Everyone froze and their hearts beat a little faster. The elephant lifted its foot and everyone closed their eyes. It stomped and the ground shook. People opened their eyes, expecting to see no sign of Tordilai. What they saw shocked and astonished them. Tordilai was there, safe and sound. People began to say that Tordilai was almost certainly a magician. It was only a matter of time 'til the emperor found out. He flew into a rage and commanded, "Present him to me immediately!"

When Tordilai was brought to the emperor, Akbar cast him a disgusted look. He turned to Munawwar, who was now serving in the Royal Guard responsible for the emperor's safety: "Is this the same rebel who used to rob your village?"

"Yes, my Lord," Munawwar answered.

The emperor turned to Tordilai. "You wretch. Do you know what this mistake will cost you? How dare you enter the *Harem Saraye* of the Emperor of Hindustan?[68] You will pay for this with your life!" he roared.

"Mercy, mercy, mercy, please, dear King," Shehi, Bhagwan Daas, and Lata cried out from afar. They had been stopped by the guards on the veranda.

"Present those who plead," said the king.

"Your Highness, mercy," Bhagwan Daas pleaded, kneeling in front of the king, "please spare Tordilai, or this young girl will be widowed before she is even married. Please forgive Tordilai."

"Bhagwan Daas, what are you asking of me? He has hurt my honour by entering my *Haram Saraye*. He must be punished for this," roared the emperor.

Shehi went to speak to Munawwar. "Munawwar bhai, Tordilai is your brother, and you are his friend. The emperor will heed your words. Please request for his life to be spared…I beg of you." She placed her *chaddar* at his feet.

The next moment, Munawwar requested the emperor to spare Tordilai's life. Surprised, the king turned to Munawwar. "Is he not your sworn enemy?"

"You are right, my Lord. However, my enmity with him is that of our tribe and is restricted to our homeland, where my sword is thirsty for his blood. But here, he is my guest and my kinsman. My tribal duty makes it a compulsion for me to save his life."

"My word is set in stone; it cannot be reversed. I reject your plea as inappropriate, and I order you to execute this guest of yours."

---

68 *Harem Saraye:* The women's quarters in the palace.

"Zill-e-Illahi, the embers of honour in my blood are still warm.[69] My sword will not be reddened with the blood of my brother. Nor can anyone harm him as long as I am here. This is a question of tribal cachet. My hands are tied. I request you once again, for the final time, please spare Tordilai. For the crime for which he has been sentenced to death, please present *the Sat-Lara Haar* to this young Pakhtun woman. I offer you my head for it."

Munawwar was now toying with sentiments of royalty by fringing upon a noble sense of honour. "Whilst your boldness is condemnable, I appreciate it. So, I hereby order Tordilai to be freed, and the queen's *Sat-Lara Haar* to be given to this Pakhtun maiden. After that, Munawwar is to be publicly executed this instant," the king announced, whilst adjourning the Durbar.

Tordilai and Shehi fell to Munawwar's feet. "Munawwar, my brother, what did you just do? How will we face the tribe?"

He helped them both up and hugged them. "Shehi, my dear sister, here stands your husband. May your union be filled with blessings. Allah has blessed me with success. Tordilai, my brother, I have been very cruel to you. I consider myself fortunate to be able to pay for my sins, even if it is with my blood. I hope you no longer harbour any hatred in your heart for me."

Bhagwan Daas and Lata sent off their guests doused in tears. Their boat set off from Attock, floating on the fierce and violent waves of the Indus. They disembarked near Khairabad. After that, they began to walk. The lovesick couple had to camp overnight in a forest near Akora before setting off again the next morning.

Just before midnight, Shehi's throat parched with thirst. Around her was the eerie wilderness cloaked in pitch-black darkness and the desperate search for water. Tordilai wandered around in search of some freshwater for her. Amidst the desolation, he stumbled upon a cluster of tents of the Kuchi nomads, nestled at the foot of the mountain. Approaching the encampment, Tordilai was met with a cacophony of barks of the guard dogs. Akin to ravenous wolves, they lunged at him. Startled awake by the commotion, the Kuchis, fearing a bandit raid, swiftly armed themselves with swords. In the veil of darkness, a flurry

---

69   *Zill-e-Illahi:* "God's Shadow," figuratively used as a title by Mughal Kings.

of blades descended upon Tordilai, inflicting countless wounds before he could even blink, injuring him greatly.

As dawn broke and Tordilai failed to return, Shehi's anguish grew. She began to search for him. She, too, saw the tents from afar and headed towards them. Drawing closer to the distant encampment, she stumbled upon the lifeless figure of Tordilai bathed in a crimson pool of his own blood. Shehi's heart shattered into a million fragments.

"Tordilai, my beloved Tordilai…" she whispered as she embraced his cold, motionless body. The whispered words of a haunting realization spread amongst the Kuchis like wildfire. "Tordilai, the bandit Tordilai…"

Rushing to witness the aftermath of their actions, their voices trembled with regret as they beheld the tragic scene before them. "Oh, good heavens. What have we done?" As they reached Tordilai's cold corpse and pried Shehi away from his icy embrace, they realized that she, too, had departed this world, following her beloved into the otherworld. A wave of grief swept over the nomadic community nestled by the river. They were weighed down with the anguish of the sudden and unjust deaths of not one, but two innocent souls. As they grappled with the loss, thoughts turned to the solemn task of burying the departed couple, a solemn procession of Akbar's soldiers silently passed by, bearing the weight of a funeral procession. Upon learning of Tordilai's murder and Shehi's tragic passing, they collected their bodies and took them along with them.

The Mandarrs and the Yousafzais stood side by side, united in the face of the tragedy. Both tribes bore deep wounds inflicted by the same arrow that pierced their eyes and the same sword that cut their souls. Tears welled in their eyes. These three souls, who had bravely sacrificed everything in the name of love, honour, and courage, were laid to rest in the very grazing ground where the soil had once been irrigated with the blood of Mandarr and Yousafzai warriors.

8

THE DEO AND THE PRINCESS

ONCE UPON A TIME, in a kingdom nestled amidst green hills and rolling meadows, there reigned a king whose heart overflowed with love for his two precious daughters. As he prepared for a journey to visit his royal acquaintances in a neighbouring land, he gathered his daughters close and inquired, "My dear ones, what gifts shall I bring you upon my return?"

The younger daughter, her eyes sparkling with excitement, requested for all sorts of toys and trinkets. But it was the elder daughter who captured his attention. "Father, I desire a *dupatta* of smoke,[70] a *kameez* of fire,[71] and a *shalwar* of flames," she said.[72]

The king was surprised at the rather unusual request. However, when he was finished with his trip, he shopped a whole cartful of toys for his younger one. He also asked his chamberlains to find out where he could get a *dupatta* of smoke, a *kameez* of fire, and a *shalwar* of flames. He was

---

70 *Dupatta:* The veil which is a part of the Pakhtun ethnic ensemble—a piece of cloth, usually 1 m by 2.5 m, traditionally worn to cover the head, but now it is also worn around the neck or over the shoulder.

71 *Kameez:* The shirt which is a part of the Pakhtun ethnic ensemble. It resembles a tunic, typically reaches the knees or lower, and is slit from the waist to the lower end.

72 *Shalwar:* The trousers which are a part of the Pakhtun ethnic ensemble. It resembles loose, baggy trousers that taper at the ankles.

told that such an outfit could only be found at the *Deo Bazaar*.[73] The king went to the *bazaar* and found a *Deo* shopkeeper, whom he asked for the outfit.[74] As the *Deo* was packing it, the king asked, "How much will that be?"

The *Deo* smiled. "You may take it for free, for now. The price for this *jorra* is that whomsoever you are taking it for, you shall have to give her to me."[75]

Upon hearing this, the king became alarmed and went on his way. When he went back to his capital and gave his younger daughter all her gifts, she was very happy; however, the older one was upset. She sulked all day long, which made her father very sad. Throwing a tantrum, she told her father, "I will go with the *Deo*, but I want that dress! You should have brought it for me."

He eventually gave in to his daughter's persistence and travelled all the way to the neighbouring kingdom again. Making his way straight to the *Deo Bazaar* and, to the very same shopkeeper, he said, "I shall give you my daughter. Give me the *jorra*."

The *Deo* gave him the package and handed the king a bagful of mustard seeds. "Scatter these on your way back home. When they flower, I shall follow the trail. We shall meet then, on a day it is drizzling. Then I shall come and take your daughter," he instructed.

The king agreed and left a trail of mustard seeds on his way back to the palace. Now, a few months went by and the seeds began to flower. The king began to worry more and more by the day. One morning, when the sky was cloudy and light rain began, the king's heart was in his throat, for he was expecting the *Deo* to arrive.

True to his word, the *Deo* did indeed arrive the same day. "Your Highness, I am here. You gave me your word. It is time to keep it," he said.

The king called his daughter, but when she saw the *Deo*, she became extremely frightened. "I'm not going with him," she cried. The king was now caught in a situation. He asked the *Deo*, "If she doesn't want to accompany you, how can I force my daughter?"

---

73 *Deo:* The Persian *Div*, known as the *Deo* in several languages in Pakistan, is a supernatural being, gigantic in size, and often evil.

74 *Bazaar:* Marketplace.

75 *Jorra:* The term used to refer to the complete ethnic outfit, including the shalwar, kameez, and a dupatta.

The *Deo* answered the king, "Do not fret, your highness. Take her for a picnic tomorrow. You will see a yellow flower, that will be me. When she comes towards it, I shall take the girl away."

The king told his daughter to prepare for a walk the next morning by the riverside. Whilst they strolled, she saw a beautiful yellow flower. "How pretty that is, *baba jaan!*" she exclaimed.[76]

"Run along, go break it. Let's take it back with us," her father told her.

As soon as the princess went near the flower, its leaves took her into its embrace and she felt herself being tugged into the water. Soon, she found herself in an area where the *Deo* lived. The *Deo* had the princess surrounded by riches and comforts beyond measure. However, despite the luxury, even though the *Deo* neither touched nor frightened her, he forbade her from venturing beyond the palace walls. Thus, despite her lavish surroundings, she remained a captive within her gilded cage.

As the days stretched into weeks and months, the princess discerned a peculiar pattern in the *Deo's* promises of return. When he said he would be back home soon, his absences could even go on for as long as six months, while when he declared that he would be travelling for months, he would reappear soon. Aware of the enchantments woven into the house, she understood that the *Deo* could hear every whisper within its walls, binding her further to his control.

It so happened that a few weeks later, the *Deo* told her, "I am going out. I shall be back in a while." In the garden, as the princess swung on the swing, a hungry stray dog appeared at the door seeking food. Seizing the opportunity, she swiftly slaughtered and skillfully skinned it. She set a trap, suspending the dog's meat on the swing and positioning a large *karahi* filled with oil beneath.[77] As the swing moved, the blood dripped into the *karahi,* creating a hissing sound. Between the creaking of the swing and the sounds of cooking, she hoped the *Deo* would not figure out she was gone, at least for a while anyway. Cloaked in the dog's skin, the princess made her escape.

---

76 *Baba Jaan:* "Father dear."

77 *Karahi:* A karahi traditional cooking pot, similar to a wok but with steeper sides and two handles, used for deep frying, as well as making an array of curries. It's typically made of cast iron or stainless steel and retains heat well, allowing for high-temperature cooking.

Breathless and weary from her frantic flight, the princess stumbled upon a dwelling, her clothes stained with mud and blood. Hastily, she made her way to the nearby river, where she cautiously shed the dog's skin and began to bathe. What she did not know was that she was being watched. There was no one nearby, but in the city, a prince standing in the window of the palace tower had noticed. As she clads the skin once more, he wondered why a girl would put on such a strange disguise, so he ordered his guards to capture the dog.

When they brought the dog before him, he commanded them to leave. With a stern tone, the prince addressed the disguised princess, "I know you aren't a dog. I know there is a person inside. Talk to me."

When he was met with silence, he responded with a single lash of the whip, after which the princess swiftly discarded the dog's skin, sobbing as she revealed herself to the prince. Entranced by how beautiful she was, the prince himself momentarily forgot about all else as his gaze lingered upon her delicate features.

As she continued to cry, it broke the spell of his fascination. "What is the meaning of this?" he questioned softly. "Why have you chosen to conceal yourself as a dog?"

Trembling, the princess recounted the tale of how she had been captured by the *Deo* and how she had escaped. The prince listened intently, his expression shifting from curiosity to empathy as he absorbed her words. "You have endured much, dear princess," he murmured.

With gentle reassurance, he took her trembling hands in his own. "Fear not, for you are safe now," he whispered. "You are welcome within the walls of my palace where no harm shall befall you."

Tears of gratitude welled in the princess's eyes as she felt the weight of her burden begin to lift. "Thank you," she whispered, her voice barely above a breath.

As the hours passed, the *Deo's* suspicions grew as he continued to hear the rhythmic creaking of the swing and hissing of the *karahi*. "Why has she been on the swing all day, and whatever in the world is she cooking which hasn't been prepared in all these hours?" he thought to himself.

When he hastened back to the palace and learnt that the princess had escaped, he set off to track her down by sniffing her out. Arriving in the same city, the *Deo* sensed that the princess might be hiding within the palace walls. Aware of the festive atmosphere in the city, he cunningly shape-shifted into a peddler, his basket overflowing with

دیو اور شہزادی

the most exquisite bangles ever crafted. With a guise of innocence, he sought permission to enter the palace grounds.

From behind the curtain separating the *mardaankhana* and the *zenankhana*,[78] everyone from the women of the royal household to the *kaneezs* extended their wrists eagerly,[79] and the *Deo* deftly slid a dozen bangles on each of them from his basket.[80] As the women took their turns, the *Deo* became increasingly apprehensive about the princess. The last in the queue, she finally stepped forward, her hand outstretched, the *Deo's* heart quickened with recognition. He tugged at her and, with a hushed tone, he whispered to her, "I shall come and take you away tomorrow. Be ready."

The princess rushed to the prince, her heart heavy with fear, and poured out her distress about the *Deo's* return. "He has found me and he shall not spare me. I don't want to die!" Tears streaked down her cheeks as she cried.

The prince gently wiped away her tears. "Please don't worry, my dear princess," he reassured her. "Let me think of a plan. Together, we shall outsmart this *Deo* and ensure your safety."

When the *Deo* came to the palace, the prince told him, "There she is," pointing to the princess through the window of the palace tower. "Go and take her. She awaits you," he said.

Now, the prince had the stairs in the tower replaced by wooden rungs which went 'round and 'round in circles. He ordered the steps to be kept very small so the *Deo* would have to go around the spiral multiple times before he reached the top. Buckets brimming with poisoned water were placed at three intervals so the *Deo* could drink his fill. With each laboured breath, the *Deo* ascended. Yet, as he reached the third bucket, weariness weighed heavy upon him. "Come down," he called to the princess, his voice laced with fatigue.

The poison tightened its grip, sapping the *Deo's* strength. She then seized her chance and pushed him from the power window with a single

---

78 *Mardaankhana:* The men's quarters.

79 *Zenankhana:* The women's quarters.

80 *Kaneez:* A member of the harem who is not a family member or wife. Whilst these girls were taken as slaves, their status was more like ladies-in-waiting, and not that of imperial concubines. In Islam, the son of a kaneez is an equally legitimate heir to the throne.

THE DEO AND THE PRINCESS

kick. The *Deo* plummeted to his end, the prince's trap, ensnaring its prey and securing the princess's freedom at last. The *Deo's* corpse was sent back to the Land of the *Deozaat,* who were told that he had fallen to death.[81]

The princess then went off on a journey to reunite with her long-lost parents. Once she had found them, she told them all about her harrowing ordeal. Now that, between the prince and his intelligence and the princess her courage, the *Deo* had been defeated, it became a tale. Soon after, the prince wasted no time in gathering a grand caravan and arrived at her father's palace with the *baraat.*[82] With joyful celebrations, he and his kingdom welcomed her as his bride, and they lived happily ever after.

---

81 *Deozaat:* Plural for Deo.

82 *Baraat:* The procession brought by the groom to wed the bride and take her with him.

9

ADAM KHAN DURKHANAYI

THE PICTURESQUE LANDSCAPES OF Swat, full of foliage, sprawling pastures, and meadows adorned with daffodils, were captured within the angelic melodies as Adam Khan's fingertips, brimming with *raag*,[83] strummed his *rabab*.[84] It seemed as if thousands of *Houra* had begun to sing and hundreds of koels and cuckoos began to tell the tales of longing and loneliness which ignited the daffodils, made the grazing grounds weep, and reduced the youthful energy of the emerald valleys to mere ashes.[85] His tunes ensnared fair maidens in a trance, halting their steps and erasing all memory of home, oftentimes leading to their earthen pitchers tumbling from their heads, shattering like their dreams. The *alaap* of romantic *tappay* echoed through their

---

83 *Raag:* A melodic framework for improvisation in classical Pashto. It is unique to the Indian subcontinent; no equivalent concept exists in Western classical music.

84 *Rabab:* A plucked string instrument. It is a part of Pashto folk music and is also the national musical instrument of Afghanistan. It is also used in traditional music in Balochistan, Sindh and Punjab.

85 *Houra:* Plural for *Hoor.* In Islamic belief, a *Hoor* is a beautiful, maiden promised as a reward to the righteous in paradise. They are described as pure, flawless, and beautiful beings, who shall provide companionship in the afterlife.

souls,[86] entwining with their hopes like wounded birds drawn into *raqs-e-bismil.*[87]

The fame of Adam Khan's enchanting melodies, his youthful vigour, pearly eyes, glowing wheatish complexion, the face of a fictional character, extremely attractive features, and the height and strength of a *Shamshad* tree had spread way beyond Upper Baz Daraye to all of Swat.[88] People of the valley envied his villagers. They used to say, "Malik Hassan Khan has such good fortune and luck. Allah has blessed him with wealth, land, and a son like Adam Khan."

Adam Khan was the apple of the eye of his tribe, and every young woman in the village was secretly in love with him. Their hearts were tangled with the strings of his *rabab*. But Adam Khan did not even meet their gaze. There was no one in his heart. His *ishq* was his *rabab*. He spoke to it, whispered his secrets to it, caressed it, his fingers played with its strings nearly all the time. The voice of his tunes was forever in search of an eternal melody. He had not yet found the woman who tugged at his heart more than his *rabab*. He closed his eyes, flowing in the stormy seas of the music he made in search of a woman prettier than a *jalperi*,[89] more enchanting than *Zohra* and *Mushtari.*[90] This woman had engraved herself on his heart and mind—who he wanted to be the queen to reign over his heart, who haunted his dreams, was a secret he

---

86 *Alaap:* Vocals before the song, no lyrics, common for Qawalli and Classical music in the region

87 *Tappay:* A form of poetry in oral tradition, in both Pashto and Punjabi; *Raqs-e-Bismil:* Literally, the movement of an animal just after a butcher slaughters it—in literature, it is used with sufi connotations, signifying tormented in extreme longing.

88 *Shamshad:* Buxus Wallichiana.

89 *Jalperi:* A mythological creature, half-woman and half-fish, absorbed into Pakistani folklore from Persian lore. Whilst she looks like a mermaid, her characteristics are quite different.

90 In Urdu poetry, *Zohra* (Venus) and *Mushtari* (Jupiter) symbolize beauty and grandeur, respectively, often used to illustrate the splendour of the beloved or the vastness of the universe. *Zohra,* representing the goddess of dawn, evokes themes of love and allure, while *Mushtari* signifies wisdom and majesty. Their celestial presence enriches the poetic imagery with layers of romantic and philosophical meaning.

آدم خان، دُرخانئی

told no one. Every moment he spent creating music was to honour the thought of this woman, to roam in her gardens, and to finally meet her.

His parents were living for their son. Now, they only had a single wish: to bring a bride for Adam Khan. But Adam Khan's wedding could only happen to the woman of his imagination. He flatly refused to get married. His parents, unaware of the background, asked his friends, who told them that he would marry the queen of his dreams. Adam's parents became concerned, thinking that he might have gone mad, owing to his passion for playing the *rabab* day-in and night-out.

One day, when Adam Khan was engrossed in playing his *rabab*, a sound fell on his ears which felt as sweet as nectar. He instantly became attentive. An old woman had come over as a guest from neighbouring Baaz Daraye Payyan and was busy chatting about the beauty of a maiden in her village: Taus Khan's only daughter, the gorgeous Durkhanayi. Adam felt affectionate towards the old woman, their guest, convinced that she had come from *Diyar-e-Mehboob*.[91] He believed that all which the old woman had said could only be true about his lover. After that, Adam Khan began to describe Durkhanayi's appearance to the old lady. When he mentioned the mole on her left cheek and the small scar on her forehead, the old lady said, "I swear you have seen Durkhanayi."

"No, I haven't, *khala*.[92] My dreams are true, my love is eternal, and my *ishq* is as pure as streamwater."[93]

"Ah!" the old woman let out a cold sigh. "Alas! All of this is in vain. Durkhanayi is engaged to a Khan of Payao." The old woman's words turned Adam Khan's world upside down. Delusion cast a shadow on him. He became even more obsessed with his *rabab* and played so beautifully that its strings almost found a tongue.

They say the fire of love never burns one. The old woman went back to her village and recounted Adam Khan's dreams to Durkhanayi. The old woman was too astonished for words when, in response, Durkhanayi narrated some of her dreams to her and mentioned Adam Khan's appearance, as well as the heartwrenching music of his *rabab*.

---

91 *Diyar-e-Mehboob:* "House of the Beloved"

92 *Khala:* Literally, "maternal aunt"; also used to address older women who may be around your mother's age or her friends.

93 *Ishq:* The highest stage of love.

Every night, in her dreams, Durkhanayi found Adam Khan with his *rabab* sitting by a lakeside. As soon as the tune touched its highest octave, Durkhanayi, like a *peri*,[94] danced in the skies and disappeared into the melody. When Adam Khan used to separate the *mizrab* from his *rabab*, Durkhanayi woke up with a start from her divine dream with the sound of his *rabab* continuing to ring in her ears.[95]

The old woman took the message of Durkhanayi's love and a present of flowers to Adam Khan. Upon hearing this, Adam felt as if he had been jolted awake and whiplashed. He began to play his *rabab* even more with a zeal he had never known before. She also told him that soon Durkhanayi would come to Upper Baaz Daraye for a wedding.

And then, at the wedding ceremony, Adam Khan did not only show off his talent. He wanted to convey his passion, love, and *ishq*. He wanted to melt and burn for the woman in his heart. It was as if someone had cast a spell on the entire gathering—a spell of love. When his gaze found Durkhanayi and he saw the queen of his dreams in the flesh, he realised that she was even prettier than he had imagined. Adam's feelings breathed life into the strings of his *rabab*. He played the tune of love for his beloved in her very presence.

After seeing Durkhanayi once, Adam's state continued to worsen by the day. His cure was with Durkhanayi. His confidants and his friends, Mehru and Babu, could not bear to see him like this, so they carried off Adam to *Diyar-e-Mehboob*. One night, beneath the blanket of stars, the two lovebirds met. They greeted each other with pearls of tears and a flood of sobs, singing a song of cold sighs. After exchanging greetings, they observed *khiraj e muhabbat* with a moment of silence.[96] When the clouds of sighs dispersed, the rain of tears began. Both horizons of love and *ishq* smiled. "Oh, you princess of my dreams. 'Til when will you keep wandering about? Come, become a part of me like the melodies of my

---

94 *Peri:* A winged creature, exclusively feminine, known for being gentle, kind, and beautiful.

95 *Mizrab:* Also known as a zakhma, is used for several Iranian and Indian string instruments. For a Sitar, a mizrab is worn on the finger of a sitar player. It is a plectrum made by hand from a continuous strand of iron used to strike the strings of the sitar.

96 *Khiraj e Muhabbat:* An ode of love.

rabab. Entwine yourself with my heart like its strings. Come, become one with me like the *mizrab* on my fingertips," Adam said.

"My lover, my musician of a lover, I, too, eagerly await to immerse myself in your world. Without one another, we are incomplete, like the *rabab* and its music, the *mizrab* and the strings. Oh, my dear moon, the world is like a dark night for me. I search for you everywhere, like the *chakor*, but all I find is traps everywhere."[97] Durkhanyi responded, holding his gaze.

"But my beautiful Darkho! Your engagement? Your wedding? Will my rabab be snatched from my hands? Will I be suffocated and the melodies of my alaap and tappay be put to sleep—the sleep of death? Will the soul of my tunes be strangled? Will my rabab be handed over to some Julaha?[98] Is this true, Durkhanayi?"

"My gorgeous Darkho. My beloved musician—stop singing out-of-tune songs. Do you not have faith in your rabab anymore? A rabab is not the only thing you own. You also have a gun. If the mizrab cannot do the job, it can always be replaced with a cartridge. This is a requirement for the Yousafzai Pakhtuns—it is a test of courage and strength. I am for you, and you are for me. No one can take me away from you. A rabab can break, but unskilled fingers cannot play a fine tune."

The spinning of the stars in the sky wrecked the night full of romance like a gust of wind. The two hearts had not even finished confiding in one another when the rooster called out. The sheep tied up in the courtyard of Durkhanayi's house began to bleat. Adam Khan and Durkhanayi instantly became alert, as if they had been shaken awake. A curse escaped Durkhayi's lips, "Oh, the sheep of my father, may you get ulcers in your throat. You have parted my beloved from me." The two exchanged rings and parted like the sun and the moon.

The fire had been lit in both hearts. Durkhanayi, feigning sickness, lay herself down on a charpoy. She thought that, if she is ill, her wedding might be called off, or she might be able to buy herself some time anyway. However, the elderly woman of the village believed that she would regain her health as soon as she was wed. And so, the move backfired

---

97 The words *chand* and *chakor* are used together. *Chand*, the moon, *chakor*, a nocturnal bird which spends its entire lifetime staring at the moon and dies pining for it. It symbolises the loved and the beloved.

98 *Julaha:* The Weaver Cast.

and her wedding date was moved up. Amid the sounds of the *dhol* and the *surna*,[99] her *doli* was lifted—as was the *Janaza* of beauty,[100] her heart,[101] and her dreams.[102] She was writhing in pain in her *doli*, like a crane with clipped wings or an injured duck.

When she moved to her new prison, her husband's house, she truly fell ill. The *Hakeems* there believed it to be tuberculosis.[103] Whilst they treated her, Durkhanayi smiled. She knew that the ache in her heart would not subside with *dawaa daru*.[104] "Yeah, right. It is T.B. What would you know of *ishq*? And what treatment could you possibly have for it?" she used to think to herself, laughing at the doctors in secret. When the medicine did not work, Durkhanayi was sent back to her parents.

"Durkhanayi has gone to the home of the adversary." The news shook Adam Khan's feelings and he nearly lost his wits. For once, he understood what it meant to be *Majnun*.[105] His *rabab* had been snatched from him, his *mizrab* had been stolen, and his honour had been attacked.

"Durkhanayi fell very ill and has been sent back to her parents. She is now a guest...only Allah knows how long she has." This news rubbed salt into his wounds, it disturbed what was left of his sanity. Adam's parents were very upset to see their son in such a sorry state. Soon, his father confided in one of his closest friends, Meermayi, and they decided that Durkhanayi would be brought to Adam Khan—if not amicably, then by force. Meermayi and Hassan Khan besieged Taus Khan's home with their parties of armed men. A feud broke out and, after a lot of hard work, Adam Khan found his pearl of destiny. However, fate was watching, smiling—it had other plans.

---

99 *Dhol:* A type of local drum.

100 *Surna:* A local double-reed instrument.

101 *Doli:* Literally, a palanquin made of wood in which women used to travel. It is also customary for the bride's brothers and cousins to carry her in a *doli* to bring her to the venue of her wedding, marking her final day at her paternal home.

102 *Janaza:* The funeral procession in Muslim tradition.

103 *Hakeem:* A Hakeem is a wise person and healer specializing in herbal medicine, with expertise particularly in Vedic and Islamic medical traditions.

104 *Dawaa Daru:* Literally, medicines and wine. It is a phrase used metaphorically to explain that something has no cure.

105 *Majnun:* Being a madman in love; a reference to the tale of Qays and Layla.

When Taus and the Khans of Payao realised that it was impossible to recover Durkhanayi with their swords, they used wealth as bait. Meermayi, despite being well-off, fell for the trap. He sacrificed all those years of friendship for gold, just as he sacrificed Adam Khan as his beloved. Durkhanayi went back to her gilded cage. One moment, her tears formed a *Sheesh Mahal,* and the next moment, it shattered into a thousand pieces, but the sounds went unheard.[106]

Adam Khan's *rabab,* once lost but now found, had slipped through his fingers once more. There seemed to be no point in searching for it anew. It would be akin to chasing a flickering flame amidst settled ashes or yearning to hear the love-laden melody of a koel silenced forever. However, Meeru and Babu loved Adam Khan too much to lose their friend. They decided to bring back both his Durkhanayi and his *rabab* to him.

The next day, Meeru, Babu, and Adam Khan, dressed as *faqirs,* made their way to *Diyar-e-Mehboob.* Outside the village, near the *mazaar* of Shaheed Baba, they lit a fire and sat around it.[107] Within moments, the news spread like wildfire throughout the village that three *dervishes* had come to visit them. People rushed to the mazaar. Soon, it was teeming with people, resembling a little *mela* of sorts, asking them to pray to Allah for their sake.[108] They also gave away amulets and talismans to the people. Lovesick Adam Khan prayed for everyone and instilled hope in everyone, but there was no one to return the favour for him...that was until the old woman, Adam and Durkhanayi's confidant, found him and told him, "My son. You are young, and you are Pakhtun. You must not lose hope. Do not let your courage falter. Durkhanayi is yours, fear not. You shall have her one day."

---

106 *Sheesh Mahal:* The Sheesh Mahal is a famous architectural landmark in Lahore, Pakistan, a palace built entirely of glass. It is built with the light and mirror effect. The hall is constructed in such a manner, that even if a single ray of light enters, then it gets replicated in the mirrors, while the entire hallway gets enlightened.

107 *Mazaar:* A shrine or tomb of a revered Islamic saint or religious figure, often a site of pilgrimage and devotion. It serves as a spiritual centre where devotees gather to seek blessings, offer prayers, and pay respects to the saint's memory.

108 *Mela:* A fair usually included games, a circus, and shops selling wares.

Word of the *dervishes* also reached Taus Khan. The old woman went to his house and said, "Khan! *Khuda* and his *dervishes* have everything.[109] People say these *dervishes* are great men. Go to them. Perhaps their prayers will be answered and Allah will be merciful to our little girl, our twig of flowers. Allah can even bring the dead back to life!" When Taus Khan agreed, the old woman went to Durkhanayi to deliver the good news to her. "My child, the flower which fell from your orbal has been found. Be careful with it and put it in your hair. The winds are strong—a storm is brewing. If you lose it this time, you will never be able to find even a single petal of it."

With a heart beating loudly and uncertain footsteps, Adam Khan made his way to *Dar-e-Mehboob*. The romantic melodies of his *rabab* rushed through his veins. He reached his destination of dreams, plucking flowers, running his hand through the foliage, hopping, and skipping around.

Durkhanayi, the willowed Daffodil of Swat's Nargistan, the withered flower and the leaf struck by autumn, was lying on her bed. When their eyes met one another, tears rained from their eyes. Within seconds, the lovesicks told one another a thousand tales of the ache of separation. The flower of Durkhanayi's beauty was like a thorn in Adam Khan's soul. His hand clutched at his chest; his tongue failed him and he fainted, letting out a piercing cry. Taus Khan's hawkish eyes, forever observant, understood what had ensued. At first, he wanted to finish Adam Khan off with his sword in a single blow and chop him to pieces. However, the old woman held his hand. "It would be wise to bury this incident here and now, in a way that the job is done and you are not blamed for it."

When Adam Khan regained his senses, he found himself on the cold floor in a dark room. Taus Khan was furious, swinging his sword. He yelled, "Leave my village immediately."

Adam Khan felt as if someone had taken him to paradise and chucked him out, as if he had been made to return thirsty from the raging sea, as if he had reached out to break a flower from a garden to set it in his pagri, but his hands had been broken and he came back, or rather, was brought back to his village. His soul still wandered near *Diyar-e-Mehboob*. He was but a skeleton in Hassan Khan's house—a body, like a *rabab*

---

109 *Khuda:* Literally "God." In this context, it means Allah. *Khuda* is the pre-Islamic word for "God." In Pashto, unless it is a religious context, the word Khuda is used to refer to Allah instead.

without music. He began to hate everything in this world—everything beautiful, even his *rabab* and its melodies.

One day, as he was lost in thought and his eyes were searching for his beloved Darkho in the distance, he saw his *rabab*. His eyes became full of rage, so he fetched an axe and chopped up his *rabab* into pieces. It was no longer his beloved; it was his enemy.

His condition got worse by the day and soon, Hussainn Khan realised that his only son, his heir and the next chief of the tribe, would be lost, so he became restless. No treatment, no medicine, no *taweez* would cure him.[110] Finally, Husainn Khan decided to arrange for Gulnar, the prettiest girl in the village, to meet him. He hoped it would sort out the matter, make him forget Durkhanayi and perhaps make a dried-up spring gush forth once more.

Gulnar was beautiful indeed. With her rosy cheeks and dark hair plaited tightly, the *paizwaan* which danced on her lips, [111] and a string of flowers adorning her *orbal*, it was as if she was the princess of daffodils.[112] However, Adam Khan was not impressed. His standard of beauty was that of the heavens, the *houris*, and the angels. Everywhere he looked, he could only see Durkhanayi. He saw her in a mirage, calling out to him everywhere he went, and when he used to walk over to her, she used to disappear, leaving a stain on his chest. The longer he was separated from his beloved, the more his madness took over.

Finally, one day, the words "Adam Khan is no more" wreaked havoc on Baaz Dara. Some said, "Our musician is dead." Others said, "The truthful lover is gone." Durkhanayi's *rabab* had been silenced forever. The melodies went silent in Baaz Daraye and wailing began instead.

She was lying on her bed as her dreams kept her company. In the entire village of her father, it was only the old woman who knew of Durkhanayi's pain and never left her side. However, no one listened to the poor old woman. Durkhanayi's mother no longer felt affection for her daughter, it was as if her heart had been replaced with stone. The honour of the family and the tribe overpowered whatever affection her

---

110 *Taweez:* Inscriptions from Islamic tradition worn around the wrist or the neck, used as a talisman and sometimes as a curse.

111 *Paizwaan:* A specific kind of nose ring—large, and attached to a chain, held by the hair.

112 *Orbal:* Pushto for forelock, a bang of hair.

parents had for her. One day, she dreamed that she was roaming about in a beautiful meadow with her friends when she heard the tune of a *rabab*.

Following the sound, she saw Adam Khan, in a boat made of silver, playing his *rabab*. Like a mermaid, she walked over the waters of the lake, and Adam Khan held her hand. "My beautiful Darkho, I shall never let you go again. Stay with me. We will build our village here. Let's live on this boat and never worry about anything ever again." She smiled at him. Just as he kissed her forehead, the lake morphed into a sea and a fierce storm broke out. The boat capsized, and Durkhanayi woke up with a scream.

The old woman was sitting by her side on her charpoy. She tried to calm her down, but all Darkho could muster was a whimper, "Adam. Adam Khan. I saw him drown. Did he make it out of the storm?" The old woman began to weep. "My child. Adam Khan has been sacrificed on the altar of the stubbornness of your parents. He is no more. He spent his last moments, in pain, calling out for you." Darkho slumped back into her pillow, face down, sobbing. For several minutes, she kept sobbing. When she ceased to cry, the old woman tried to lift her head. Durkhanayi let out a whisper, "Adam Khan." and she, too, went silent, forever.

10

BEHRAM AND
PERI GULAB BANO

ROM THE MOUNTAINS OF Kif came down Safed,[113] the King of
the *Deozaat*, to visit the kingdoms beyond his and the veil.[114]
Wandering around the land, he decided to take a stroll through
a forest. He saw a small party of huntsman giving chase to a deer. The
young lad leading the party was strikingly handsome, and Safed felt
something for him deep inside his bones. Safed was struck and felt like
he would never know contentment in his life unless he possessed the
boy. After following them around for a while, Safed learned that he was
Prince Behram.

Safed shape-shifted into a beautiful mare with snowy skin and a neigh
like thunder and crossed paths with the prince every now and again to
grab Behram's attention. Struck by the beauty and the finesse of the
mare, Behram gave the orders to capture it. Safed, graceful and docile,
waited 'til he was saddled and bridled. However, as soon as the prince
hopped onto the mare's back, Safed galloped far, far away, so quickly
that the world seemed to whoosh past Behram and stopped when he
had taken the prince back to his palace in his kingdom.

---

113 *Safed:* Refers to the colour, white. Safed is also the King of the Deozaat
in the local mythological tradition. He is referred to as "The White One"
because he is described to be so.

114 *Deozaat:* Plural for *Deo;* the Persian *Div,* known as the *Deo* in several languages in Pakistan, is a supernatural being, gigantic in size, and often evil.

بہرام اور پری گلاب بانو

Safed tried his best to appease Behram by showering him with favours, treasure chests full of gold coins and precious stones, lots of servants, the finest clothes, and magnificent chambers.

Eight days later, Safed came to Behram and told him, "I shall now leave you for eight days. I must go and attend my brother's wedding. You, however, will remain here. But I am giving you this key. It will allow you to visit the palace patio. No one has seen it 'til today, apart from myself, so when you go, go alone, and remember to lock the door again when you return." Handing Behram the keys, he set off for his brother's palace.

The following evening, Behram decided to go see the garden for himself. It was beyond anything that he had ever imagined, let alone seen! Beautiful fountains bubbling into pools lined the edges of the garden and a pavilion of jasper inlaid with precious stones stood in between. The trees bore sapphires, rubies, and emeralds for fruit. As he sat down, he watched on as the fountains threw up a glistering, golden spray, which made the most enchanting reflections in the pools. Just then, four milk-white doves flew onto a tree and took the shape of four *peris* as they settled by the edge of a tank of crystal-clear water.[115] Their beauty left Behram a little dazzled.

The fairies undressed, daintily dived into the tank with a plop, and began to bathe. As they were bathing, one of them said, "I had a dream. In my dream, I saw that one of us will be parted from the rest."

They stepped one by one out of the water and robed themselves. It so happened that the prettiest *peri* from the four, Gulab Bano, could not find her clothes. Meanwhile, the others, having finished dressing, turned themselves into doves again and flew away. She called out to them, "It is what has been written for me. We part here, and we shall never meet again. My destiny awaits me here."

She looked around and her gaze became fixated on the pavilion, where Prince Behram sat on the steps. She fell in love with him at first sight; she felt as if her heart was no longer hers. Now, it was the prince himself who had stolen the *peri*s clothes and hidden them. He had seen her, and she had caught his eye. He knew that if she got her clothes back, she would take the form of a dove and fly far, far away from him.

---

115 *Peri:* A winged creature, exclusively feminine, known for being gentle, kind and beautiful.

He offered her another dress and looked away as she changed. The two lovers remained in the garden for eight days, 'til Safed returned.

Upon seeing huge chains which hung from his waist, Behram began to tremble with fear. Safed reassured the prince, saying, "Why do you fear, do you not own all I possess?" Anyhow, the *Deo* ordered the musicians to play and girls to dance to the tunes to try to beguile the young prince and to lift his spirits. Behram could not see the dancing girls, although he could hear the tunes. "Do you see them?" asked the *Deo*.

"I do not," replied the prince, "the girls and the musicians are invisible, but I do hear the music and the tinkling of anklets."

"I will give you some antimony. It belonged to our king, *Hazrat Suleman*.[116] Bring it close to your face and allow it to touch your eyes," Safed told him. Prince Behram obeyed and suddenly, he saw the whole place filled with troops of dainty maidens, performing exquisitely to the music of *rababs*[117] and *tablas*.[118]

Now, Gulab Bano, the *peri* Prince Behram had fallen in love with, happened to be Safed's wife. Despite knowing everything which had happened, Safed told Behram, "Take Gulab Bano and take everything which belongs to me if you wish." That is how much Safed loved Behram. Behram took the *peri* for his bride, and they began to live happily together in the palace Safed had given Behram.

One day, the *peri* felt homesick, so she asked Behram, "Please let me go visit my parents, I miss them very much. I promise to come back to you." So, the prince returned her *peri* robes to her, she turned into a dove, and away she flew. When her parents found out that she had fallen in love with a mortal and married a child of a man, they became furious. They imprisoned her in a cramped-up house, in a gloomy, subterranean

---

116 Hazrat Suleman is the Prophet Suleman (A); or Solomon. In Islamic tradition, he is believed to have also ruled over the Jinns, besides humankind and the animal kingdom.

117 *Rabab:* A plucked string instrument. It is a part of Pashto folk music and is also the national musical instrument of Afghanistan. It is also used in traditional music in Balochistan, Sindh, and Punjab.

118 *Tabla:* A pair of hand drums. Since the eighteenth century, it has been the principal percussion instrument in local folk and classical music, where it may be played solo, as an accompaniment with other instruments and vocals, or as a part of larger ensembles.

city. Time went on and on, but Gulab Bano did not return. Behram began to pine for his beloved, and his sorrow began to weigh down on his shoulders. Safed, too, grew melancholic and sad seeing his youthful, cheery friend so desolate. When Behram could no longer take the pain of separation, he pleaded with Safed. "I must follow her, I need to find her, I shall not return without her," he cried.

"Have you made your decision, are you sure you want to go?" Safed asked him.

"I can no longer live," said the prince, "without her."

Safed gave the prince three things to take along with him on his journey—an invisible cap, King Suleman's antimony, and some of his hair—as Behram set out on his way.[119] After several days, the prince arrived at the subterranean city, only to find it clouded with darkness. Unable to find his way, he rubbed his eyes with the antimony. Lo and behold! Every nook and cranny, every path and track appeared in his view. Upon asking a few passers-by for the whereabouts of Gulab Bano, he found out that she was imprisoned in a lofty tower with one hundred iron doors.

The prince made his way to the tower and put on the magic cap. The cap not only made him invisible, but it also made the hundred iron doors fly wide open! He ran inside, his heart racing, thrilled at the thought of seeing her again, his princess, his *peri*, his Gulab Bano. He took off his cap once he was inside and rushed into her arms. They remained together for many days.

However, a woman can rarely ever keep a secret. It was not long before Gulab Bano whispered to some of the maids who she liked to give the good news to her friends, and how good fortune had walked to her, even amid banishment. The news began to spread like wildfire and soon reached the ears of her father. He put together a party of *deozaat*, and headed straight to the tower, only to find the prince and the *peri* fast asleep in her bed.

Horrified, they decided to finish the prince off for good, crying, "Come, let us kill him!" The hue and cry aroused the prince from his slumber. Judging the gravity of the situation, he whipped on the magic cap and turned himself invisible. He then held a lock of Safed's hair over the flame of an oil lamp. As the smoke rose, a thousand squadrons of

---

119 A reference to the Prophet Suleman (A) or Solomon.

deozaat appeared at once, as did Safed himself. A fierce battle followed, but the enraged and humiliated father was forced to surrender and give up his daughter to the prince. After that, Safed, Prince Behram, and Gulab Bano happily returned home in triumph.

As it had been a few years since Behram had been away from his kingdom, he had begun to feel a little lonely without his people and felt homesick. His longing grew and grew, 'til he became determined to go back home. Although it made Safed very sad, the *Deo* king allowed the prince to leave with the *peri* princess.

Gulab Bano transformed herself into an enormous bird, and the prince mounted on her back between her wings, and within a few moments, they had arrived at the capital of Behram's kingdom. There, the prince disguised himself as a hermit, while the *peri* changed into a dove. Then he entered the city and called on his old nurse. The old woman recognised the prince at once! He warned the prince that one of the viziers had seized the kingdom and was ruling in the king's stead. "And where are my wives?" asked Behram.

"He took three of your wives for himself. For her disobedience, the fourth has been imprisoned in a pit, where she bore a son. She is fed the leftovers of his hounds." The *peri* had taken her real shape for the time when the prince was staying with his nurse. One day, news reached the palace to the illegitimate king, that a woman who possesses grace, elegance, and beauty unlike any other woman on earth had been seen at the lodgings of the old woman.

Without a second thought, the evil king rushed to the dwellings of the nurse and seized Gulab Bano. "Come with me at once!" he ordered her.

"Oh, king! Allow me to change my clothes first." The king nodded. Leaving him waiting by the door, Gulab Bano entered her bedroom and put on her magic dress. As soon as she donned her special outfit, she shape-shifted, taking the form of a beautiful dove, and flew out of the window. She flew as fast as her little wings would carry her, far, far away, whilst the king returned to his palace, vanquished and confused.

When Behram returned to the lodgings of his nurse, he inquired, "Where is my wife?"

"She is gone," the woman informed him. "The vizier came to take her away."

Without a second thought, unaware that Gulab Bano had escaped, in his fury, Prince Behram took out a few strands of the *Deo's* hair and held it in a flame once again. Instantly, thousands of *deozaat* armed with clubs and swords rushed to his aid. The city was taken, and the vizier and the three wives who had been disloyal to Behram were put to the sword. The fourth wife was restored to her place as the queen. Behram lived in the palace, ruling justly in the companionship of his fourth wife.

Although he was always good and kind to her, his heart yearned for Gulab Bano, the *peri* princess. He began to wander around his city, the forest, and the palace as melancholy overpowered him. People began to say that he was nearing madness. He searched in vain for the woman who was the love of his life but had flown to the house of her parents, only to never return.

On the other hand, Deo Safed also grew tired of his longing for his friend, so he set out to look for Prince Behram. Once he found Behram's kingdom, he whisked Behram away to his palace, where he also brought back Gulab Bano to him. Behram recovered from his madness and spent the rest of his life happily ever after, sometimes with Gulab Bano in the mountains of Kif, and sometimes in his capital with his faithful wife. But at last, one day, he left his mortal wife for good, never to return home again, and presumably joined *Peri* Gulab Bano 'till the end of his days.

11

MOMIN KHAN SHIREENO

MANY CENTURIES AGO, IN the village of Rohistan, there lived two very popular and extremely powerful Khans. Blood brothers, the older one was the *Sardar* of the tribe and had seven sons, the oldest of whom was known as Zabardast Khan.[120] The younger one had no children.

One day, he was lost in thought, looking sorrowful, when his older brother probed him about what was worrying him. He tried to brush away the matter. However, being an intelligent man, the older brother guessed what the matter was. He consoled his younger brother, "Nothing is scarce for Allah. One day, He shall make you rich with the wealth of offspring."

Coincidentally, the tree of expectation bore fruit for the wives of both brothers in the same year. Both performed *Sajda-e-Shuker*.[121] The older brother told his younger brother, "I promise you, that if I have a girl, and you have a baby boy, I shall give my daughter to him. If you are blessed with a daughter, and I have another son, we shall bead our pearls in the same string."

Days passed by, and finally the day came when both the brothers loaded their rifles, awaiting news. They hoped to be ready to celebrate

---

120 *Sardar:* Head of the Tribe.

121 *Sajda-e-Shuker:* Prostrating in prayer in front of Allah with the intention of thanking him for something; particularly when you have prayed for something for a long time.

with aerial firing for whichever one of them had a son. The older one was blessed with a daughter and the younger one was blessed with a son. To celebrate, they fired rounds upon rounds, as a father and an uncle, to celebrate this welcome news. Both were overjoyed. The names Shireeno and Momin Khan were suggested for the children. After that, both the brothers announced their decision to the entire clan: that Momin Khan and Shireeno were promised to one another. They're not just cousins—they're also engaged to be married.

The two frisked about when they were little. They used to play together, eat together, and even throw childish tantrums when they wanted to nap together. Both the brothers were very happy to see them get along so well. At last, *Malak al Mawt* snatched away the brothers from the tribe.[122] Momin Khan and Shireeno felt the loss of their fathers very deeply. In mourning, they wailed and sobbed 'til their throats became sore and they became overwhelmed with exhaustion due to grief.

After their father passed away, the sons of the older brother began to fight amongst themselves for the leadership of the clan. All seven brothers were contesting for it. When the *Jirga* was called, the elders of the tribe said, "We shall unanimously accept whatever you guys decide amongst yourselves."[123]

Momin Khan, too, presented his claim to the *Jirga:* "After my uncle, my father would have been the *Sardar*. Now that he is no longer, it makes me the rightful inheritor of the *pagri*."[124] Because Momin Khan was the most intelligent, capable, and virtuous among his cousins, half the clan sided with him. The other half chose to side with Zabardast Khan, both of whom became de-facto chiefs of each half the tribe. Momin Khan paid a dear price for the *Sardari*.[125] Zabardast Khan and his brothers began to seethe with jealousy. They simply could not stand his popularity. Momin, however, could not care less about what his cousins think.

One day, his mother tried to make him understand the gravity of the situation. "Momin, my son, your cousins harbour nothing in their hearts but malice, jealousy, and enmity. They are planting thorns in your path. Zabardast Khan takes great pride in his six brothers; he will crush you

---

122 *Malak al Mawt:* The angel of death.

123 *Jirga:* A council of tribal elders.

124 *Pagri:* A type of headgear worn by men in Pakistan.

125 *Sardari:* Leadership of the tribe.

like an ant. Send the elders of the tribe to Zabardast Khan to discuss your marriage to Shireeno with him, or you shall regret it."

Had Shireeno's name not been mentioned, Momin Khan would not have paid much heed to his mother's words. He thought that something would need to be done for Shireeno. So, he prepared a *Jirga* of the old and well-respected elders of the tribe and sent them to Zabardast Khan. When the *Jirga* asked Zabardast Khan about Shireeno's marriage, he outrightly denied everything. He said, "Neither did our father give Shireeno to Momin, and nor are we ready to do such a thing."

The *Jirga* told him that his father had announced it in front of the entire clan. "All of us are witnesses that it is so. It is why the entire tribe is here, in front of you, as a *Jirga*. If you go against Pakhtun custom and tradition and send back a *Jirga* unsuccessful, it will not bode well."

Zabardast Khan realised that the situation could escalate, so he said, "I will accept this proposal, and give Shireeno to Momin Khan on one condition. My father's silver shield weighs one *mann*. It has been in our family for centuries. Momin Khan is to provide twelve such shields, twelve *mann* of silver, as Shireeno's bride price."[126]

When the *Jirga* accepted the condition, Zabardast Khan gaped at them open-mouthed. He was not expecting the *Jirga* to accept such an absurd demand. "Neither will there ever be so much, nor will it ever happen," he thought to himself. However, now his hands were tied. He had made a promise, and a Pakhtun cannot go back on his word. He happily saw off the *Jirga*.

When the elders of the tribe informed Momin Khan of the decision, his face went red with anger. "His father gave Shireeno away for free—and the brothers? They want to sell her. Shameless. Cursed be their honour. But from where shall I bring twelve *mann* of silver? This means I shall have to leave my family, homeland, and tribe behind, travel to Hindustan, work there, and find a way to produce twelve *mann* of silver to marry Shireeno. But whatever happens, I shall go," he announced decisively.

Momin Khan began to prepare for travel. Someone passed the news to Shireeno, and her world was enveloped in darkness. She gave her brothers the slip and sneaked out quietly to Momin's house. "Oh, the crown of my head, you are preparing for travel, but to whom are you

---

126 *Mann:* A local measuring unit, about forty kilograms.

entrusting this garden full of flowers to before you leave? What if a cursed gust of autumn wind destroys it?" she sobbed.

"This garden is entrusted to my *Khuda*, and He is its guardian.[127] If autumn tries to destroy it, I shall be back to chop its hands off. Shireeno! Your brother has asked for twelve *mann* of silver in exchange for you. Now I will come back from Hindustan with this silver and marry you."

"Oh, my childhood friend Momin! You are going to Hindustan, but I have heard that the girls there are very cunning and clever. They enchant young men with magic. What if they entice you and steal you from me? How will you face the clan then? A Pakhtun never let go of his honour and his chastity. Momin Khan! Do not give your cousins a chance to mock you."

"My beautiful Shireeno, all the girls in Hindustan are my sisters. They can never entice me. Their charm can never compete with your beautiful face and your rosy cheeks." With these words, he spurred his horse forward, and his steed began to speak to the winds.

Shireeno laid the pearls of her tears and the flower petals of her prayers in his path. She said, "Momin Khan, my beloved, the Sardar of the tribe, has set off on his horse. There is a stream of tears rolling down my cheeks. You did not even turn around to glance at my *sheen khaal* even once, the girls of Hindustan do not adorn their cheeks with it. [128] If any one of them so much as dares to look at you, I will scoop out her eyes with a spindle. My locks and my *sheen khaal* are entrusted to you. The treasure chest of my kisses is locked, just for you, and it shall remain locked. Eid only comes after fasting for an entire month of *Ramzan*."[129]

Outside the village, everyone gathered to see off Momin Khan. The elders of the tribe tried to convince him to stay back, but he said, "I shall go, and fulfil the condition the *Jirga* has accepted, or else, my tribe will lose its honour in front of my cousins."

---

127 *Khuda:* The pre-Islamic term of "God" and is now used to refer to Allah in various ethnic languages in Pakistan, including Pashto; originally a Persian word.

128 *Sheen Khaal:* Geometric green-blue tattoos on the chin, cheeks, mid-brow, and forehead of young. For Pashtun women, a symbol of beauty, that makes use of natural ingredients only.

129 *Ramzan:* The ninth month in the lunar Islamic calendar in which Muslims fast from dawn to dusk.

Raidi Gul Khan, an old and very loyal friend of Momin Khan's, travelled with him. The days and the nights passed by, as did a lot of towns and cities. Where are they going? They had no idea. They had not yet decided on what their precise destination would be. At last, they reached a city in Hindustan where custom dictated that everyone veiled their faces, men and women alike. Raidi Gul said, "Cover your face, Momin. You're handsome, and we don't want your fair face causing mischief."

Momin Khan did so and, in the *bazaar*, he crossed paths with the royal guard.[130] Seeing it, his heart became full of lust and envy—he wished that he, too, had a retinue. With his thoughts tangled, he lifted the veil from his face. Suddenly, his face caught the eye of a guard. Impressed with how good-looking the young man was, in this distraction, his foot bumped into something, he stumbled, and his lance fell out of his hands, lodging itself in his stomach. Seeing this, Radio Gul quickly fixed Momin Khan's veil and hurried out of the *bazaar*, finding a caravanserai to stay at.

The incident of the guard was no small thing. Within moments, the news spread like wildfire throughout the city. When he was investigated and the guard recounted what had happened, word reached the king, who ordered this stranger to be presented at his court immediately. When the government officials came to the caravanserai in their search for Momin Khan, he greeted them very hospitably. When they showed him the Shahi Farmaan, he presented himself as soon as he could in the royal court, along with Raidi Gul. Whilst the magnificence of the durbar and the finesse of the palace impressed Momin and Raidi, Momin's good looks left all, even the king, awestruck. The Shah asked Momin to sit beside him and asked him about his whereabouts. He told him that he has travelled from the northwest and is the son of so-and-so Malik. The king was pleased to hear this and hosted him in the palace as a royal guest. Whilst he was comfortable, Momin missed Shireeno—it was all that bothered him.

One day, a *Peer*, clad in green, came to visit Momin Khan in his dreams. "Get up and try your hand, *pehelwani*."[131]

When he woke up, he thought to himself that there must have been a good reason for such a dream. So, the next day, he requested the Shah

---

130 *Bazaar:* Market.

131 *Pehelwani:* A traditional art of athletics and a form of martial arts which originated in Iran.

to order one of the *pehelwans* at court to wrestle him.[132] The Shah smiled and said, "Momin Khan, you are my guest, I do not want you to get injured. I don't think you can fight the seasoned *pehelwans* at our court. God forbid, if you break a bone or a rib, it shall cause a scandal." Momin Khan insisted anyway and, finally, the Shah gave in and called in a *pehelwan*.

People gathered around to see the spectacle. When both of them went down into the *akhara*, the king became very concerned.[133] He was afraid that Momin Khan would end up getting hurt, so he prayed for his victory. The people were shocked to see Momin Khan put his arm around the back of the royal *pehelwan*, lift him over his head, and spin him around. He slowly set down the *pehelwan* on the sand and the king was grateful that Momin had not ended up with a broken bone. The king was also glad to have found a *pehelwan* at his doorstep.

Momin Khan was given a place at the durbar to the Shah's right. Now, he began to yield considerable influence in court. One day, a letter was presented to the Shah, who did not wish for Momin Khan to see it. However, when Momin insisted, he showed him the letter, and when he read the letter, he became furious. He got up and said, "How dare someone ask our king for tribute? I will not stand for us paying taxes to anyone."

The Shah told him that they were happy to pay tribute. As long as it kept the peace, there was no need to fight. But Momin Khan said that it would not happen on his watch, and he would raze the enemy to the ground. The king allowed Momin and Raidi to set off after Momin refused to heed anyone's words. The following day, they left early morning.

When they reached the city of the king who had asked for taxes, he first went to a goldsmith and ordered horseshoes made of gold for his horse. At first, the smith thought that the young man was joking. He only got to work after Raidi Gul gave him a stare and asked him, "Do you think of us as jokers? Get to work before my chief picks you up and slams you on the ground."

Amid the noise and chatter of the *bazaar*, Momin Khan saw a beautiful maiden riding a camel. However, she was crying. "Help! Help! Please

---

132 *Pehelwan:* A fighter trained in Pehelwani (also spelt as *Pahlavani*).

133 Akhara: An open-air traditional wrestling ground; an area for physical exercise or practising wrestling.

save me from my father's tyranny," she called out. People looked at her sympathetically, but said, "Dear Princess, we would help you, but it is not our right, now that you have a fiance."

Momin Khan's heart softened and asked the goldsmith what the matter was. "Unfortunately, an *azdaha* has found the road to the city.[134] It requires the sacrifice of a girl and a camel every day. If we fail, it comes into the city and wreaks havoc. Today, it is her turn to be sacrificed. That is her fiance, Wazirzada, tall but a coward."

Seeing all this, Momin Khan missed Shireeno. He could almost see her in front of him, calling out to him, as she sobbed. His eyelashes also dampened at the thought. He was lost in his thoughts when the princess passed by the goldsmith's shop. She called out for help again, and the thread of Momin's imagination snapped. "I will protect her. She's another helpless woman, just like my Shireeno," said Momin Khan, and rode after the camel.

As soon as they reached outside the city gates, the cameleer let go of the camel and turned back. Momin Khan rode again and grabbed hold of the camel's rope. The princess thought that the *azdaha* might have shapeshifted. She screamed and fainted, falling off the camel. When she regained consciousness, she found Momin Khan standing there, just as before. She calmed down a little, and Momin Khan told her, "Don't fret, *Khatun*, I am here to save you.[135] The *azdaha* shall not swallow you or anyone else, not today. Go hide in the thicket. I will wait here for the *azdaha*. If I fall asleep, wake me up. Alright?"

Momin Khan rested his back against a large boulder. The princess began to feel affection for him. "This young man is so handsome…how fearless does one have to be to fall asleep like a child even in the jaws of death? He shouldn't be resting on rocks," she thought. "I should try to return the favour," and she rested his head on her thighs.

Meanwhile, the sound of nasty hisses and rustling fell on her ears and she saw the *azdaha* crawling towards her in the distance. Her blood went dry and she was too frightened to even scream. Her senses were overcome with fear and she froze. Tears began to roll down her cheeks, which fell on Momin Khan's face, stirring him from his slumber. Finding his head

---

134 *Azdaha:* A mythical being with the head of a dragon and the body of a serpent. Sometimes, it also has wings.

135 *Kahtun:* Literally, "woman," used as a title (like "Lady so-and-so").

in the lap of the princess, he was very angry, but seeing the *azdaha*, he jumped up to his feet. The *azdaha* was heading towards him, foaming at the mouth and hissing loudly. Momin Khan tied his sword to his foot and, when the *azdaha* attacked him, he slid his leg into its mouth. The *azdaha* tried to chew on it, but the more it chewed, the more the sword sliced through its mouth—soon, the *azdaha* fell cold, cut up into two. Momin Khan suffered no injuries and when he called out to the princess, she found the *azdaha* dead. Momin Khan sliced away a thin strip of the *azdaha's* scales from its head to its tail. He told the princess, "Get back on the camel and go home. Should someone ask who killed the *azdaha*, tell them it is the one who has its skin."

After this, Momin Khan went back to the goldsmith. The princess sat on a cliff and began to wait. She was expecting someone from the palace to come check up on her. Back at the Royal Palace, everyone was mourning the princess. Everyone believed that, by now, the *azdaha* must have swallowed her whole. Her mother's heart began to bleed for her daughter, so she asked one of the servants to ride outside the city and fetch a last memento of the princess that may have been left behind. When the servant saw the princess alive and well, he was surprised, but when he saw the *azdaha* lying near her, he was frightened out of his wits and began to run for his life. The princess laughed at his cowardliness and called out, "You coward! This is the *azdaha's* corpse. Come back."

In the Royal Harem, a wave of happiness washed over every nook and cranny. The wailing ceased. The king thought that the princess had failed her duty and returned mid-way. He chided her for failing her people, but the servant appeared at the doors of the harem and bowed. After asking for permission to speak, he said, "The slave did his duty and slain the *azdaha* into two. Your good fortune has shined. Here is your daughter and the camel, both safe and sound in front of you."

When the princess heard this, she lost her temper and said out loud, "*Baba Huzoor*,[136] this coward did not fight the *azdaha*.[137] The one who killed the *azdaha* is the man who has a string of its scales with him."

"Lies! White lies! Both of you think me for a fool. I want evidence—prove it to me that the *azdaha* is dead. And where is this man who slayed it?" raged the king.

---

136 *Baba:* Father, also used as a title for aged men.
137 *Huzoor:* A title of respect, used for prophets, saints, and kings.

The princess said, "The braveheart who spared our Sultanate from this curse is at the goldsmith's workshop."

When Momin Khan was presented to the king, he said, "*Badshah Salamat*, it is I who hunted down the *azdaha* and saved the princess.[138] For evidence, here, I present to you a string of its scales."

The king looked at Momin Khan gratefully. "What a brave young man you are. Ah! Only if there were a few like you in my kingdom too. No one has the right to the hand of the Princess anymore. I gift you my daughter, a piece of my heart, and half my sultanate."

"*Badshah Salamat*, I am grateful to you for your kindness, that you think of someone like me worth so much. I do not want your Sultanate, nor do I wish to marry the princess. I have a request, however—you ask the neighbouring king for a tribute. Please don't do so anymore, because it is unfair," said Momin Khan.

The king said, "That tribute is a payment for the *pehelwans* we have given to him."

"My King, forgive me. I have tested them. Calling them *pehelwans* is an insult to the art and skill of *pehelwani*."

"I figured as much. Not even they could get rid of the *azdaha*."

"Do not worry, you are our *Mohsin*.[139] We shall forgive the tribute for your sake. However, you mustn't refuse the princess."

Momin Khan could not do much, so he agreed. After the wedding, when he and the princess were together, he said, "Dear Princess. I am helpless in front of my heart. I cannot love you. I have promised Shireeno, and a man does not go back on his word. Please forgive me. Let this sword be the judge between you and me. If I extend a hand towards you, it is your right to do as you please with me. Or else, this sword, like the *azdaha*, can also finish you."

"The crown of my head, your wish is my command. In your happiness, I will find mine." The next day, Momin Khan set off with the *Maafinama* for the tribute back to his king, leaving the princess behind at her father's.[140]

---

138 *Badshah Salamat:* A greeting for a king which includes a prayer for peace and for them to reign long.

139 *Mohsin:* The one who helps others.

140 *Maafinama:* Official letter of forgiveness (literal) in this case, a letter to waive off tribute.

After Momin Khan left the village, the whole tribe was at odds with his cousins. Zabardast Khan and his *zabardasti*[141] were getting too much to handle, so they protested against him. He and his brothers began to insult the elderly and turn away the well-respected. They controlled the clan with tyranny, and after they threw Momin Khan's mother out of her home, seizing the house, as well as the rest of the land, a revolt was just around the corner.

An orphan child in the village, Majtayi, who had been adopted by Momin Khan's mother, was a shepherd for a Khan of a neighbouring village. One day, the cattle ended up walking into Zabardast Khan's fields. His shepherds were as mean as he was, so they beat poor little Majtayi black and blue. When Majtayi came back crying to his mother, she held him close to her chest and consoled him, "My son. Zabardast and his *zabardasti* have not spared your mother either. Go, go after your brother to Hindustan. Find Momin Khan and tell him that your mother craves the simplest of necessities in life. She would have died unless the tribe had not given her refuge." With that, Majtayi also left his village.

After he reached Hindustan, by chance, he ended up in the territory of the same king who was hosting Momin Khan. When Momin brought the *maafinama*, the king greeted him with great respect, and celebrations were held throughout the entire kingdom. Momin Khan was over the moon to see his brother. He asked, "My brother, how is my village? Is my Shireeno well? How is my beautiful, dear mother doing? Tell me, how do my orchards fare?"

When Majtayi narrated Zabardast Khan's tyranny, Momin Khan's fury knew no bounds. His hand instinctively reached out for his sword, and he rose. "My king, please grant me your permission to leave. My honour is under threat."

"Go along, you have my blessing. Take as many men with you as you need. I shall send reinforcements later," said the king.

"Thank you, my king. But the three of us are enough. My cousins aren't worth more." The king ordered the royal treasurer to fill up seven sacks of gold and silver to send with Momin Khan. The royal servants gathered everything and set off to accompany him.

---

141 *Zabardasti* has been added for the semantics. *Zabardast* means amazing, whilst *zabardasti* means forcing someone to do something.

After Momin left, the princess became very lonely. She stopped eating and sleeping and sobbed all day and all night long. The king became very concerned. She said, "*Baba jaan,* please permit me to go after my husband."[142] The king, unable to stop her, sent her off. The princess travelled with her maidservants, not one or two, but thirty-nine of them. She also took along with her chests full of gold, silver, and jewels.

After she reached the palace of the king who was hosting Momin Khan, she was heartbroken to learn that he had left for his homeland. She, along with her servant girls, lost her temper and began to throw a tantrum, going about the palace asking for the whereabouts of Momin Khan. His former companions greeted her with great respect, and she began to wait restlessly for her beloved.

A little way from his village, Momin Khan set up camp. He left his companions there and rode to his village alone. Zabardast Khan kept a very strict eye on poor Shireeno. He was extra careful, suspecting that she might run off to Hindustan to look for Momin. At night, all seven of her brothers used to lay their charpoys around her.

When he entered, night had fallen. The entire village was asleep. An eerie silence had enveloped the surroundings. On occasion, the howling of jackals would break the quiet, making it feel even more sinister.

Momin Khan went straight to the door of his cousins. He tied his horse outside to a tree and jumped over the wall. He saw that his moon was surrounded by clouds. Shireeno was fast asleep. Momin lost control and threw himself around her, planting kisses on her cheek. She got frightened and let out a scream. The following moment, all her brothers lunged at Momin Khan, and the screams of "Thief! Thief! Thief!" woke up the neighbours.

Zabardast Khan blindly attacked Momin with a knife, striking rashly with all the force he could muster, which lodged itself in Momin Khan's liver. Momin lost consciousness. He did not fight back, nor did a word or a cry escape his lips. When Zabardast Khan bent down to remove the veil from his face, Shireeno recognised him instantly. She fainted. Zabardast Khan thought that Momin might have brought a party of soldiers along with him. When they went outside to see, Momin's horse neighed loudly. They sprinkled water on Shireeno's face. When she

---

142 *Baba Jaan:* "Father dear."

regained consciousness, she began to laugh like a madwoman. She laid her red *dupatta* over Momin Khan.[143]

Someone told Momin Khan's mother that he was back, and she should come quickly to see him, lest he goes back. Even though she was overjoyed to hear that he was back, she was extremely upset at the fact that he had gone to see his cousins before coming to meet her. She said, "I did not know Momin Khan would become so shameless after he returned from his travels that he would stay with these cousins of his, who threw his mother out of the house, abandoned and all alone. Momin, I shall not forgive you a single drop of my milk."

As soon as she entered the house, she found Momin Khan bathed in blood. She began to strike herself on her head. "Oh dear! I thought you would return from Hindustan with gold and silver utensils, fine silk, pashmina shawls, and sacks full of coins. Instead, you lie here, wearing Shireeno's *dupatta*. Your cousins hosted you well, didn't they? Not even one, but they struck you with seven knives." Momin Khan was whimpering and did not have the strength to speak. He signalled with his hand, calling Shireeno and his mother to him. When they came close to him and to one another, he whispered, "I relish this painful wound in my liver because it was not a *ghair*, but my cousin who struck me."[144] with these words, Momin Khan gave his life to the Creator of the World.

When Zabardast Khan heard that Momin had died from his blow, he lost heart. He called his sister, kissed her forehead gently, and said, "My sister, my stubbornness destroyed your whole world. Forgive me." Just as he finished talking, he took the knife and stabbed himself in his liver. "Carry my *Janazah* with Momin Khan."[145]

When Momin Khan did not return for a long time, his companions became concerned. It was nearly dawn. The princess decided she could not wait any longer and headed for his village along with her maidservants. However, on her way, a shepherd told her what had happened. Her head began to spin, and she nearly stumbled off her horse, but her friends

143 *Dupatta:* The veil which is a part of the Pakhtun ethnic ensemble—a piece of cloth, usually 1 m by 2.5 m, traditionally worn to cover the head, but now it is also worn around the neck or over the shoulder.

144 *Ghair:* A stranger, outsider, or not from amongst you; it can be used for someone outside the family, tribe, or even a foreign country.

145 *Janazah:* The Muslim funeral procession.

protected her. When she woke up, she headed towards Momin Khan's house. She had only travelled a little when she saw his *Janazah* in front of her. Behind the procession was a beautiful young woman, wailing, and almost going insane with grief. The princess stopped the procession and said, "Because Momin Khan has died chaste, his *Janazah* shall be lifted by virgin maidens."

Dressed in black, thirty-nine beautiful young women lifted his corpse on their shoulders. Shireeno called out loud, "Momin Khan kept his word. Hindustani women did not manage to entice him. He did not fall a prisoner to the cuffs of their long hair. He truly treated them like his sisters," and then hugged the princess and began to weep.

Both had lost their dreams, hopes, and the man who had their heart. When Momin Khan was about to be lowered in his grave, the princess said, "He shall be buried by the hands of chaste women as well." Then the princess and Shireeno laid him to rest.

When they loosened the shroud to see their beloved one last time, the princess fainted. Shireeno climbed out of the grave, guffawing like a lunatic. The maidservants tried to lift the princess out of the grave, but her soul had already gone to Momin Khan. After his grave was sealed, the maidservants laid all the precious fabrics they had on his grave and sprinkled the gold and silver coins on it.

A very fervid Shireeno began to scoop the coins in her little fists and throw them at her brothers. "Oh, men of greed, this is why you sent Momin Khan away, did you not? You wretches. He brought a lot more than what you asked for. Now take it and bury it with Zabardast Khan," she began to scream and beat her head against the boulders nearby.

The maidservants tried to stop her the best they could, but she began to wail. "The Princess, being a Hindustani woman, remained loyal to Momin Khan. How can I, being Pakhtun, be disloyal to him?" Amid lamentation, Shireeno gave up her life before the sun went down that evening.

مومن خان، شیرینو

12

JALAT MEHBOOBA

IN THE DIMLY LIT *Hujra*, where the tendrils of smoke wove intricate patterns in the air, seated in a circle, their faces illuminated by the soft glow of oil lamps, the members of the gathering listened intently as the melody of the *rabab* filled the room.[146] The tale of Jalat and Mehbooba echoed through the chamber. Each strum of the *rabab* seemed to breathe life into the characters.[147] As the music swirled around them, voices rose and fell, intermingling with the haunting strains of the instrument. Each member of the gathering took their turn, reciting couplets which spoke of love and courage. And then, as Jamal *Rababi* plucked the strings and delivered the final couplet, silence descended upon the *Hujra*.[148]

Atlas Khan's voice cut through the air, "Ghondia...*chillam?*"[149] Smoke billowed from the fireplace, thickening the already impure air as smoke

---

146 *Hujra:* The Hujra is a traditional all-male space, a designated outhouse, where friends and acquaintances can come visit. Culturally, Pardah is observed in Pakhtun culture, which is why men who are not relatives, do not enter the home. It is like the modern-day drawing room, only that it is detached from the main building of the house.

147 *Rabab:* A plucked string instrument. It is a part of Pashto folk music and is also the national musical instrument of Afghanistan. It is also used in traditional music in Balochistan, Sindh, and Punjab.

148 *Rababi:* One who plays the rabab.

149 *Chillam:* A smoking pipe used in Pakistan, Afghanistan, Iran, and India.

the *chillam* joined in. Murad, adjusting the mustard oil lamp, remarked, "Babar *kaka* is absent today."[150]

"He'll show up. Lately, he's been practicing *Wazifa* after *Isha* prayers,"[151] Karmay reassured.[152]

"Let him come today; we'll hear the tale straight from him. This old man's been avoiding us every single day," Murad grumbled. Meanwhile, Babar Kaka entered the *Hujra,* coughing, his fingers tracing the beads of his *tasbeeh.*[153] "Babar Kaka, close the door," commanded Murad, as greetings of *"Khush'amdeed"*[154] and *"Pakhair raghlay"*[155] echoed in the *Hujra.*

Murad asserted firmly, "Tonight, Babar Kaka, it's your turn to tell us the tale of Jalat and Mehbooba."

"Children, it's awfully late now. Another time, perhaps," Babar Kaka hurriedly replied, attempting to evade the request. However, his words were drowned out by a chorus of "no, no" from the assembled group.

Ghonda interjected, "Even if the sun rises, we're listening tonight, Babar Kaka."

"Fine then, gather 'round," Babar Kaka relented, yielding to their insistence. "But remember, not a single blink," he warned, tucking his *tasbeeh* into his *khaddar*[156] *kurta* pocket and clearing his throat.[157]

There once was a king known as Na-Muslim. He had a daughter whose beauty rivalled the sun and the moon. She was named Mehbooba. However, this king was cruel and oppressive. Despite having many wives, he despised the birth of daughters. Whenever news arrived of a newborn daughter, his fury knew no bounds and often resulted in the tragic end of many infant lives, strangled by his own hands. When Mehbooba came into the world, she was so heart-warmingly beautiful that all of

---

150 *Kaka:* The Pashto word/title for uncle (typically paternal uncle), but also used to address any man significantly older than you.

151 *Wazifa:* A regular litany practiced by followers and comprising Quranic verses, hadiths of supplication and various Duas.

152 *Isha:* The fifth prayer of the day in Islam.

153 *Tasbeeh:* A rosary of prayer beads used by Muslims.

154 *Khushamdeed:* Urdu word for "welcome."

155 *Pakhair Raghlay:* Pashto greeting.

156 *Khaddar:* A type of woven cloth worn in winter.

157 *Kurta:* A variant of the kameez, recognised by the difference in collars.

جلات، محبوبہ

the king's wives decided to protect her from his tyranny. Very tactfully, they convinced the king that she was born lifeless and secretly hid her away in a cellar. There, Mehbooba was raised, hidden away from the world's gaze. It is said that both the Chinaberry tree and a girl-child grow up quickly.

As Mehbooba blossomed into a young woman, she occasionally ventured out of the cellar and into the palace when the king was away on hunts or journeys. But upon his return, she was swiftly hidden away once more.

One day, as God would have it, while Mehbooba was innocently laughing and frisking around in the palace, the king unexpectedly returned, catching the queen off guard. Frantically, she hid Mehbooba in the storeroom, arousing the king's suspicion. Upon discovering her, he was astonished. Compelled to explain, the queen confessed the truth about Mehbooba, much to the king's fury over the secrecy of his wives. He immediately ordered Mehbooba's execution.

Yet, in the stillness of the night, as the king lay in his chambers, Mehbooba appeared before him, stirring a long-forgotten paternal affection. Startled, the king embraced her, only for her to vanish into thin air, leaving behind a mere illusion. It was at that moment that the king's heart softened, and he rescinded the execution order. Instead, he decreed for Mehbooba to be confined to an underground maze within the palace. Despite her imprisonment, she was showered with every luxury and comfort. The king forbade his wives from any mention of Mehbooba's marriage, threatening to punish them by pulling their tongues out, should he hear such talk.

The king's decree was swiftly carried out, and the maze was constructed with intricate complexity, ensuring no soul could navigate its twists and turns. Accompanied by the king himself, Mehbooba was led into the labyrinth, where her father bestowed a tender kiss upon her forehead before bidding her farewell.

"Were the maze builders truly skilled, Babar Kaka?" Ghonda inquired.

"They were masters of their craft, but you know how they were rewarded for their service to the king? They were all slaughtered, ensuring their silence," Babar Kaka revealed solemnly.

"And then what happened, Babar Kaka?" everyone asked simultaneously.

"What happened...what else could happen? Precisely that happened which Allah willed," Babar Kaka responded cryptically.

One day, Mehbooba secretly navigated her way through the labyrinth and ascended to the palace roof for a stroll. There, she caught the attention of a passing *faqir*, who was taken aback by her presence.[158] Though Mehbooba eventually retreated indoors, the *faqir* lingered.

Just then, the king's royal carriage passed by. He saw the *faqir* loitering around the palace. Enraged by the disrespect, the king had the *faqir* arrested, subjected to brutal beatings, and sentenced to death.

The *faqir*, named Malameer, managed to escape his imprisonment and fled the city under the cover of night. He did not rest until he had left the country of Mehboobanagar. He found refuge in the neighbouring kingdom, reigned by King Khoonkaar, who had seven young, handsome, and valiant sons.

Upon regaining his strength, Malameer began extolling Mehbooba's beauty to all, young and old alike, causing the tale to spread like wildfire across the land. Just as the scent of musk cannot remain hidden within the deer's naval, the truth inevitably comes to light.

Despite never setting eyes on Mehbooba, the prince, King Khoonkar's eldest son, lost his heart to her. Driven by the tug of love pulling at his heart, he set off to claim her as his own. But upon arriving in Mehbooba's city, he discovered that princes from distant lands had gathered, each vying for a chance to win Mehbooba's hand.

The king, fraught with worry, pondered over the difficult situation. Rejecting suitors from neighbouring kingdoms risked sparking conflict, yet accepting a son-in-law was a notion he couldn't bear. After much deliberation, the king devised a cunning plan, shirking responsibility for its consequences. In the palace gardens, a great drum was placed, signalling a challenge to all suitors. To win Mehbooba's hand, they must navigate a treacherous maze where she resides. Success meant marriage; failure meant death at the hands of royal guards.

The announcement drew Mehbooba's suitors to the drum like moths. Ready to burn in the flames of love, it was almost as if they had come with burial shrouds wrapped around their heads, in readiness for sacrifice. But the maze proved impossible. In somewhere between a week to ten days, over twenty young men met their fate at the edge of the executioner's sword. Faced with the grim reality, the remaining suitors relinquished their desires, choosing survival over futile pursuit.

---

158 *Faqir:* A wandering Muslim ascetic who lives solely on alms.

"The path of love is fraught with challenges, children," said Babar Kaka, his voice strained with a cough. "You will do yourself well to stay clear of it."

Among the princes who met their end in pursuit of Mehbooba was King Khoonkar's eldest son. When news of his demise reached the palace, the second son resolved to try his luck with fate. However, the union with Mehbooba was not destined for him either. Thus, one by one, each of King Khoonkar's six sons met their end at the altar of Mehbooba's beauty.

King Khoonkar's youngest son couldn't bear the loss of his six brothers. Anguish burned in his eyes as he packed his belongings, determined to journey to Mehboobanagar. King Khoonkar cherished him dearly, Jalat, the youngest prince, and tried his best to dissuade him. He was the most handsome among all his brothers and was an extremely intelligent young man.

Despite his father's opposition, Jalat did not budge. "Father," he declared, "I shall either return with Mehbooba by my side or I shall avenge my fallen brothers. Do not mistake me for my foolish brothers." With these words, he mounted his white stallion, its hooves thundering like lightning as they sped towards Mehbooba's country.

Upon hearing of King Khoonkar's tragic loss of his six sons, when Malameer saw Jalat at the city gates, he stopped him and offered his assistance. "My prince," he implored, "Allow me to accompany you. I shall serve you well."

Jalat agreed, for he, too, needed a companion, and together they ventured forth. Upon arriving in Mehbooba's land, Malameer told Jalat not to beat the drums just yet. Instead, Malameer disguised him as a humble *faqir* to keep him from being recognised. They then wandered the city streets, trying to locate the entry point to the maze.

Alas! What does love not to afflict on people? Qais, too, was a prince. However, Layla's love turned him into *Majnun*.[159]

As fate would have it, one day, a coquettish lady-in-waiting of Mehbooba went to the market to buy some *Ittar*.[160] There, she chanced upon Jalat. She froze in her tracks at the sight of a jewel wrapped in rags. Upon returning

---

159 *Majnun:* Being a madman in love; a reference to the tale of Layla and Majnun (Qais).

160 *Ittar:* An essential oil derived from botanical or other natural sources.

to the Haram Saraye, she narrated tales of how charming Jalat was in a way which stirred unrest in Princess Mehbooba's heart.[161] Desperate to catch even a glimpse of him, the servant girl proposed a plan. She suggested holding a charity at the palace gates for all the *faqirs* in the city.

Countless *faqirs* thronged the gates of the Haram Saraye, awaiting alms. From a gazebo, Princess Mehbooba observed the scene from the *Jharoka*, her eyes scanning the crowd in search of the purpose behind her orchestrated event.[162] The lady-in-waiting signalled to the left, where a humble figure sat beside a pillar. "This is the *faqir*, Your Highness," she whispered.

As their eyes met, she swooned, and a sudden dizziness overcame the princess, causing her to faint. Frantically, the servant girl attempted to revive her with some *lakhlakha*.[163] When the princess regained consciousness, her heart had taken a hit. With pleading in her voice, she held the servant girl accountable. "You are responsible for this affliction," said Mehbooba. "For Allah's sake, find a cure." For once, her words were not a command but laced with a plea.

You know, love robbed even Aristotle of his sanity—so what was the poor servant girl supposed to do? But when Allah chooses to bless someone, the seas part for them, and mountains move themselves out of their way.

Malameer discovered a notable goldsmith in the city. This goldsmith's mother crafted a flower crown with gold wires each day, presenting a fresh one to Mehbooba every day. Meanwhile, the goldsmith himself, Mohmandi, fashioned jewellery for the princess. Malameer thought to himself, "We are sorted."

The following day, he brought Jalat to Mohmandi's shop. Malameer also managed to convince Mohmandi to take Jalat under his wing and train him as an apprentice in the art of Goldsmithery. Being age-fellows, Mohmandi and Jalat quickly developed a strong bond. The two soon

---

161 *Haram Saraye:* The royal palace which houses the women's quarters.

162 *Jharoka:* A kind of window found in local architecture. The Jharokha is a stone window projecting from the wall face of a building, in an upper story, overlooking a street, market, court or any other open space. The net, made of stone, has smaller holes inside, and larger holes outside—you can see outside, but you can't see inside properly.

163 *Lakhlakha:* A special kind of fragrance used as a cure for fainting spells.

became very good friends, and Mohmandi began to consider Jalat to be his brother in just a few days.

Jalat's charm soon became the talk of the town. Tons of women and girls were drawn to Mohmandi's shop and even to his home after closing hours. Hoping to catch a glimpse of the prince, they often broke their necklaces, *jhoomers,* and bangles as an excuse to visit Mohmandi's shop.[164] Mohmandi's fortune flourished as his business boomed, and his fondness for Jalat grew stronger with each passing day.

One day, while Mohmandi's mother was running errands, she returned to find that Jalat had already prepared a flower crown for Mehbooba. Impressed by his skill and intelligence, she praised him and delivered the crown to the princess. The princess was surprised when she saw the crown. "This is not your handiwork, is it, mother? Tell me, who made it?" she inquired. The old woman panicked. "My daughter, who is visiting from her in-laws, made this," she lied.

"I want to meet your daughter. Bring her with you tomorrow," commanded Princess Mehbooba. The old woman nearly lost her wits upon hearing this request. She didn't even have a daughter to bring. Returning home, she recounted the situation to Jalat and asked, "Son, what should we do now?" Jalat comforted her and then went to Malameer to explain the predicament.

Malameer was overjoyed. "Believe me, your luck has begun to turn," he assured the prince.

The next day, Malameer disguised Jalat as a young woman, dressing him in women's clothes and applying *Surma* and rose tint.[165] Mohmandi and his mother were astonished when they saw Jalat. He looked every bit as beautiful as a princess.

"*Bismillah.*[166] Let's go," Jalat said, and Mohmandi's mother led the way.

The princess told Mohmandi's mother, "Your daughter shall stay here tonight. Come take her tomorrow." The princess enjoyed the Mohmandi girl's company so much that she didn't sleep. They kept talking all night. From time to time, she became suspicious of some of Jalat's actions or things he said, thinking, "This can't be a girl." But she dismissed it as

---

164 *Jhoomer:* A large headpiece worn at either side of the forehead.

165 *Surma:* Also known as kohl; is a traditional eye cosmetic used in South Asia, the Middle East, and North Africa.

166 *Bismillah:* "In the name of Allah"—Muslims say it before they begin a task.

her suspicion. Once, she even asked the girl, "Girl, I think I've seen you somewhere."

Jalat's gaze fixed itself on the floor. He said, "Even I feel the same. But is it so? What of us poor people, and then you, even the stars and the moon have not gazed at you."

Mohmandi's mother couldn't sleep all night; she was worried. She feared Jalat might have been killed by now. She felt as if her blood was drying.

The next morning, she was wary but took the flower crown to the princess anyway. Afraid, she stepped into Mehbooba's room. She was relieved to see Jalat alive and Mehbooba happy. The princess praised her daughter and gave her a lot of presents before sending her away.

This meeting added fuel to the fire. Jalat became increasingly restless. He stopped going to work and stopped eating. Mohmandi became very worried to see him in this state. Then finally, one day, Jalat narrated the whole story of his love to Mohmandi and said to him, "You have called me your brother. You will help me, or else I will go beat the drums. I am willing to lay down my life for the princess."

When Mohmandi found out that an actual prince was staying over at his house, he couldn't believe it. He also thought that he would be guilty if an innocent life was lost. Also, people will shame him if he cannot be of use to his brother. So, he thought of a plan.

Mohmandi was not just a goldsmith, but also a skilled artisan and painter. He could craft sculptures from wood with such precision that they looked lifelike. One of his creations was a magnificent, life-sized lion made from ebony wood. It was so realistic that anyone who saw it would be fooled into thinking it was a living beast. To add to its realism, Mohmandi installed clockwork inside the lion. When spun, it would move around and roar just like a real lion.

With pride in his craftsmanship, Mohmandi decided to present the lion to the king. He brought it to the royal court and spun it before the entire assembly. The sight of the wooden lion roaring amazed and entertained everyone present, earning Mohmandi applause and appreciation from all.

The king, impressed by Mohmandi's skill, rewarded him generously. News of Mohmandi's artistry spread throughout the city. Word also reached Princess Mehbooba. Intrigued, she expressed her wish to her father to see the lion for herself. Upon her request, the king ordered Mohmandi to send the lion to the Haram Saraye so that Princess Mehbooba could admire it in person.

"You wretch, Ghondia, he's falling asleep. Pass over the *chillam*," Babar Kaka grumbled, with a frown on his forehead. Ghonda jolted awake and began to roll the tobacco between his palms. Babar Kaka took two or three long drags and coughed, clearing his throat. After that, he retrieved a packet of *naswar* from his kurta, placed a pinch in his right cheek, and continued.[167]

"Then, as Allah would have it...what was I saying, Karmaye?" Babar Kaka inquired.

"You were telling us that the princess wanted to see the spectacle of the lion," Karmaye responded.

"May Allah bless you with steadfast faith," Babar Kaka replied, offering a prayer to Karmaye.

Mohmandi gave Jalat a high five and said, "My dear brother, get ready now. Be careful and keep your wits about. I will get you to Mehbooba," he said gleefully. "After that, you're on your own." Mohmandi helped Jalat into the lion's belly. He then handed over the lion to Mehbooba's ladies-in-waiting.

Mehbooba enjoyed the lion's antics all night until she grew tired and fell asleep. Quietly, Jalat crept out from the lion's belly, taking the princess's ring and shawl with him. Later, as Mehbooba stirred, she noticed her missing ring and shawl. Confused, she searched but couldn't find them. Frowning in puzzlement, she lay back down in bed.

Just then, she saw the lion split into two, and a young man crept out of it and sneaked up towards her. Upon seeing him, Mehbooba recognized him as the same *faqir* mentioned by the servant girl, who had come to the Haram Saraye for alms. It was also the same man who had disguised himself as a woman and as Mohmandi's sister.

Mehbooba's lips quivered beneath her nose-stud as she grasped Jalat's hand firmly. "Thief! Confess the truth. Who are you, and why are you here?"

With sincerity in his eyes, Jalat poured out his heart to Mehbooba, revealing his love for her and exposing the tyranny of her father. For the first time, Mehbooba learned of the innocent lives sacrificed in her name, fueling her disdain for her father. Opening her own heart to Jalat,

---

167 *Naswar:* A moist mixture made from sun and heat-dried tobacco leaves. These are added to slaked lime, ash from tree bark, and flavouring. It is consumed by stuffing a pinch inside the cheek or beneath the lower lip.

the princess confessed, "I cannot rip my heart out of my chest for you to see, but your love resides in every corner of it."

As Jalat prepared to depart, Mehbooba instructed him, "Beat the drums tomorrow and enter the maze without fear. I will meet you at the first crossroads."

The following day, the lion was returned to Mohmandi, and Jalat joyfully recounted the events to Mohmandi and Malameer. As planned, Jalat beat the drums, and he was adorned with flower garlands by the king's servants before entering the maze. Victory awaited him as Mehbooba greeted him at the first crossroads. Embracing each other, they shared their love through the rhythm of their heartbeats, lingering in conversation for a while.

Jalat found Mohmandi waiting with a fine steed as he escaped the labyrinth with Mehbooba. Without hesitation, the two mounted and spurred it into a thunderous gallop. As the horse's mane danced in the wind, their hearts pounded faster. Instead of presenting themselves to the king, Mehbooba's father, they had chosen to defy him and elope instead.

Upon learning of their escape, the king's fury knew no bounds. He dispatched his soldiers in pursuit, but Jalat and Mehbooba vanished without a trace. Returning to his city, Jalat delivered Mehbooba to safety at his *Haram Saraye*. News of their reunion spread rapidly, bringing joy to the hearts of many. "Father," Jalat urgently called out, "Na-Muslim is at our heels. They'll soon attack our kingdom."

The king, alarmed, responded, "Prepare the forces swiftly. Beat the war drums."

King Khoonkar's forces outnumbered Na-Muslim and his men by far. Both forces met each other on the battlefield. A fierce fight followed. Dead bodies began to pile up on the ground. Bloodstreams began to flow in the soft earth. Many of King Na-Muslim's soldiers were killed, and the rest fled in retreat, abandoning the fight. The king was injured and arrested. Mehbooba couldn't bear to see her father in such a sorry state, so she obtained a life pardon for him, and he was respectfully escorted back to his kingdom.

The love between Princess Mehbooba and Prince Jalat blossomed like a flower and a bumblebee. In celebration of their union, the king hosted a grand wedding, marking the beginning of their happily ever after.

"May Allah fulfil our wishes and dreams just as He did for them."

13

KHADI BEBO

THE KINDRED SPIRIT OF youth can only be truly understood and reciprocated by another youthful soul. In its entirety, encompassing emotions, extremes, and all that lies between...whether it blooms amidst the lavish trappings of velvet beds and ornate curtains or flourishes beneath the open canopy of green fields and endless skies, its essence remains inherently beautiful and profoundly simple.

As Khadi and Bebo ascended the mountaintop to gather firewood, Bebo's face, fair as the moon, would glisten with perspiration, resembling the radiant seeds cascading from a ripe pomegranate. Her beauty, heightened by labour, was a sight to behold. Khadi, entranced, would pause in his woodcutting, his axe suspended mid-air, as he gazed upon her, captivated. Often, Bebo used to playfully cry out "Jackal, jackal!" shattering their idyllic moment and scattering the delicate threads of Khadi's imagination.

In a quaint village nestled in Qandahar, tales echoed of two brothers, Wali Muhammad and Ali Muhammad, scions of affluent households, each holding sway as the esteemed Malik of their *Kandi*'s.[168] Khadi was the son of Khan Wali Muhammad, and Bebo, the daughter of Ali Muhammad.

Little did anyone imagine that these two dusty blossoms, frolicking together in childhood innocence, would one day rise to fame akin to

---

168 *Kandi:* Name of a Pakhtun tribe.

the legendary lovers, Layla and Majnun.[169] Who could have foreseen that the same children fashioning miniature mud homes today, only to gleefully destroy them, would one day succumb to the same fate as their transient creations, crumbling under the weight of their passions? Love would be their guide, *Prem nagar,* their destination, and death, their inevitable destiny.[170] "For their union, death is the decree, Ah! Such poignant closure, for all to see."

As they transitioned from childhood into youth, their innocent affection blossomed into *ishq.*[171] Entranced by the sway of their emotions, they became ensconced within the rhythmic pendulum of love's swing. To them, this swing represented both the vibrant colours of a rainbow and the vast expanse of a galaxy.

One serene day, as the two lovers returned from their woodcutting expedition, they sought respite beneath the sprawling shade of a mighty tree. Bebo, overcome by weariness, drifted into slumber, her ebony locks dancing with the gentle caress of the breeze, framing her fair countenance and flushed cheeks. She looked like a *Hoor* of the earth.[172] Enraptured, Khadi found himself ensnared by a spell he could not resist. Succumbing to the urge, he tenderly planted a kiss on Bebo's rosy lips, igniting a tempest within the sleeping maiden.

Startled awake, Bebo seethed with anger, as if a she-snake had been stirred from deep sleep. Her fury erupted like a dormant volcano. She shook with anger as she reprimanded Khadi. This is not the reaction Khadi was expecting. He pleaded for forgiveness from his beloved—*ishq* beseeched *husn* for clemency.[173] However, *ishq* had hurt Husn's honour. Despite his earnest apologies, Bebo remained unmoved. She rose and walked off.

Overwhelmed by Bebo's apparent disregard, Khadi decided to depart from the village that very night. Swiftly gathering his belongings, he set

---

169 This is a reference to the tale of Layla Majnun and the madness as a result of unrequited love.

170 *Prem nagar:* The street of the beloved.

171 *Ishq:* The highest stage of love.

172 *Hoor:* In Islamic belief, a *Hoor* is a beautiful, maiden promised as a reward to the righteous in paradise. They are described as pure, flawless and beautiful beings, who shall provide companionship in the afterlife.

173 *Husn:* The extremity of beauty.

off into the wilderness. As soon as Bebo learned this, she was consumed by regret and set off to follow him. She apologized, expressing deep remorse for her neglectful behaviour. She implored him to change his mind, however, he remained unmoved, leaving her behind, her cries echoing in the night air.

After Khadi's departure, Bebo found herself in a state of melancholy. When her mother inquired about her distressed demeanour, Bebo initially attempted to evade the topic, but eventually, she relented and recounted the entire incident to her mother. As Khadi wandered aimlessly, his mind consumed by thoughts of his beloved, fate led him to encounter a caravan near Dilaraam village. When the *Mir* of the caravan saw a handsome young man traversing the desert all by himself with nothing but barrenness for miles around, he stopped the caravan and extended a gracious offer of employment to Khadi.[174] Initially hesitant, Khadi was moved by the kindness of the *Mir* and ultimately accepted the opportunity. As the caravan resumed its journey, Khadi found himself in the unfamiliar territory of Isfahan.

In Khadi's absence, Bebo's condition deteriorated with each passing day, much to the distress of her father, who, witnessing his beloved and only daughter's sorrow, set off in search of Khadi Khan. However, his efforts proved futile. Bereft of Khadi's presence, Bebo languished like a parched bird, her days filled with longing and emptiness. Every morning, she stood at the entrance of Dilaram village, awaiting the arrival of caravans. She inquired about Khadi Khan from every passerby. Yet, she returned home every evening disappointed.

A ray of hope pierced through the darkness of despair one fateful day. From a passing caravan, a messenger arrived bearing a letter from Khadi Khan. As Bebo clutched the missive in her hands, it was as if the barren garden of her life had suddenly blossomed with the arrival of spring. In the letter addressed to his father, Khadi Khan wrote: "In Isfahan, I have risen as a distinguished merchant. Yet, amidst my success, Bebo's memories remain my most cherished treasure. Alas, she is cruel, which is why I do not wish to return to my homeland."

This letter had breathed a new life into Bebo. She dictated her response, "Khadi, my love, I am yours, and my heart belongs to you alone. Since

---

174 *Mir:* Title for the leader of a tribe/caravan.

you left, I have not adorned my *orbal* with flowers…for whom should I adorn it?[175] Return swiftly, or else you shall not find me alive."

Khadi Khan's father prepared to travel to Isfahan. A misty-eyed Bebo handed over the letter she had written for Khadi Khan to her uncle. Khan Wali Muhammad reassured her, "My daughter, do not fret. I shall bring him back along with me, or else I shall not return either."

After several years of separation, the father and son reunited in Isfahan. They poured their hearts out to one another—holding each other responsible for their grievances and lamentation. When Khadi Khan read Bebo's letter, tears streamed down his cheeks uncontrollably.

One day, while Khadi and his father were seated in their opulent *haveli*, engaged in casual conversation, Wali Muhammad persuaded Khadi to return home.[176] However, Khadi tearfully responded, "*Baba jaan*, I have no homeland left.[177] Bebo was my only refuge; in her embrace, I found my sanctuary. But she harbours no space for me in her heart. If I am destined to burn, what difference does it make whether it's there or here? The closer a moth is to the flame, the more intense the pain."

"No, my son. You've misunderstood. Bebo doesn't even wish to continue living without you. If you don't return home, both Bebo and your uncle will kill themselves. I promised Bebo that I shall bring Khadi."

His father's words breathed new life into Khadi, igniting an immediate readiness to return home. As he drew nearer to his homeland, the blaze of love within him intensified. Upon reaching Farrah, fate intersected his path with the Mir of his caravan, fresh from Hindustan. Urging Khadi Khan forward, the *Mir* entrusted him with a mission: to retrieve assets worth a staggering one hundred thousand rupees left behind. Though the shore beckoned, Khadi Khan refused to quench his thirst for home; he simply had to see Bebo before venturing forth again.

Declaring his intent to first visit his village and then embark on the journey to Hindustan, Khadi Khan arrived ahead of his father, knocking upon his uncle's door. Met by Bebo's mother, he was met with suspicion. "Who are you?" she inquired. "I am but a traveller, a guest seeking work.

---

175 *Orbal:* Pushto for "forelock," a bang of hair.

176 *Haveli:* A house or mansion built in the traditional architectural style of the region.

177 *Baba Jaan:* "Father dear."

Might I have a sip of water and a moment with the *chillam?*"[178] Bebo's mother, sensing familiarity, instructed her daughter to attend to the visitor.

As if guided by an unseen force, Bebo rushed to the door, her heart leaping with recognition even before she laid eyes on him. Hastening back with water and preparing the chillam, her joy was palpable. Yet, in her excitement, she inadvertently burned her fingers while adding coal, prompting a moment of reflection. "Ya Allah, was this flame not Khadi Khan's love? Why then does it now sear me?"

Observing Bebo's mishap from outside, Khadi Khan's heart swelled with affection. "My Bebo, so caring, even to the point of burning her fingers for me," he remarked. These words were like a salve on her wound.

With the chillam in hand, Bebo approached, murmuring softly, "I shall touch the *chillam* with my *paizwaan*, thus Khadi's lips shall meet mine."[179]

In an instant, an indescribable attraction drew Khadi and Bebo together, binding their chests and lips in an irresistible embrace. With tender care, they exchanged necklaces of tears of joy, their intimate moment veiled by the cloak of the beautiful, deep purple night.

Before parting, Khadi extracted a promise from Bebo to meet him again that very night, then reluctantly made his way back to his dwelling, his heart alight with anticipation. As Bebo was going to Khadi's house, she was stopped by her father. "You are betrothed to him now. It is improper for you to visit his home. People shall gossip," he admonished.

Meanwhile, Khadi remained vigilant, eagerly awaiting his beloved's arrival throughout the night. Yet not a whisper signaled of Bebo's presence. Khadi waited like this for three consecutive nights, each one weighing heavy on his heart. Desperate for a solution, Khadi's parents reached out to Bebo, hoping her influence might sway him. Perhaps love would yield to beauty...however, despite Bebo crying a flood of tears and pleading to Khadi that she was sorry and why she could not have come to see him, passion did not succumb to the beloved's plea. His heart softened and he hugged her but refused to change his mind.

Bebo said, "If you are leaving, then leave a mark of yours somewhere, so I can look at it, and console my wounded heart." Khadi dug up a

---

178 *Chillam:* A smoking pipe used in Pakistan, Afghanistan, Iran, and India.
179 *Paizwaan:* A specific kind of nose ring—large and attached to a chain held by the hair.

small mound of dirt and left an imprint of his right hand on it. After that, his horse began to fly.

After travelling for many long days and nights, Khadi Khan finally reached Quetta, where the Mir's brother, Baaz Muhammad, lived. Baaz Muhammad greeted Khadi Khan with warm-heartedness. He also invited Khadi to stay over at his place for a few days. However, Khadi declined politely, saying that he needed to pick up the assets and depart for Isphahan as soon as possible. However, Baaz Muhammad said, "It is not the tradition of Pakhtuns to send off a guest without sacrificing a lamb or two."

Afraid of offending his host by turning down his hospitality, Khadi agreed to stay, albeit reluctantly. One day, Khadi Khan was sitting by himself, lost in Bebo's thoughts, when a young woman with hair as dark as midnight falling all the way to her hips, as beautiful as a *Hoor*, entered his room. As soon as she came in, she brazenly addressed him, "My dear father's guest, who are you, and where have you come from?"

"I have come from Isfahan; your uncle has sent me here to run an errand for him. My name is Khadi Khan. O my host, what is your name?"

"My name is Shireeno. O handsome young man, you are very attractive."

"Pardon me, I do not quite understand what you mean."

"You are like a magician. My heart wishes to keep staring at you."

"Oh…you are getting romantic, and saying affectionate things, just like my Bebo."

"The flower of my *orbal*, my heart is now your prisoner. How will I be able to live without you now?"

"Listen to me, my sister. I am leaving tomorrow. And speaking of such things is inappropriate anyway."

"Khadi Khan, words like this shall not do. Now, you shall either stay here or you will take me with you."

"Please stop talking nonsense, and leave."

"Khadi Khan, my heart is no longer mine."

"Look, someone will overhear us. Please leave. I shall see you near the walls of the fort in the evening."

Using this excuse, Khadi Khan got out of the tricky situation with Shireeno and began thinking about how he could quickly leave Quetta. He knew that the only escape from Shireeno's claws was to depart from her city. In the evening, he asked for his leave from Baaz Muhammad Khan. However, Baaz told him that he would fetch the assets from his village the following morning, and Khadi could leave the day after. When Khadi Khan expressed his desire to go along with him, Baaz declined his request, telling him it would not be pragmatic for him to accompany him.

The next morning, Baaz Muhammad Khan set off for his village. Khadi thought that, now that beautiful *balaa* would suddenly come to his room anytime now.[180] He decided it would be wise to leave the house and go out somewhere. Whilst he was mulling over all this, the beautiful *balaa* truly did appear out of nowhere and knocked on his door. Today, she had prepared a whole *dastarkhwan* with a variety of very tasty dishes for Khadi Khan.[181]

"Khadi Khan, what kind of Pakhtun are you? Pakhtuns stick to their word. I spent all night waiting for you in the shade of the walls of the fort."

"I was helpless, Shireeno. There wasn't much else I could have done. Your father was with me. I will come today, for sure."

"Alright, you enchanter of a guest. Come, eat, and then we can shower one another with love."

"Shireeno! I haven't made *Wuzu* yet,[182] nor have I said *Namaz*.[183] Why don't you wait here? I will be back." said Khadi, and he left for the mosque. After he finished his prayers, he stayed there for a while, not wanting to return. Eventually, he fell asleep. As Khadi napped, Shireeno kept patiently waiting for him to return. When he didn't come, she went to the walls of the fort. Just outside the mosque, beneath the shade of a large tree, she saw Khadi fast asleep.

Shireeno walked to the mosque. She did not call out to him, afraid of being ignored and, hence, disrespected. However, she filled up a bowl of water and threw the water at his face. When the droplets of water fell onto his face, Khadi woke up. Shireeno quietly signalled to him with

---

180 *Balaa:* Evil spirit, calamity, misfortune.

181 *Dastarkhwan:* A white cloth is spread out on the floor upon which food is laid out. Floor settings are the norm in Pakhtun culture; tables and chairs have come into use very recently. The word can be used to refer to both the tablecloth or the entire meal laid out.

182 *Wuzu:* Ritual ablution performed by Muslims before prayer, involves washing the hands, face, arms, and feet.

183 *Namaz:* Essential Muslim prayer, performed daily at prescribed times, is the second of Islam's five pillars.

her henna-adorned hands to come home. Khadi Khan pretended not to see anything. He shifted sides, turned his back towards Shireeno, and closed his eyes again. She chewed on her lips with fury.

In the evening, when Baaz Muhammad returned from his village, he was surprised at not finding Khadi at home. Shireeno informed her father that Khadi was sick and was resting in the mosque. When Baaz came to the mosque looking for Khadi, he found out that Khadi was truly ill.

The next day, when Khadi Khan received what was entrusted to him and took his leave, he was thankful to Allah for keeping him steadfast. Even though he was sick, when he set off and felt himself getting even weaker on the way, he continued travelling. Near Dilaram, just before noon, he stopped his horse near a *jhonpri* and nearly passed out from exhaustion as soon as he dismounted.[184] He felt thorns on his tongue due to thirst. For a while, he lay there, helpless…not a soul was around. By chance, a traveller passed by. Khadi Khan asked him to take a message to his village and to inform his family of his sickness.

All hell broke loose in the village when the news of Khadi Khan's sickness reached them. Before everyone else, it was Bebo who rushed her horse and found Khadi. However, before she found him, Khadi's soul had departed, in search of Bebo. She shook him, "Khadi Khan, why are you not waking up? I am here to take you to the village. Get up, please get up. Come on, let's go. Wake up. Please don't be upset with me anymore. Talk to me." However, Khadi Khan had become silent, and this time, for good. He had done what he said he would do.

Everyone in Khadi Khan's village gathered in Dilaram. They had brought the *Jirga* to him.[185] However, his only answer to them was silence…after all, without asking for his permission, the *Jirga* took him back to the village. However, the procession was taken amid crying, wailing, and *Nohas*,[186] rather than the sounds of the *naqqara*[187] and the *dammam*.[188]

---

184 *Jhonpri:* A small hut made of mud roofed with thatched straw.

185 *Jirga:* A council of tribal elders.

186 *Nohas:* Poetic lament about a tragedy, has the historical and social milieu of Islamic, Arabic, and Persian culture.

187 *Naqqara:* Kettle drum.

188 *Dammam:* Large double-headed drum played especially in mourning processions.

When Khadi Khan was lowered into his grave, Bebo requested the *Jirga* to allow her to step in and look at Khadi one last time. Even though this was against the norms, seeing her sorry state, the elders of the village allowed her to do so. She climbed down into Khadi's grave and threw herself around his cold corpse. She screamed and cried; first, her voice went hoarse, and then, she went silent. Her father tried to reach out and help her up. However, instead of Bebo, there was only her dead body there.

14

MUSA KHAN GUL MAKAI

LIFE MIRRORS THE DANCE of a stream: water glides and swirls in waves, at times serene, at times turbulent. Youth intertwines with streams; or, more so, youthfulness has woven the spirited current, the uproar, and the thunderous surges, into its very soul. This storm is heightened by the rugged, serrated peaks of Kohistan, where ancient secrets slumber, veiled within the mountains and the tales of its dwellers, whispered by winds that carry the echoes of ages past.

Amid the streams of Kohistan and the carefree spirit of the mountain youth lies the essence of beauty and love. It is the love of Musa Khan and the beauty of Gul Makai that defined the peaks and valleys of their romance. Who could have foreseen that the *madrassa* of the village,[189] Speentareen, would be home to a tale akin to that of Layla and Majnun?[190] Perhaps this is why the streams of the mountains snake down from their peaks to bow their heads as they flow past the village, paying homage to this very tale with their endless waves.

Speentareen's Layla, Gul Makai, Shah Mast Khan's only daughter, was enrolled in the *madrassa* of *Mullah*, Shams-ul-Islam.[191] Amid a crowd of children, both boys and girls, Gul Makai used to shine like the light

---

189 *Madrassa:* A place of education; not necessarily religious, unlike the modern connotation of the term in English.

190 This is a reference to the tale of Layla and Majnun, and the madness as a result of unrequited love.

191 *Mullah:* A Muslim cleric.

موسیٰ خان گل ملکئی

of the sun and the moon. Gul Makai's cousin, her paternal uncle's son, Sohail, who was also her fiance, studied in the same *madrassa*, but she did not so much as cast a glance at him. Gul Makai was the soul of the *madrassa*. All the students loved her. Then, one day, a new student joined the *madrassa*—Isa Khan's only son, Musa Khan, was the apple of the eye of the Yousafzai clan. He was the sole heir of his father's fiefdom, the region of Swabi.

As soon as Musa Khan set foot into the *madrassa*, Gul Makai embraced him wholeheartedly. She found her gaze wandering from her books to Musa Khan. She bit on her pale pinkie finger as she stared at him.

After Musa Khan joined, the school became so much livelier. Musa Khan was extremely intelligent, very handsome, kind at heart, and a thorough gentleman—he quickly became friends with everyone. Soon, everyone at the *madrassa* became fond of him, particularly Gul Makai, who had lost her heart to him. Musa Khan and Gul Makai soon became the hero and heroine of the *madrassa*. As they grew closer to one another and their love bloomed so much so that they could not spend a moment without one another, they also became the hero and heroine of the world of *ishq*.[192]

One day, Musa Khan and Gul Makai were engrossed in play near the streamside, along with Sohail. Gul Makai danced about, carefree. Before she knew it, the powerful waves and the thunderous stream enveloped her in their embrace. As the harsh waves clashed against the delicate form of Gul Makai, Sohail raced towards the village, crying out, "Help! Help!"

Musa Khan leapt into action, diving into the tumultuous waters to rescue Gul Makai from the jaws of the murderous waves, guiding her safely to shore. Emerging from the waters, they were greeted by the sight of the entire village assembled along the banks, witnessing the heroic deed. Shah Mast Khan, overcome with gratitude and relief, took Musa Khan in a warm embrace. "My brave Pakhtun son, I expected nothing less from you. You have saved my daughter's life."

Everyone began to praise Musa Khan's courage and bravery. Sohail, on the other hand, was awfully ashamed and embarrassed. Now, Musa Khan had become a sore sight for him, and he began to consider him

---

192 *Ishq:* Highest stage of love.

an adversary—particularly as far as Gul Makai's attention and affection were concerned.

To try and redeem himself, he challenged Musa Khan—to aim for a sparrow mid-flight with a slingshot. Before the face-off began, word spread around amongst everyone. One day, after lessons, students thronged the grounds of the *madrassa.* Sohail deftly fitted a stone into his sling: one...two...three....

Yet, each time, his aim missed its mark. Each time, the sparrow would flutter around him in circles, its wings carrying it higher and higher, reaching for the skies and the horizon.

Gul Makai's heart began to beat faster. The colour drained from the faces of the rest of the students, as they all prayed for Musa Khan to win. Everyone truly wished that Musa Khan did not fail in his aim. Gul Makai picked up a white pebble from the earth, blew *Bismillah* on it, and handed it over to Musa Khan.[193] The next moment, the grey little sparrow fell to the ground from the open skies, whimpering. The boys hoisted Musa Khan on their shoulders, and Gul Makai had tears of happiness in her eyes.

The sting of defeat only fueled Sohail's sense of rivalry, igniting a fiery desire for revenge within him. After much contemplation, he devised a cunning plan. He went to his mother and told tall tales of Gul Makai and Musa Khan's forbidden romance. The old hag, in turn, wasted no time in fanning the flames and narrated the fabricated tale straight to Gul Makai's mother. When Shah Mast Khan learned of this from his wife, his wrath knew no bounds. The very same day, he barred Gul Makai from attending the *madrassa.*

Speentareen's nightingale had been caged by Shah Mast Khan. For how much longer could Musa Khan endure such injustice? The thought of attending the *madrassa* became unbearable; its walls seemed to close in on him. Lost in thoughts of her, he wept for his beloved day-in and night-out, the ache of separation gnawing at him. Meeting her was impossible. However, Musa Khan came up with a plan. He persuaded Gul Makai's servant girl, Salaaro, to carry a letter to his beloved. When the reply arrived, Musa Khan's heart overflowed with joy and longing. Each word and letter penned by Gul Makai carried within it a storm of love, affection,

---

193 *Bismillah:* "In the name of Allah"—Muslims say it before they begin a task.

and tenderness. He clung to the letter, tracing its contours with trembling fingers, pressing it to his eyes and lips each time he reread it.

As the letters went back and forth, both restless souls found some solace. But how long could this secret remain hidden? Love forges its path like mercury. One day, Musa Khan wrote a love letter for Gul Makai and placed it in his book, intending to give it to Salaaro for delivery. However, on his way back from the *madrassa,* the envelope slipped from his book and unfortunately fell into Sohail's hands. Now, Sohail prayed for an opportunity like this. He hurried to Shah Mast Khan, presenting him with the letter and saying, "Khan, things are spiralling out of control. Please think of something quickly. Otherwise, we will not be able to face anyone."

Shah Mast Khan was already furious. This letter added fuel to the fire. It was decided that Musa Khan would be killed in the *madrassa* whenever they got a chance. As soon as Salaaro became privy to this plot, she rushed to warn Musa Khan and sent him back to his village before the plan could be executed.

When Shah Mast Khan arrived at the *madrassa* with his comrades and discovered that Musa Khan was not present, he seethed with anger. Determined to retaliate, they devised a plan to launch an announced attack under cover of the night on Musa's village. However, upon reaching the village, Shah Mast Khan could not believe his eyes when he found Musa Khan and a large number of men awaiting their assault. Outside the village, there was a fierce and bloody fight. As the battle raged on, it became evident to Shah Mast Khan that victory was slipping from his grasp, prompting him to consider retreat as the more prudent course of action. Amidst the chaos, Sohail was arrested. Musa Khan wanted to execute Sohail, but he managed to plead for mercy and convinced Musa Khan of his loyalty moving forward, ultimately earning a reprieve from his captor's wrath.

Several months passed since this incident. The tribal elders intervened, and Isa Khan and Shah Mast Khan came around to being on good terms with one another again. However, this had no impact whatsoever on Musa Khan's and Gul Makai's relationship. The two kept burning in the fire of separation—two restless hearts could find no way possible of a union, but they believed that one day, their time would come...they had faith that, one day, they would be successful. Gul Makai had Musa

Khan's whole heart, just as he had hers. There was no power in the world which could estrange them.

One day, Musa Khan's shepherd was tending to his goats and entered the grazing grounds in Shah Mast Khan's village. Sohail saw him, took along some friends, and ganged up on him. They roughed up the poor shepherd, beating him black and blue, and chased him out of the village. The shepherd went straight to Musa Khan to complain. Hearing of this, Musa Khan's rage knew no bounds—he picked up his sword, belted his scabbard, and set off. Sohail was still roaming in the fields when Musa Khan saw him. He had almost met his end at Musa's sword when he placed his head on Musa Khan's feet. He swore that he had not recognised the shepherd. Noble-hearted and brave, Musa Khan forgave Sohail again.

This incident had the elders thinking once more. However, by now, the matter had become so serious that no one could think of any solution. Sohail went to Shah Mast Khan, who was in search of a chance to avenge his defeat. He narrated the incident to his uncle in such a way that he successfully managed to manipulate him to marry Gul Makai to him, as soon as possible. The date for the *baraat* was fixed, and Musa Khan was invited alone.[194] It was decided that, in the midst of celebrations, his chapter would be closed for once and for all.

'Til when was Gul Makai's true lover going to remain oblivious to such plotting? He accepted the invitation, and, apparently, came to attend the wedding alone. However, he had brought along a handful of brave young men, armed to the teeth, in secret, who hid in the fields, waiting for their *Sardar's* signal. [195]

The decision of the date of the wedding was a message of death for Gul Makai. She did not know what to do. Heart in heart, she was contemplating suicide. At that moment, Salaaro appeared, and whispered something in her ear, which made Gul Makai's eyes sparkle instantly. Her heart began to dance with happiness, and she became lost in daydreaming about a beautiful future.

The festivities reached their zenith. The *Hujra* bustled with activity, alive with the vibrant energy of the *Lakhti* dance.[196] An amicable

---

194 *Baraat:* The procession brought by the groom to wed the bride and take her with him.

195 *Sardar:* Leader of the tribe.

196 *Lakhti Dance:* Pashtun folk dance.

challenge over *Wailain* ensued.[197] The aroma of hookah, filled with dry tobacco, lingered in the air, casting a heavy veil over the *Hujra*. The lids of *naswar* boxes flickered open and shut as pinches of *naswar* found their place between people's lips and cheeks with each passing moment.[198]

Musa Khan was sitting alert to one side with an air of honour and nobility. When the music and dancing reached their peak, he got up slowly and slipped out of the *Hujra*. He found Gul Makai waiting for him in Shah Mast Khan's backyard, just behind the *Burj*.[199] She wanted to say something, but Salaaro said, "*Bibi*, this is no time to talk.[200] You must make haste." Musa Khan's horse neighed and began galloping away at the speed of light. Beneath the shroud of the night, the sound of weeping and wailing echoed from Shah Mast Khan's home. The lively beats of the *dhol* and the melodic strains of the *shehnai* abruptly ceased,[201] suffocated into silence as if smothered by an invisible hand.[202] Someone came and said, "The bride has gone missing."

Upon hearing this, a hushed stillness enveloped the gathering. Everyone was frozen in disbelief. Sohail's gaze swept across the *Hujra*, searching for Musa Khan in vain. He instantly understood what had transpired. Musa Khan urged his horse onward, pushing it to its limits. Every muscle in the animal's body strained with exertion, its sweat leaving a trail in its wake. It was as if a tracker had marked their trail. But their efforts seemed futile against the oppressive night, where even the outlines of their own hands were lost in the ebony void. Suddenly,

---

197 *Wailain:* A practice of throwing money into the air during a singing/dance performance. The bride and the groom's sides often engage in a competition of who throws the most. At weddings, the money on the floor is collected by the performers and kids and given away to charity.

198 *Naswar:* A moist mixture made from sun and heat-dried tobacco leaves. These are added to slaked lime, ash from tree bark, and flavouring. It is consumed by stuffing a pinch inside the cheek or beneath the lower lip.

199 *Burj:* A tower—traditionally, Pakhtun houses have one, or more than one. Family feuds were common, and it served as a lookout post.

200 *Bibi:* "Lady of the House"—a word adopted from Persian. It is also used as a surname, and as a title (e.g. Lady so-and-so), but is added after the first name (e.g. Gul Bibi).

201 *Dhol:* A type of local drum.

202 *Shehnai:* A clarinet-like instrument specific to the Indian subcontinent.

disaster struck as the horse stumbled over an imposing boulder, collapsing in its fatal fall.

Reacting swiftly, Musa Khan shielded Gul Makai behind the shelter of a towering tree. Before he could fully prepare himself, Sohail and Shah Mast were already upon them. Brandishing his sword, Musa Khan bravely fought the enemy, standing firm against the odds all by himself. However, a powerful blow by the enemy brought him to his knees. Just as Sohail raised his sword to finish Musa Khan for good, Gul Makai seized a rock and hurled it at Sohail, disarming him. She leapt forward and deftly retrieved the fallen sword, swiftly incapacitating Sohail with a single powerful blow.

Just then, Musa Khan's reinforcements arrived. The skirmish escalated into a ferocious melee, littering the ground with fallen combatants. In the chaos, Shah Mast Khan and his dwindling band of followers were forced into a hasty retreat, leaving behind a scene of carnage and defeat.

Gul Makai gently tended to her beloved's wounds, her heart heavy with worry and her prayers fervent with hope. She beseeched Allah, making countless vows, until finally, the day arrived when Musa Khan regained his health and did his *ghusl*.[203]

That day, as he sat with Gul Makai in a picturesque garden in his backyard, they savoured each other's company, surrounded by the fragrance of blooming flowers. Gul Makai, radiant as a rose in full bloom, gazed at her beloved with adoration, her eyes fixed upon him, his enchanting face like the moon. Musa Khan broached the subject of marriage, but Gul Makai responded with a firm condition, much like a boulder blocking a path. "You will have to convince my father."

Hearing this, it was as if the sky had fallen on Musa Khan's shoulders. He told her that this was a very difficult condition and Shah Mast Khan would never agree. "Whatever happens, he will need to be convinced. Or else, this thorn shall always prick my heart, and our happiness will remain incomplete," she told him.

At last, Musa Khan had to give in to his beloved's stubbornness. With a *Jirga* of well-respected tribal elders and his father, he went to call on Shah Mast Khan.[204] Isa Khan addressed Gul Makai's father, "Shah Mast

---

203 *Ghusl:* A specific type of bath Muslims take to purify themselves, including after prolonged sickness.

204 *Jirga:* A council of tribal elders.

Khan, I, Musa Khan's father, accept defeat. I am here to beg you for my son's life. Please take him in as your son."

Shah Mast Khan could do little to resist the tribal *Jirga's* request. He raised Musa Khan from his feet and gave him a warm hug.

The apple of the eye of the Yousafzai clan, Musa Khan, and Speentareen's *peri-like* Gul Makai were heading towards the bed chambers adorned for the newlyweds when they heard Salaaro.[205] "Stop!" she commanded. "You owe me an award before you leave."[206]

Musa Khan and Gul Makai chuckled at Salaaro's mischief. Gul Makai came forward and adoringly pinched her cheeks like her little sister, and said, "Here is your due."

---

205 *Peri:* A winged creature, *Hoor* exclusively feminine, known for being gentle, kind, and beautiful.

206 In Pakhtun tradition, it is very normal to ask for a present or an award when you help someone with something. It does not, however, imply that Salaaro is actually asking for something. If she actually did, it would be rude. Helping your friends is a love language, it is not transactional, you know you will be paid in kind when the need and the time arises. This practice reflects a broader influence of Persian customs on the social etiquette (*Tehzeeb*) in Pakhtun society. Historically, both Pakistan and Afghanistan have been integrated into several Persian empires. Additionally, indigenous empires from these areas, such as the Ghaznavid and the Mughal empires, also displayed strong Persianate cultural characteristics. This cultural interaction, as a result, has significantly shaped local cultural and social norms over the span of several hundred, if not thousands of years. Take for example, the Iranian custom of "*Taarof*"—the rules or framework put into place by the Persian custom, are a part of social ettiquete. It is followed to varying degrees, across ethnic lines in both Pakistan and Afghanistan, also merging with other local customs.

15

FATEH KHAN RABIA

HE POSSESSED ABUNDANCE BEYOND measure, and nothing was ever scarce for him. Allah had provided him with everything a man could have asked for. Wealth and riches, honour and glory, a country, and a Sultanate. Despite the grandeur, sadness lingered on his face, and his heart felt like it was being crushed under tonnes of grief. There were endless gold and jewels in his treasury, he was the king of the mighty sultanate of Qandahar, and the ruler who reigned from the formidable fortress of Bost—however, there was nothing which could bring peace and contentment to his heart.

The absence of an heir to his throne was distressing. This realisation of this struck him like a lightning bolt falling onto a tree when one day, in the mirror, he noticed a single silver-grey strand in his thick black beard. He became very worried. He began to think he would pass on from this world without achieving anything at all. His crown and his throne will be captured by people, and after he dies, there will be no one to take his name or carry on his legacy.

This realisation made him lose the will to live his life. He handed over state affairs to his viziers; he left his royal palace, the royal throne room, and even his royal chambers, and moved to the courtyard, spending most of his day in isolation, both angry and in pain.

As Allah would have it, one day, a *faqir* called out at the doors of the royal palace.[207] The servants, as usual, were just about to leave some alms

---

207 *Faqir:* A wandering Muslim ascetic who lives solely on alms.

for him in his *kashkol,* but the *faqir* was different—he did not wish for alms.[208] He wanted an audience with the king! The servants presented the *faqir's* request to the king, however, he refused to meet him. When the *faqir* was informed that the king had declined, he called out once again, "I do not want charity. I want to meet the king, the king who goes by the name of Aslam Khan."

When the king heard this, he became furious. "What is this insolence? Who dares to call me by my name? Bring this disrespectful man to my presence this instant." he snapped. The *faqir* was presented. The king, infuriated, inquired about the reason for this disdainful behaviour.

"My king, I am not one of those *faqirs* who beg for gold and silver. I am a *faqir* of purpose, not of uselessness. I do not aim to merely keep my stomach full. I am not here to ask you for anything, rather, I am here to give you something. I am here to cure you of your utter hopelessness. I am here to give you the gift of life and teach you how to live. Ask, oh sorrowful soul, what do you wish to ask for?"

Deeply impressed by the *faqir's* courage and bold words, he orders a chair inlaid with gold for the visitor. However, the *faqir* flatly refused. "We *faqirs* are nomads, we call out in humble voices and move on," he said. "We find life in movement, not in idleness. This land, country, and its people belong to Allah. Listen, oh king, for we know what your heart truly desires. Pessimism is a habit which does not befit men."

The *faqir* handed over his cane to the king. "Here is my walking staff. Take it and go outside to your apple orchards. Hit an apple tree with it, once, but only once. Collect all the apples which fall from the tree from your first blow. Give one to your wife to eat and distribute the rest amongst whomever you wish. The true desire of your heart shall be fulfilled." Saying this, the *faqir* took his leave and departed.

The king, surprised, sat there, pondering for a while. After contemplating, the king decided to heed the *faqir's* words, thinking to himself, "Perhaps Allah, in His infinite mercy, will breathe life into this desolate wasteland and grant it the blossoming of spring amidst the barrenness of a sorrowful existence."

He strolled into his garden and struck an apple tree. Sixty apples fell at once. Gathering them all, he followed the *faqir's* instructions. He gave one of the apples to his wife to eat, another to his concubine, and

---

208 *Kashkol:* Begging bowl used by *faqirs.*

a third to the vizier's wife. The rest were distributed amongst everyone at his court.

Now, speak of miracles. Everyone who ate the apples was blessed with children, most of them being baby boys. The king's wife and *kaneez* both bore him sons, who were named Fateh Khan and Karmaye.[209] The vizier was blessed with a beautiful daughter as radiant as the moon—Rabia. He was overjoyed and began to take interest in the affairs of the state once more.

In celebration, the city was lit up for three days, and everyone was a guest of the king. It was announced that a school would be built for these children. The king also decreed that their upbringing would be paid for by the royal treasury. And so, all these children began to live and study together. Amongst them, Fateh Khan was considered a *Sardar* of sorts.[210] Karmaye was both Fateh Khan's half-brother and his confidant. He was a very mischievous child. He often played strange, and sometimes, dangerous tricks, which would get the prince and his friends into hot waters.

One day, Karmaye was in the mood for mischief. He gathered all his friends and armed them with slingshots. After that, he took them a little way from the riverbank and asked them to hide there. Soon, a group of girls passed by to fetch fresh water, and he asked everyone to fix pebbles into their slings. For some time, they laughed and chattered amongst themselves. They were frisking about in the waters, playfully spraying one another, making their glass bangles collide in soft twinkling sounds. When they finished filling up their earthen pitchers and balanced them on their heads, Karmaye asked his friends to aim for the pitchers and shoot. Tarraak…tarraak…tarraak—all the red-brown pitchers broke one by one, leaving the girls drenched in water from head to toe, making their vibrantly coloured clothes stick to their bodies. They ran away screaming and yelling. Karmaye was amused.

The people of the city complained to the king. Even though he was very upset, there was nothing much he could do, besides reprimanding

---

209 *Kaneez:* A member of the harem who is not a family member or wife. Whilst these girls were taken as slaves, their status was more like ladies-in-waiting, and not that of imperial concubines. In Islam, the son of a *kaneez* is an equally legitimate heir to the throne.

210 *Sardar:* Leader of the tribe.

the children. He had leather pitchers made for the women. Now, when Karmaye heard of this, he armed his friends with bows and arrows instead of slingshots. Soon, the girls arrived at the riverbank. Their lively laughter and singing broke through the air.

> *"Today our pitchers will defeat the slingshots,*
> *Our pitchers will turn the faces away of the stones.*
> *Today our enemies will be slapped in the face,*
> *If they have any shame, they should drown in the waters of this river*
> *The water's surface mirrors a lesson's firm decree."*

Amid celebratory laughter, anticipating triumph over a handful of rowdy children, and the tingling of anklets and bangles, they lifted the pitchers with their fair arms, and blushed palms on their heads. Before they could blink, a volley of arrows flew, and each one found its mark on a pitcher. The girls yelped "Oi Allah!" in unison, which sounded romantic to the young boys, and they found it to be incredibly comical and entertaining.

Fateh Khan and Rabia had gotten along since early childhood. They were never separated from each other. Their bonding was the talk of the town and found its way to everyone's tongue. People remembered them as Shireen Farhad. Once, Rabia fell sick. Fateh Khan almost lost his wits. He never left her side and kept sitting beside her charpoy. Karmaye Khan taunted Fateh, "What kind of man are you? Afraid for a woman? If we had two or perhaps four more young lads who are as compassionate and as loving as you, the world shall become an utter wreck!" But Fateh's love stood firm as a mountain, unmoved by Karmaye's words.

The fire of love was burning on both sides. Once, Fateh Khan did not return from a hunt as scheduled. It worried Rabia so much that she ordered a servant to fetch her a horse. Just as she was about to set off, she spotted a cloud of dust and dirt on the horizon. Soon after, Fateh Khan's black horse emerged, drenched in sweat, bringing relief to Rabia's anxious heart.

The innocent early days passed as quickly as the spring, and the *Qayamatkhez* fall of adolescence stepped into the courtyard of Rabia's life.[211] Fateh Khan's desires also began to awaken. A myriad of unfamiliar emotions which they had been strangers to surged within them, teasing

---

211 *Qayamatkhez:* As cruel as the Doomsday/Last Day.

their senses. Customs and tradition stood between them like a wall, and Rabia had to become *pardahnasheen,* as was the established norm.[212] As a young woman, she could not mix and interact freely with men outside her family anymore.

Neither one of Fateh Khan's parents was happy about how close he was to Rabia, and how frequently they interacted with one another. First, they were thinking of Nazneen, their niece, as a potential daughter-in-law. Besides, discord with his vizier dissuaded the king from considering his daughter, Rabia, to be his son Fateh Khan's bride.

Whenever Karmaye saw Rabia, his heartbeat nearly stopped. It was as if a serpent had taken his heart into its grip. He had fallen in love with her, head over heels, but he did not have the nerve to confess to her. Even if he had done so, Rabia would have flat-out refused. Her rejection would have stung like a slap on the cheek. He began plotting to sever the relationship between the two lovebirds. Fateh Khan's mother thought of Karmaye as a blessing—she knew that if anyone could separate the two, it was him. She also knew that if Karmaye tried, Fateh Khan could choose to marry Nazneen.

Karmaye Khan and his stepmother meticulously wove a web of deceit—each strand designed to ensnare Fateh Khan and Rabia. Fateh Khan invited Nazneen over to stay as a guest and explained to her the part she needed to play. This was the first step in executing the plan.

When Nazneen came over to stay as a guest, Karmaye said to Fateh Khan, "*Bhai jaan,* Nazneen is one in a million.[213] Shouldn't you consider her, once at least?"

But Fateh Khan was indulging in, and captivated by, the thoughts of another. He paid no heed to Karmaye. However, Karmaye was not one to lose heart and accept defeat so quickly. Put off by his comments, Fateh went along with him for a stroll into the palace gardens anyway, albeit unwillingly. Nazneen was there, walking amid the flowers and picking them, in full character—looking both pretty and elegant. When she saw Fateh Khan, she greeted him with "Salam" in a rather peculiar way, but he did not pay much attention to her and turned to walk away instead.[214]

---

212 *Pardahnasheen:* A woman who observes purdah, either by religious or cultural practice.

213 *Bhai Jaan:* "Brother dear."

214 *Salam:* Muslim greeting, "Peace be upon you."

فتح خان، رابیا

Just then, Nazneen shrieked, "Ow! Stupid thorn!" Fateh Khan, chivalrous as he was, concerned, rushed to her. He laid her down on the soft, velvety hearth, placed her head in his lap, and began to look for the thorn in her delicate fingers. Karmaye saw his plotting work and wasted no time in finding Rabia. He began to narrate an exaggerated tale of how Fateh Khan and Nazneen had fallen in love with each other.

"This simply cannot be," Rabia said. "You're lying to me," she snapped at him.

"There is no point questioning something which is crystal clear anyway. Rabia, go outside and see for yourself," he responded.

And when Rabia went to the *jharoka* in her room and saw Fateh Khan and Nazneen, she found Karmaye's words to be true.[215] Seeing Nazneen resting her head in Fateh's lap felt like she had been stabbed in her heart and the dagger had been twisted. It shattered her. Hate began to replace the love she had for Fateh Khan, and when he came to see her, she flatly refused.

Fateh Khan was shocked—he was wondering what the matter was. Once again, Karmaye found his chance and did not intend to let it go. He instigated Fateh Khan against Rabia. "She has lost her mind. The needless praise, affection, and love you shower her with has made her arrogant. She hardly cares about you. Who does she even think she is?" Although Karmaye's words had Fateh Khan rethinking his feelings for Rabia and had sowed the seeds of discord—to forget her was impossible for him. She lived within him, just like the soul lives in the body.

Karmaye's schemes began to reveal their ugly colours. He managed to convince the king that Fateh has broken off his affectionate relationship with Rabia and is not only interested but in love with Nazneen. The royal drums were beaten, and Fateh Khan's and Nazneen's marriage was announced. Now, apparently, the way had been cleared for Karmaye. He went to see the vizier and narrated him a make-believe take of Fateh and Nazneen's affair. The vizier took offence and believed the marriage announcement was tantamount to disrespect for him and his daughter.

---

215 *Jharoka:* A kind of window found in local architecture. The *Jharokha* is a stone window projecting from the wall face of a building, in an upper story, overlooking a street, market, court, or any other open space. The net, made of stone, has smaller holes inside and larger holes outside—you can see outside, but you can't see inside properly.

Now, the pearls of his destiny were in Karmaye's hands. Karmaye sent Fateh Khan's mother, the queen, to Vizier Shah, to ask for Rabia's hand for her stepson, and her father accepted the proposal.

When Fateh Khan saw the world around him spin at a hundred-and-eighty degrees so quickly, he lost his heart. He announced that he would not marry Nazneen. However, the news of their marriage being fixed had spread like wildfire. On top of that, Karmaye announced that he would be bringing Rabia home very soon. Rabia took both developments extremely poorly.

She became a portrait of sorrow, her form draped across the bed like a wisp of mist clinging to the ground. With her face buried in the pillow, she wept torrents of tears, stringing together a necklace of sorrow. Amidst the echoes of her grief, she sought solace in playing melancholic melodies on her *rabab*, her fingers dancing upon the strings, weaving heartbreak into haunting tunes that echoed through her silent chambers. On one side Rabia, and the other, Fateh Khan, both were engulfed in the searing flames of separation. Their hearts beat in unison, yearning for each other's presence, with no room for any other soul to trespass their thoughts.

Finally, one day, Rabia sent a letter to Fateh Khan through her *kaneez*. She wrote:

Has your honour met its demise? You promised me forever—a bond forged in love and destined to withstand the trials of time. Do you wish to see someone else caress your Rabia's paizwaan? You will do well to remember that even if your self-respect and shame no longer endures, I am still courageous enough, and your Rabia will swallow this paizwaan of gold whole, until my dying gasp, lest other dares to touch it. My love, we only die once. In an honourable death lies the essence of a Pakhtun woman's life.[216]

Fateh Khan's heart bore testimony to the truth: Rabia was not the woman the whispers painted her to be. Her message breathed into him a new life. He sent the *kaneez* back with a message: that Rabia would meet him at the back entrance of her pavilion, just as the first call of the rooster.

---

216 *Paizwaan:* A specific kind of nose ring—large and attached to a chain held by the hair.

When Fateh Khan reached Rabia's backdoor at the crack of dawn, as per his promise, he saw her dressed in an all-white ensemble, a *kameez*, *partug*,[217] and a *chaddar*,[218] appearing as beautiful as a *Hoor* from heaven. Fateh had not come alone. He was accompanied by a handful of his friends, armed to the teeth. They took Rabia and rode away.

Karmaye was left behind, his palms burning with frustration. Shocked and seething with anger, he grappled with the realisation that what was almost within his grasp had been snatched away from him. Powerless to do much about anything on his own, he sought refuge in the halls of power, marching straight to his father, the king, and stoking the flames of his fury once more. Yet, even as Karmaye pleaded for action, he found his father consumed by despair, torn apart by the distance separating them from his beloved son. The king demanded the immediate return of the prince and issued an urgent command to his soldiers to coax and win over Fateh Khan to come back home.

The king's emissaries scoured the breadth and depth of the kingdom in relentless pursuit of the prince. For three days and three nights, they traversed rugged terrains and dense forests. At last, they discovered the prince and his retinue encamped at some place.

When Fateh Khan and his friends heard the thundering hooves of approaching horses, they thought that the king had dispatched his soldiers to arrest them. They decided to meet them with force and charged at the approaching soldiers. However, they soon found out that the king's men were not there to arrest them, but to persuade them to return home. With this revelation, the skirmish came to an abrupt halt. It was unanimously agreed upon that they would spend the night together at that very spot and set off on their journey back home the next morning.

Karmaye's evil mind reasoned that if the prince returned home, he would face punishment for his actions. Therefore, Karmaye plotted to prevent Fateh Khan from returning to the palace. Under cover of darkness, he untied all the horses and drove them into the village fields. Silently, he wielded his sword, swiftly dispatching two sentries stationed

---

217 *Partug:* A type of shalwar and is the lower garment (like trousers) which is baggy, gathered at the ankles, and tied around the waist, creating folds.

218 *Chaddar:* A large piece of cloth, used to wrap around the body and veil the face by women.

around the village. This disturbance stirred the village into chaos and caused a ruckus.

Thousands of armed men mobilised and followed Karmaye's lead. Taking cover behind a tent, Karmaye watched as the enraged villagers attacked Fateh Khan's unsuspecting men, who were asleep. Many soldiers lost their lives in the ambush, while others valiantly fought back. However, Karmaye saw this chaos as an opportunity. He stealthily entered Rabia's tent, where she lay sleeping. Binding her wrists and ankles, he gagged her with a cloth. Intent on abducting her, Karmaye was intercepted by Fateh Khan, who had been alerted to the situation. In a swift motion, Fateh Khan struck Karmaye down with his sword, ending the treacherous plot.

As Fateh Khan's men fell one by one in the brutal conflict, he found himself increasingly isolated on the battlefield. With death looming perilously close, he cast a fleeting, yet impassioned gaze toward Rabia, his eyes aflame with longing. "Fateh Khan, I cannot bear to live on after you...depart if you must but kill me with your own hand before you go," Rabia spoke to him, half-whispering, half-whimpering, her eyes filled with tears.

Fateh Khan, drenched in crimson hues, took his sword and stepped forward. Fateh Khan gently unclasped Rabia's gold *paizwaan*, pressed a tender, lingering farewell kiss upon her ruby-coloured lips, and drank deeply from the well of love in her eyes. "I desire neither another *paizwaan* nor the touch of another's lips, not even that of a *Hoor*, Rabia. I refuse to let you depart alone. I shall bathe in this blood with you." And, with these words, Fateh Khan's sword descended on Rabia's throat just as swiftly as one swallows water.

Soon, this devoted lover crossed paths with his beloved in the afterlife, meeting his end amidst the chaos of battle. When Shah Aslam Khan heard the news of his son's martyrdom, his vision blurred, darkness closing in around him until he collapsed unceremoniously, falling face-first from his throne. As his subjects rushed to his aid and lifted him upright, it became painfully clear that his soul had flown away from the cage of its earthly vessel.

ڈر بی بی ڈر

16

DUR BIBI DUR

ONCE UPON A TIME, a young farmer was passing by a field. An old woman was trying to lift a sack of dried cow dung. She calls out to him for help. As he lifts the sack of dried dung for her, a small white speck of broken popcorn reveals itself. "Woah! This is so pretty. It looks like the tooth of *Dur Bibi*," says the woman.[219]

"Dur Bibi? Who is that?" asks the young lad.

"Dur Bibi is a girl. She lives across the seven peaks, alone, with her mother. No one has ever seen her, yet she is known for her beauty. Her skin is the colour of milk; her teeth gleam like gems; she has beautiful, big eyes, the colour of the sea; and hair the colour of honey," the woman narrated.

"I will go meet this girl," thought the farmer to himself. He headed home, packed himself a duffel bag, fetched his moneybox, and told his mother that he was off on a mission—he has a girl to find.

"I shall either come back with her or I shall not come back at all," he informed his mother assertively.

He set off on his journey and crossed the first range of peaks on his way to where Dur is rumoured to live. After that, he called out "Dur Bibi, can you hear me?" He heard no answer.

---

219 *Bibi:* It means "Lady of the House" —a word adopted from Persian. It is also used as a surname and as a title (e.g. "Lady so-and-so") but is added after the first name (e.g. Gul Bibi).

He made his way across the second mountain range and called out once again: "Dur Bibi, can you hear me?" Once again, he heard no answer.

He crossed the fourth, fifth, and sixth peaks, calling out each time, but no one answered his calls. When he crossed the seventh peak, he heard a girl's melodious voice singing a tragic song. "My mother eats humans and picks their bones. Do not come in front of her, for she will pick your bones clean."

Ecstatic, unafraid, he called out again. "Let down your hair from your window beautiful, so my heart is assured that you can hear me."

The girl sang again, "Who are you? Do not come near me, my mother is a cannibal, she will make a meal out of you."

Regardless, the farmer headed straight for her house. The girl told him, "My mother has a habit. When she says she is going to hunt far away, she is usually somewhere nearby, but when she says I shall be home quickly, she often crosses the mountains."

"Today, she said she will wander far, so I'm expecting her home early, you should hide," she continued.

Dur had nothing in her house other than a ragged, patched sheet. She offered it to him. He digs a shallow hole in the ground, lies down in it, and covers it up with the rag. Dur sits down in the furthest corner and puts her fingers to good use, finishing a piece of crochet she had started earlier.

When her mother came back, she immediately said, "I sniff human." The girl tried to calm her mother down.

"No, no, it's just me, and my things. You're mistaken," she said.

Dur's mother took a walk around the house and voiced her concerns again. "No, I smell an outsider here."

"Mother I just told you, it's just me and my things. Have me if you want to eat a human," Dur Bibi said as a matter of fact.

"I would eat myself before I ate you. I would rather die, my child," replied her mother.

Unconvinced, Dur's mother kept going around the house, visibly uncomfortable. The conversation continued 'til nightfall, with the mother suspecting a non-human around and Dur trying to brush it off.

The next morning, Dur's mother told her that she is off to hunt; she will be nearby though. Dur Bibi was relieved to know that she has gone far away, across the mountains.

Now, this tale is from a time when even things could talk. She told her newfound saviour that first, "we should make lots of popcorn and fill up all the utensils in her house, for they spy for her mother and keep her informed of all her activities." Together, they made popcorn and filled up every glass, plate, and pan they could find to make sure they cannot speak. As fate would have it, they forgot about a mud pitcher, which was broken. Even though they filled it up, a hole in the bottom rendered their effort to keep it quiet useless. Anyhow, Dur Bibi cut off her little finger and put it behind the shower curtain before she escapes.

When Dur Bibi's mother returns, she called out, "Dur dear, where are you?"

Dur's finger spoke back to her, "I'm in the shower, Mother!"

A while later, her mother called out again. "Hurry up!"

Her finger talked back once again. "I'm in the shower!"

Her mother kept roaming around the house, getting increasingly exasperated with Dur. She finally pulled away the curtain to find Dur's finger. She started to scream, "Where did my daughter go, oh no!"

The broken mud pitcher told her, "A thief took her away."

Without a second thought, she ran out of the house to catch the thief and recover her daughter. She picks up her pace 'till she nearly caught up with them. Dur and the farmer set up a huge pile of needles in her path and continue running.

Barefoot, Dur's mother crossed the pile in immense pain, with her feet bleeding profusely, only to find another pile blocking her way: a pile of soap. Slipping, sliding, and struggling, she made her way across it. Her difficulties hadn't ended. The next obstacle which waited for her is a pile of salt. Already hurt from the needles and the wounds stinging from the soap, the salt rubbed into her wounds, burning her skin, but she crossed the salt nevertheless. She met her end, as the final pile is one of the matches. She tries to crossed the burning pile, but to no avail, and burned to death.

As the danger passed, near a lake, the farmer asks Dur Bibi to wait for him, whilst he brought his mother and his family and friends for the *baraat*.[220]

---

220 *Baraat:* The procession brought by the groom to wed the bride and take her with him.

The girl agreed, and whilst she waited, a bald, old, ugly woman finds her. She tells the girl, "Your husband-to-be has sent me. I will prepare you for your wedding." The girl agreed. Nearby, in the lake, she offered to wash Dur Bibi's hair before she takes a shower. Whilst Dur is taking a bath, the woman pushed her into the water. Unable to swim, Dur drowned. Rather than dying, she transformed into a Chinar tree right in the centre of the lake. When the farmer returned with the wedding procession, he failed to understand where his bride went. This abomination of a woman, with pale skin and marks on her face, was certainly not the girl he had left here! The procession was also worried.

Anyhow, he convinced his family that Dur had become so ugly crying her heart out, waiting for her beloved's return. They got married and soon had a child. The evil woman wanted Dur Bibi to find out that she now had a child with the man Dur loved, the man she stole from him. So, she told her husband of a *Chinar* tree in a lake and asked him to fetch wood from that tree to make a cradle for the baby.[221] Her husband did as she asked. However, Dur would have none of it. The moment they put the baby in the cradle, the baby boy would wail and scream. As soon as they picked the child up, it would calm down. Dur Bibi's soul in the wood of the cradle was hell-bent on making the cradle uncomfortable for the child, so she used to pinch the baby.

The woman decided to break the cradle and use it to repair the panelling of the doorway into the house. Funny as it sounds, the panels on the door used to leave a flower on the ear of the farmer every time he passed beneath it. As for the old woman, she used to get a tight slap! Tired of the nonsense, the evil woman takes off the wood and stokes a fire. As the wood of Dur's tree burned, the wood sniffed and sobed. The woman disposed of her ashes in a faraway field of melons. Out of Dur's ashes grew a small melon. An old man with his grandchild were touring the field. Everyone had taken the ripe, yellow melons. The child ran in excitement to the small melon, which popped out of nowhere.

"Let's take this one home, Grandpa. I don't want to go home empty-handed! We can put it where we store wheat, it will ripen, eventually." His grandfather agreed. One day, the long box of tin began to shake. The melon ripened into a young woman!

---

221 Chinar: Old-world sycamore; Platanus orientalis.

Upon her request, she was given a pair of clothes. She told them her story and how she wants to meet a certain farmer. Her hosts agreed to take her along and drop her off at the house of the farmer. She told them not to tell him the truth just yet, so they tell the farmer that she has come from far away and needs refuge. The farmer granted their request.

Although he thought she looked like Dur Bibi, he didn't ask her since she didn't speak to him much. One day, he came and asked her, "I am off to the market to get some things for my wife and my kid. Do you need something?"

"Please bring me a doll," she asked. Curious about why she wants a doll, he brought it for her anyway, but after he gave it to her, he waited outside her room, eavesdropping on her. Aware of this, Dur wasted no time. She hugged the doll and starts telling the doll her story, every word, from the start to the end.

Hearing the events and how unfair his wife had been, he became furious. However, he did not react immediately. He went to her and asked, "Would you like red metal or white metal?"

She assumed he is talking of gold and silver. "Red metal please," she said, secretly becoming very happy.

Her husband had other plans. He heated a metal plate enough to make it glow red, picked up his wife, and put her on the plate. She burned to death, while Dur and the farmer lived happily ever after.

17

YOUSAF KHAN SHERBANO

IN THE EXPANSE OF lush pastures, hundreds of bleating goats yielding creamy milk, and fields ablaze with the golden promise of harvest resided Hussain Kaka. Despite his abundance, melancholy shadowed his days, for he harboured a deep yearning unfulfilled: the absence of offspring. Though prosperous and generous, his heart ached with the barrenness of the fruitless orchard of his life. He longed to witness the joyous laughter of a child echoing through his house, to behold a little one frolicking amidst his gardens, a rightful heir to his legacy.

Each glance in the mirror at his greying hair and beard made him sigh with sorrow. Six decades had passed, but the walls of his home had not yet a single note of childish laughter. He dreaded the thought of his fertile lands passing into the hands of his paternal cousins. Yet despite his inner turmoil, he maintained an air of strength and cheer, offering a gentle smile in response to sympathetic people who brought up the subject. "It is the will of Allah. What do we know of what is best for us?"

Together, with his wife, he went on pilgrimages to the shrines of many revered saints and Pirs, to pray, and to make *mannat*.[222] And then, one fateful day, the news he had long awaited reached him—the tree of his wishes was on the verge of bearing fruit, flooding his heart with joy beyond measure.

---

222 *Mannat:* Owing to Allah to give away a specific amount of charity or praying a certain number of rakat's of non-obligatory prayer (Nafal) if what you have prayed for is accepted.

Finally, the long-awaited moment arrived, and Hussain Kaka's life became bliss with the arrival of a beautiful baby girl. He named her Bunadayi. Despite the dismissive murmurs of his detractors who deemed a daughter inconsequential compared to a son as an heir, Hussain Kaka cherished her as if she were worth a hundred sons, his heart brimming with gratitude. And it seemed as though nature, pleased by his appreciation, granted Bunadayi a precious gift the following year—a baby brother, radiant as the moon. That day, Hussain Kaka celebrated to his heart's content with ceaseless aerial firing, later joined by his family, friends, and acquaintances. The cacophony of gunfire had distant observers wondering if a feud had erupted between rival tribes.

The newborn baby boy was beautiful, earning him the endearing moniker *Yousaf the Second* —Hussain Kaka decided to name the child Yousaf after all.[223] As swiftly as a gust of wind, Yousaf's childhood days passed, and soon his father sent him to the *madrassa* for education. Now, adorned not only with handsome features, but also with the jewels of knowledge, the Yousafzai clan beamed with pride at this fine and fair young man from Turlandi. Travellers bound for the Karrahmar Hills for hunting expeditions always made a stop at Turlandi, only to see Yousaf once. Hussain Kaka's *Hujra* was always teeming with guests.

Until when was Hussain Kaka going to live. Eventually, the flicker of his life dimmed. Yet, in his final moments, he found contentment. He knew that upon his passing, his hands would be tenderly clasped by his children. They would continue to offer charity in his name. Beside his lifeless form, his daughter would lament *"Baba, baba,"* while his stalwart son, a beacon of strength, would gently lower him into the earth. His funeral procession would be a burden to none.

Following Hussain Kaka's demise, Yousaf found himself bound by a web of newfound responsibilities. No longer could he roam freely; instead, he was tasked with safeguarding his land and property, tending

---

223 The title "Yousaf the Second" is referring to the Prophet Yousaf (A). Known as Joseph in Biblical tradition, he is believed to have been extremely good-looking. Not only Pakhtuns, but Pakistanis in general, often say "This is the second so-and-so" to describe how they feel about something. So, when a beautiful baby boy was born, it was natural for the villagers to have said something like "He is the second Yousaf" —hence, Yousaf the Second; the first one being the Prophet (A) himself.

to his orchards and fields, and navigating the schemes plotted by envious cousins. The weight of these obligations weighed heavily upon him, transforming his once carefree demeanour into one of solemnity.

With intelligence, astuteness, and a warm heart, Yousaf greeted everyone with courtesy and friendliness. He did not loiter around aimlessly like his friends and did not like it either. he did not play or sit with the loafer boys in his village. While others sought amusement, Yousaf preferred to sit aside and think. His peers began to call him "*Yakka Yousaf*" —the one who stays by himself.[224] Even though it sometimes made him lonely, eventually, he found himself a hobby: hunting.

Whenever guests came over to stay the night at Yousaf's *Hujra* before setting off to hunt, Yousaf always went along with them. He also kept two hunting dogs who accompanied him. Their collars were adorned with *ghungroo*—the tinkling of the bells announced Yousaf's arrival wherever he went.[225]

The hunting grounds were three miles away from Turlandi. Nearly halfway was another village, Shera Ghund. Sherbano was the daughter of the Malik of that village—the girl as beautiful as the moon, who glowed like the sun, was one of the thousands of young women who lived at the foot of the Karrah Mar Hills.

In the tranquil hours of early morning, as Yousaf walked through the village pathways, the melodious tinkling of his dogs' collars serenaded in the crisp air, it drew the attention of villagers. They came onto their rooftops, into the streets, and outside their *Hujras* to greet him. Yousaf exchanged pleasantries warmly, inquiring about their well-being before going on his way. One day, Sherbano thought to herself, "I must see this young man for myself—who is he?"

One day, as the chimes of *ghungroo's* pierced the tranquil morning air, Sherbano went up to her rooftop to catch a glimpse of Yousaf. At the mere sight of him, her heart was stirred with an overwhelming affection. At that moment, new desires swirled within her, performing the *attan* in the depths of her heart.[226] Love had found her, but in its embrace, she found herself lost. Body and soul surrendered entirely to him, as

---

224 *Yakka:* The one who stays by himself, a loner.

225 *Ghungroo:* Small metal bells are worn around the foot by women or put around the neck of animals as a collar.

226 *Attan:* A traditional dance originating from the tribal Pashtun regions.

Yousaf became her sole focus. Yousaf had come into her life like a bolt of lightning, which she glanced upon for a second, and then disappeared.

She stood, lost, still as a statue. If her mother's voice calling out to her had not broken her trance, she would have remained there. From that day onwards, waking up to the sounds of the bells became a routine for her—she would look at Yousaf and keep staring at him 'til he disappeared out of sight. She wished her eyes would meet his, but Yousaf did not turn around even once. It was as if he was careless with her heart. Sherbano's routine roused her mother's suspicions. Realising what was happening, she mentioned the matter of Sherbano's heart with her husband.

One sweltering afternoon, Sherbano was lying on her charpoy, counting the girders of her roof, when someone knocked on her door. Her heart began to beat faster, and she jumped towards the door. When she opened the door, an innocent young girl was standing outside. Her features and her physique starkly resembled those of Yousaf. "What happened, sister? Who are you? Come, sit." Sherbano greeted the stranger who had just popped up kindly.

"I'm thirsty. May I please have some water?" the girl politely requested.

Sherbano quickly fetched her a large glass brimming with *lassi*.[227] For some strange reason, she could feel Yousaf's scent on the girl. After having some *lassi*, the girl suddenly appeared to be a lot more hydrated and livelier. Sherbano insisted she stay for a while to rest. She could not shake off the feeling that this girl was somehow related to Yousaf, and she simply had to find out more. "Where do you come from, sister dear, why are you so exhausted? What is your name?" Sherbano probed.

"I am called Bunadayi. My brother, Yousaf, goes to hunt in the Karrah Mar Hills nearby. I pack some lunch and take food for him every afternoon. I ran out of water on the journey today and felt very thirsty, so I had to knock on someone's door hoping for help," responded the girl.

"Yousaf who? The son of Hussain Kaka of Turlandi?" Sherbano inquired.

"Yes, sister, the same Yousaf," Bunadayi told her. Upon hearing this, Sherbano's heart nearly jumped with joy.

"Bunadayi, consider this your home. You're welcome to rest. After giving food to your brother, do drop by for a chat from now on. You are

---

227 *Lassi:* A local drink made with yoghurt and water.

یوسف خان، شیربانو

blessed to have a brother such as Yousaf," Sherbano told her, happy that she had found her beloved at her doorstep.

Bunadayi began to drop by at Sherbano's every afternoon. They soon became very good friends. Sherbano would ask her about Yousaf every day. Whenever Bunadayi mentioned him, Sherbano would smile, and kittens would frisk about in her heart. When Yousaf heard of Sherbano's affection from Bunadayi, a pleasant feeling tickled his chest. For the first time, he felt like someone was entering his daily routine. The next day, when Yousaf was returning from the hunt, his restless eyes scanned every nook and cranny of the village. At one turn, his eyes froze. His gaze met Sherbano's—she, too, was awaiting him. He was greeted with a warm smile, which he duly reciprocated. All it took was one look for the fire of love to be lit on both sides. Yousaf was no longer just a hunter—he was also the hunted—by the woman with gazelle eyes.

One morning, Yousaf went off to hunt as usual. In Shera Ghund, two pairs of eager eyes greeted one another. After he reached Karrah Mar, he was busy hunting, laying snares and taking aim, but his heart was lost in the thoughts of his beloved. It was as if he was looking for Sherbano on the peaks and in the ravines. On every boulder, Farhad saw the picture of his Shireen.[228] For a second, he leapt towards it, mistaking it for Sherbano, and the next moment, he would realise that it was only the enchantment of his thoughts.

Amid this confusion, Yousaf's foot slipped over a sharp stone on the edge of the path winding around the mountain, and from Karrah Mar's peaks which kissed the sky, he tumbled into a ravine where death awaited him with open jaws. He tried to grab at boulders to steady himself, but it went in vain. As he was falling over the rocks, he managed to grab a tree branch, which broke his fall. He was hanging in mid-air, and whilst he could not hang on for long, letting go meant that *Malak al Mawt* would have not let him go either.[229]

Several hours later, the alchemist of the east began to create gold in the west as the sun began to set. The shadows began to grow longer. Sherbano, like *Zulaikha*, was awaiting Yousaf's return, as this was the time

---

228 This is a reference to the tale of Shireen and Farhad.
229 *Malak al mawt:* The title of the Angel of Death.

he usually came back.[230] Time was passing by, but Yousaf was nowhere to be seen. A few moments later, she heard the tinkling of the bells worn by his dogs and was happy that Yousaf was finally coming. However, his dogs were alone and running towards the village in angst. "Ya Allah, please let all be well with my Yousaf," a silent prayer escaped her lips.

Darkness fell everywhere, and Sherbano spent the night tossing and turning. She was in pain and extremely anxious, wondering what had become of Yousaf. All night, his dogs barked, as if they were pleading for help. She understood that Yousaf needed help. The rooster had not finished calling out, and Sherbano heard the dogs once again. She went to her roof and saw Bunadayi and her mother running after them, panting. Sherbano's patience wore thin. She joined them, her blood on fire.

Seeing Yousaf hanging in the well of Karrah Mar, his mother beat her chest, his sister pulled her hair, and Sherbano froze like a soulless statue. Yousaf was hanging, and all that stood between him and death was one single branch of a tree. "Had this tree not been here, my Yousaf would have been in the jaws of the wolf of death—and the wolf of death spares no one," thought Sherbano. This thought seemed to suck the blood right out of her. Her pomegranate-like face went pale.

Yousaf called out to his mother, reproaching her. "Mother, what happened to you, and your heart? How could it not feel my pain?"

"My son, I spent the whole night awake," his mother sobbed.

Yousaf screamed again, "Tell me, Mother, how many times did the clouds cover the moon last night?"

Yousaf wasn't satisfied with his mother's answer and asked her yet again. However, he could not see the truth in her answers. His tired eyes asked his sister the same question, and she, too, could not say anything to stop his heart from breaking. His gaze then met Sherbano's, where he not only found warmth and love, but also read countless tales of the ache of a night of separation. Her tears were full of pain and torment. Suddenly, Yousaf found hope to save himself—he knew there was someone who cared.

---

230 As she waits for Yousaf, Sherbano is referred to as "Zulaikha." This is a reference to the romance Yusuf Wa Zulaikha. This story from the Quran has been widely retold as a folktale in various languages across the Muslim world, including Pashto. In the Biblical tradition, it is known as the story of Joseph and Potiphar's wife.

Sherbano's soft, delicate hands whipped her *chaddar* off her head and threw it towards Yousaf. The love of his mother, the affection of his sister, and the force of *ishq* and attraction gave Yousaf a second chance at life.[231] His love had turned from a drop into a sea. Now that Sherbano had been seen with Yousaf, the situation needed to be handled with extreme care.

Finally, the day arrived when Yousaf's mother went to ask Sherbano's family for her hand. Now, who could refuse the proposal of Turlandi's Malik, the great Hussain Kaka's son and his only heir? Sherbano was also the only daughter of her parents, who found the match suitable. However, fate had other plans.

Sherbano's paternal cousins were not in favour of this marriage. They were thinking of bringing Sherbano home as a bride to one of the brothers, thereby gaining an upper hand on their uncle and strengthening their claim to the property of their father's brother. They told their uncle, "Sherbano is the nose of the clan, she is our honour and the invaluable *chaddar* of the women of our tribe. We will not give her away to anybody if he does not pay what she is worth." When, according to Yousafzai tradition, Sherbano's bride price was calculated, it was a lot more than all which Yousaf owned.

Both Yousaf and Sherbano were angry, but they also laughed at the mentality of these people, who are ignorant of the rules put in place by love. However, they could not do much other than bow their heads to centuries old Pakhtun traditions, and the sacred customs of their tribes. It was as if a wall of gold had been raised between *husn* and *ishq*.[232] This chasm could have only been bridged by wealth, gold or silver. Yousaf decided to take action and he prepared to leave behind everything and set off to Hindustan. His mother's heart burned at the thought, his sister cried to him to stop, and Sherbano's wishes whimpered as he left, but nothing stopped him.

Now enrolled in the military of the Mughal Emperor, Padishah Akbar-e-Azam, Yousaf soon earned a name for himself. It did not take long for him to be promoted to an officer from a soldier. His mother and his sister were helpless. Poor Bunadayi, who had been raised being showered with affection, now had to assume the responsibilities never

---

231 *Ishq:* The highest stage of love.
232 *Husn:* The extremity of beauty.

meant for her. His paternal cousins thanked the Lord that Yousaf had left. They thought, "He isn't coming back, is he now?"

A few days later, they spread the false news of Yousaf's death and then seized all the property which was rightfully his. They also chucked his mother and Bunadayi out of their home. After spending a whole lifetime being treated like princesses, the poor mother and daughter began to earn a living for themselves by serving other people. Sherbano was spending each moment burning in the fire of separation like an injured *koel*.[233]

When her father passed away, she lost whatever was left to keep her grounded. Now, her sprawling village and the endless green fields were like a coffin to her. Gossip and whispers made it to Sherbano's ears, and she realised that her cousins did not mean well for her. They intended to sacrifice her like an injured bird and take hold of her dad's property. She had a feeling they would torment her in every way possible and, to show off their tyranny, perhaps even marry her off to someone else. She shivered and swore to herself that if her hand was given to anyone else to clasp, she would poison herself.

Soon, the ill-fated moment came when Sherbano's marriage was announced amid the din of the *dhol* and the *surna*.[234] It was as if a sky of grief had come crashing down on Sherbano's shoulders.[235] She found a way to send Bunadayi a message. "Bunadayi, my sister, I have no one in this whole wide world besides you. It will be a favour if you can get me some poison. I, and my soul, shall be grateful. I do not wish to go to anyone else's home other than Yousaf. He will say, 'Sherbano turned out to be disloyal.' Here, keep my gold *paizwaan;* sell it, so that the purity of my love remains untainted.[236] Please, fetch me poison which works quickly."

Bunadayi dropped by to see Sherbano. "My dear sister, please, let me share your poison. Do not go alone. Now that my prince of a brother is not here anymore, I do not wish to live in this world anymore." She promised Sherbano to bring poison for her the following day and left.

---

233 *Koel:* A bird, the Eudynamys.

234 *Dhol:* A type of local drum.

235 *Surna:* A local double-reed instrument.

236 *Paizwaan:* A specific kind of nose ring—large and attached to a chain held by the hair.

The *naqqara* blew loudly.[237] The *dhol* and the *surna* drowned out all other noises from one's ears. On one side, large cauldrons were simmering over the stoves, and Bunadayi, unfortunate Bunadayi, was fetching water for them. With tears in her eyes and Yousaf's name on her tongue, she reproached her brother for leaving and not turning back to ask her, his sister, even once about how she was doing. Just as she was thinking all this, the earthen pitcher fell from her hands. It broke, and the cook scolded her for being so careless. Her patience was wearing thin, and she went into a corner and began to bawl her eyes out, sobbing loudly. She wiped away her tears with her grimy *dupatta*—but what did it know of the worth of these tears?

"Bunadayi, sister!" someone called out to her, and she suddenly remembered the promise she had made Sherbano. "Poison."

The thought seemed to lift a burden off her chest. Now, she would be free of her pain soon. She got up, wiping away her tears. "Bunadayi, sister, why are you crying? I'm here." When she saw Yousaf standing in front of her, she screamed, and ran towards him, flinging her arms around his shoulders. In this moment of sheer joy, she sometimes laughed and sometimes cried. "What is all this?" Yousaf asked, pointing towards the cauldrons.

"Your sister is no longer Hussain Kaka's daughter. She is a servant girl, and I am working here. All this is for Sherbano's *baraat*," Bunadayi cried.[238]

"Don't you worry? Your brother is not a nobody anymore, but a great officer in the forces of Padishah Akbar-e-Azam. I have brought along a party of soldiers; I came to visit on a holiday. Go and give Sherbano the good news. Tell her that Yousaf is here and has brought a lot of wealth with him. As for this rice, her *baraatis* will eat this very food."[239]

Just when the *Qazi* was about to begin the *Nikkah*,[240] Yousaf attacked with his men.[241] There was a stampede of sorts in the *baraat*. When people realised it was Yousaf accompanied by soldiers, they began to

---

237 *Naqqara:* Kettledrum.

238 *Baraat:* The procession brought by the groom to wed the bride and take her with him.

239 *Baraatis:* Members of the baraat procession.

240 *Qazi:* Local magistrate or judge.

241 *Nikkah:* The Muslim marriage contract.

wonder if it was a dream or reality. Amongst the enemies, anyone who tried to fight back was put to the sword. Yousaf did not want to fight the entire village. He only targeted his rivals, and after the path had been cleared, he presented himself to Sherbano with his heart pure as ever.

For a moment, the two stared at each other in silence, as if two photographs had been placed in front of one another. When the spell broke, the seashells of their eyes filled with pearls of love, and the two complained to each other about the pain they had caused.

The villagers got together and greeted Yousaf. They were happy that the one who shall keep their *Sardar's* name alive still lives.[242] Sherbano was brought to their village as the daughter-in-law of the Sardar Hussain Malik. Bunadayi greeted Sherbano as a friend and as her sister-in-law. Yousaf decided to build his world a little far away from his village: he built his house at the peak of the Karrah Mar Hills, where Sherbano's *chaddar* had saved his life. He hunted and spent his days with his beloved, in utter bliss.

One day, Bunadayi suddenly fell ill. A cold fever gripped her. Yousaf loved his sister dearly and arranged for many doctors and *Hakeem's* to treat her,[243] had several *taweez* done on her, but Bunadayi's days were finished—and she left this world to meet her Allah.[244] Life had been long, and the journey had been difficult. Bunadayi had stood by Yousaf and Sherbano throughout it, and now they had lost her. But Yousaf's world had everything, as long as he had Sherbano.

Yousaf Khan and Sherbano lived together, happily ever after. Sherbano eventually passed away, after which he resigned himself to taking care of her grave. A few days later, singing melodies in her praise, Yousaf's soul, too, broke the cage of this temporary life and fluttered away.

---

242 *Sardar:* The head of the tribe.

243 *Hakeem:* A wise man or physician who is a practitioner of herbal medicine, especially in Greek and Islamic medicine.

244 *Taweez:* Verses written and worn around the neck or the wrist as a talisman.

18

SHER ALAM MAIMOONAYI

"**T**HAT'S A HIT!" EXCLAIMED Sher Alam, releasing a stone from his slingshot.

"Tsk, tsk, tsk, what did you just do? Sher Alam…how will you answer Allah for this? You're ruthless…you just harmed an innocent bird." Maimoonayi expressed her feelings, upset, her face turning as pale as a withering jasmine flower.

"This is what should have happened to the wretch!" Sher Alam turned to her, his expression serious. "I do not stand disloyalty, even if it is a dove. Did you not see, how she was flying from one tree to the next? And him? He was getting exhausted fluttering after her." he huffed, annoyed.

"But you were going to…" Maimoonayi started to speak, but Sher Alam interrupted her.

"Yes, actually…I would have done the same to you, should you ever be disloyal to me."

"To me as well…?" Maimoonayi wailed, thumping her chest, and began to sob. "I expect nothing less from you. You're heartless."

"Oh dear, you've begun to cry. You're a woman at the end of the day, aren't you? Making a mountain out of a molehill, as usual. What's the big deal, and why would you cry about this? We play this game every day. This is how we perfect our aim anyway. Or else, when we face off with the enemy, our rifles too would miss their target on their chests. Okay now, come on, get up. Let's go and check up on your beloved little dove. Come on, my Maimoonayi, let's stop crying now, eh? Come." Sher Alam took her wrist and sweet-talked her.

159

After that, they walked over to the weeping willow tree, where the injured dove was whimpering and breathing her last breaths. The little life in her could not fight the sharp stone from the slingshot. She closed her eyes and was living through the ache of dying. Within moments, she lost her life, and large teardrops fell on Maimoonayi's flowery cheeks like dewdrops.

"Tsk, tsk, tsk…the poor thing…she was my Maimoonayi's friend. May Allah bless *Bi Fakhta*. What will happen now?"[245] Sher Alam said, smirking gleefully. "What is going to happen? Allah will grant her a place in the trees of Heaven. The poor thing was innocent. Her blood is on your hands," Maimoonayi said, her voice low as she held Sher Alam's gaze with her eyes full of tears.

"Alright, I think we've been out long enough. Let's go back," said Sher Alam. And then, the two of them lost themselves amongst the winding ways of the village.

Bajaur's sky-high peaks, never-ending mountain ranges, tall pine trees, and the light of the rising sun fell onto the top of the *Chinar* trees, colouring them with the orange hues of twilight.[246] The shrubbery stood next to the gigantic trees like quiet, frightened children. The high and low branches of the trees were heavy with the weight of *Gurgura* fruit, as if someone had passed a thread through purple, black, and blue beads in a specific order.[247]

Sher Alam, who was wearing his sling like a necklace, wasted no time taking it off and fitting a small, round pebble into it. He aimed for a tree branch heavy with fruit. Suddenly, it was as if it had rained violet and indigo gems. After that, both of them filled their *jholi* with the juicy gemstones to run and skip like fawns, giggling, all the way to the last turn of the village.

Just like that, the days turned into months, and the months turned into years, passing by in the blink of an eye. In Bajaur's cheerful village of Nawagai, the sun rose thousands of times. Thousands of nights enveloped it in their darkness or covered it with a blanket of a starry night. Maimoonayi and Sher Alam spent their childhood in this very

---

245 *Bi Fakhta: Bi,* a title for old women; *Fakhta,* "dove." *Bi Fakhta* is used as a title.

246 *Chinar:* Old World sycamore; Platanus orientalis.

247 *Gurgura:* A fruit native to Khyber Pakhtunkhwa, like the Grewia asiatica (Falsa).

village. And one day, the mud walls of the houses which dotted the village, the *Chinar* trees and the shrubs alike, the branches filled with *Gurguray,* witnessed the reflection of their adolescence in the sparkling clean streams. And believe me, it left them spellbound. Every ear was interested to hear their tale. Every eye witnessed them grow from a crescent into a full moon. In their youth, it had evolved into a thread of gold. They were not only childhood friends but were sweethearts. Sher Alam and Maimoonayi were first cousins. The siblings, Maimoonayi's mother and Sher Alam's father, were very happy to see their children grow up to love one another, even though they never expressed it.

Maimoonayi was the beauty of Bajaur's mountains, the prettiest girl in the village, the nose of her tribe, the story on every tongue, the soulful melody of every *rabab,* and the desire of every young man's heart.[248] Sher Alam was Nawagai's braveheart, tall and handsome, broadly built, a man of fine character, the apple of his tribe's eye, and the heartthrob of the village. All the young women in the village envied Maimoonayi.

It is said that "what is crushed in the mill can remain, but nothing remains of what is crushed between the teeth." The Evil Eye of the girls of Nawagai brought misfortune to Sher Alam. Suddenly, he found himself ill with smallpox. It was as if the moon of Nawagai had been eclipsed...or rather, as if acid had been splattered over the radiant sun. Sher Alam's face, as rosy as a pomegranate, was now as dark as burnt charcoal. Maimoonayi's dreams had been burnt. The flowery orchard of her life had been struck by lightning. For days, she sat beside Sher Alam's charpoy, gazing at him as he whimpered in pain. After he fell ill, Maimoonayi was always lost in thought. She used to stare wide-eyed at anyone who tried to address her.

The boat of Sher Alam's life escaped this whirlpool by a miracle. He gave away his looks but kept his life, leaving Maimoonayi feeling blessed, even amid all this. She was very happy. The day Sher Alam did his *ghusl-e-sehat,*[249] Maimoonayi distributed *Niaz* at Shaheed Baba's *mazaar* and completed her *ziarat* alongside her friends.[250] Even though

---

248 *Rabab:* A local string instrument.

249 *Gusl-e-sehat:* A bath of purity Muslims take after regaining health.

250 *Niaz:* A ritual in which food is given away as charity on shrines or other religious occasions; *Mazaar:* Mausoleum/shrine; *Ziarat:* Pilgrimage to a shrine or a holy place for Muslims.

she was very happy, she realised that her tribeswomen were uninterested in hearing her talk of Sher Alam. Now that he was no longer the handsome young man he once was, they felt disgusted when she mentioned him. Realising that they had only loved him for his looks, she knew that, now, he was hers alone.

For a long time, Sher Alam's illness was the subject under discussion at every gathering and in every *Hujra* in the village.[251] People thought that Maimoonayi would now find Sher Alam despicable. There was not a single young man in the village who was not happy at a potential chance with her and tried to marry her. Each one of them wished that this fresh flower of Nawagai adorn their *dastaar*.[252] However, everyone was mistaken. Maimoonayi's love was written in stone. At times, it even surprised Sher Alam himself. When he was ill, the doubts which had taken root in his mind slowly began to dissipate. Every ounce of Maimoonayi's existence found peace in Sher Alam's arms, even though he had become homely and hideous.

One day, when Sher Alam and Maimoonayi's marriage was announced amidst the beating of the *dhol* and the playing of the *surna*,[253] the entire village was silent with shock.[254] Eventually, they were married to one another. There was an element of surprise and taunt in everyone's eyes, and mockery on every tongue: "poison and honey in the same bowl," "a *Hoor* married to a langur," "a crown of thorns on a princess," "a branch of the gum Arabic tree entwined with grapevine" —tongues wagged ceaselessly...so many men, so many minds. Despite all this, Sher Alam and Maimoonayi began to live together in utter bliss. Their marriage was filled with love and countless happy days.

One day, Sher Alam had to leave the village to run an errand. By chance, he could not return home the same night. Maimoonayi spent the night walking on hot coals. Guests were flowing in and out of the

---

251 *Hujra:* A traditional all-male space, a designated outhouse, where friends and acquaintances can come visit. Culturally, Pardah is observed in Pakhtun culture, which is why men who are not relatives, do not enter the home. It is like the modern-day drawing room, only that it is detached from the main building of the house.
252 *Dastaar:* A type of headgear worn by Pakhtun men.
253 *Dhol:* A type of local drum.
254 *Surna:* A local double-reed instrument.

Hujra. The *rababi* was playing the *Qissa* of Prince Behram and Gul Andaam as rounds of the *chillam* were being passed around when,[255] suddenly,[256] the tobacco ran out. [257] Everyone suddenly missed Sher Alam's presence, for he always had a packet of tobacco tucked into the *naifa* of his *shalwar*.[258] There was always enough to pass around and share, keeping the *honour of the Hujra* intact. After that, Karmaye went over to his house to fetch some tobacco from Maimoonayi.

When Sher Alam returned the next day and found out that Karmaye had brought tobacco from Maimoonayi, he became very happy. He had been remembered and tobacco had been made available, or else the guests would have talked and said that in Sher Alam's absence if there was not a pinch of tobacco left in the village…he held his neck up high with pride. He tilted his *dastaar* with his right hand,[259] fixing it upon in *zari* worked under cap,[260] and Maimoonayi swelled with happiness on seeing her husband with his tilted *pagri*.[261]

Sanam Khan was Sher Alam's adversary, famed for his lack of character throughout the tribe. He tried his best to persuade Maimoonayi to leave Sher Alam, who had been attacked by smallpox, for him, but all his efforts went in vain. The infamous young man seethed with anger and sought revenge. Looking at Sher Alam made his blood prickle. However, he was a coward and lacked the courage to come face-to-face with Sher himself.

One day, Sher Alam was working his fields, but he was lost in thought. In his imagination, he saw Maimoonayi at every turn and, as soon as

---

255 *Rababi:* One who plays the rabab.

256 *Qissa:* A tale, a story.

257 *Chillam:* A smoking pipe is used in Pakistan, Afghanistan, Iran, and India.

258 *Naifa:* Where a naara, or elastic, rope-like thing is passed through to fasten the shalwar around the waist. It can be used to hide or tuck away small things. It's around an inch and a half wide; *Shalwar:* The trousers which are a part of the Pakhtun ethnic ensemble—it resembles loose, baggy trousers that taper at the ankles.

259 *Dastaar:* A type of headgear worn by Pakhtun men; tilting the dastaar is an expression of pride.

260 *Zari:* A type of embroidery done with gold thread.

261 *Pagri:* A type of headgear.

he made his way towards her, she used to disappear like a *peri*.[262] In his hallucinations, Maimoonayi evaded him every time, only to reappear in front of another tree.

"Sher Alam, Sher Alam."

Sher Alam recited "La Hawla Walaa Qoowata Illa Billa Hil Aleeyal Azeem" in his heart as he heard Sanam's voice.[263]

"Assalam-o-Alaikum," the deep, stern voice called out.[264] "I see my prince is lost in thought. Tell me, where does your mind wander?" Sanam Khan called out to Sher Alam as he threw a taunt at him.

Sher Alam ignored him. "*Dheet*. This is how he behaves anyway," he thought to himself.[265] He decided that he would not respond to the wretch, unworthy of his time and energy.

"Come, Sanam Khan, how do you do, my brother? Where are you coming from? You look tired. There is the *lassi* and there's some *roti* and onions wrapped in the cloth,"[266] said Sher Alam, greeting Sanam to get over the formalities and pleasantries.

"Ah, ah! Here you are, dipping all five of your fingers in *ghee*, showering in honey and milk, and you want to send poor me off with mere onions and *roti*?"[267] Sher Alam taunted him once more.[268] "Not really, Sanam Khan. We get what is written for us," Sher Alam responded, swallowing his anger.

"Destiny…ah…what can one say about it? Sometimes, even the angels make mistakes. They pen fate without casting a second glance at the man they are writing it for," Sanam Khan retorted with yet another insult.

Sher Alam instinctively went on guard, and his suppressed anger began to show on his face as his skin flushed red. "Why are you talking

---

262 *Peri:* A winged creature, hoor exclusively feminine, known for being gentle, kind, and beautiful.

263 *La Hawla Walaa Qoowata Illa Billa Hil Aleeyal Azeem:* Arabic phrase— "There is no power and no strength except that of Allah."

264 *Assalam-o-Alaikum:* A religious salutation for Muslims worldwide when greeting each other.

265 *Dheet:* A personality trait—the word encompasses being apathetic, lazy, and stubborn.

266 *Lassi:* A local drink, made with yoghurt and water.

267 *Ghee:* A type of clarified butter used as oil.

268 *Roti:* A type of flatbread—a local diet staple.

in riddles? Speak plainly. Hiding away like a coward is not befitting of a Pakhtun," he gritted his teeth.

"Oh, so now I'm not Pakhtun either, eh? That's rich coming from you. Absolutely shameless, aren't you? Have you taken a hard look at yourself in the mirror? Put your own house in order first," Sanam Khan retorted.

"Everyone in the village knows which one of us is shameless," Sher Alam's anger began to gush into his words.

"The village knows, oh they bloody well do. You should know it as well. It's not that you're unaware of things, you just choose to ignore them," Sanam Khan hit back once again.

"Had you not been in my fields right now, I would have taught you a lesson for misbehaving with me. Your tongue would have never run off on its own, ever again," Sher Alam tried to evade the subject.

"Why don't you go teach Karmaye a lesson first? He makes excuses and goes to visit your wife at night. What was it again? To fetch tobacco, ah!" Sanam Khan threw a poisonous arrow with his words, which hit home.

"Silent! You insolent wretch!" Sher Alam was seething with rage and shaking with fury. The blood rushed to his face and he began to take deep breaths as he stood face-to-face with Sanam Khan, their faces inches away from each other, and walked off.

"Two doves with one stone. Now, time for some fun. The snake will die, and my cane shall not break either," Sanam Khan thought to himself, feeling proud of the move he had just made.

As the bright afternoon sun cast its golden rays over Nawagai, the smoke from the *tandoors* began its dance in the air rising lazily at first, it swirled and twirled.[269] At first, the shapes were abstract, shifting and changing with the whims of the breeze. But, as the smoke climbed, it began to take on distinct forms. Serpentine coils twisted and slithered, reminiscent of sinuous snakes. Then, as if summoned by ancient tales and superstitions, the smoke began to shape itself into eerie figures, like the *Deos, Jinns, and Dayyans* before the smoke eventually dissipated into the vast blue skies.[270]

As usual, young girls and old women alike were gathered around the *tandoors*. Even though it was business as usual, something foreboding

---

269 *Tandoors:* An oven, traditionally made of mud, used to cook chapati and naan.

270 *Dayyan:* Supernatural feminine creature that drinks blood.

hung in the air. Everyone was waiting their turn like every day with their utensils full of flour. The bangles of the girls clinked, but the sounds were just noise, instead of the usual melody. Horrifying whispers had put off every heart. There was poison on the tip of every tongue as the girls giggled. The air was suffocating as if something treacherous were about to happen.

At Maimoonayi's place, a lively group of her friends had gathered. Palwasha playfully teased Chinaray, "Step aside, I need space to make my *chapatis* too."[271]

Chinaray responded with a hint of concern, "Palwasho, my dear sister, I don't have the energy for anything today. It's as if a sense of impending doom looms over us. May Allah keep us safe and secure."

Maimoonayi snubbed her, saying, "Allah, Allah, why would you feel that way? Everything will be alright."

"I think Chinaray is right. My brother is travelling. I hope he comes home soon safe and sound. I have a bad vibe about the day too," added Zarjana.

Saaza, who was cooking her chapatis on the *tandoor,* also seemed worried. "Something is wrong. I have burnt two *rotis,* and look, I have singed my hand as well," she held out her henna'd hand for the girls to see.

Just then, Maimoonayi picked up her utensils and walked over to her friends. "What is wrong with all of you today? There's no talk, no cheer, no nothing. Is this supposed to be food we're preparing for a funeral?" she tried to lighten the mood with a smile. However, she was met with silence from her friends, which she did not like.

"*Khala,*" Sheikhay looked at Maimoonayi.[272] "Don't you see? The *rotis* are getting burnt, poor Saaza has burnt her hand as well, and no one feels very chatty. Pray to Allah. May there be *khair,*" she said, wiping the sweat from her brow.[273]

Maimoonayi began to chuckle. "Khala Sheikhay, it seems to me that you are getting old and starting to lose your mind," she joked. "When did Saaza ever know how to cook *rotis?* She acts as if a prince will come and marry her, and she won't have to lift a finger for the rest of her life. Today, I was late, and she wasted so much flour."

---

271 *Chapati:* Another name for roti.
272 *Khala:* Maternal aunt; also used as a title to address older women.
273 *Khair:* The state of well-being, or all being well.

Maimoonayi turned to Saaza. "Go on, hush. Move. I will make *rotis* for everyone," she grinned.

Suddenly, the doors of the courtyard flung open as if someone was trying to break in. "Sher Alam *Lala?*" all the girls exclaimed together, fixed their *chaddars* to cover their faces, and meekly hid behind the wall.[274]

Maimoonayi, surprised to see Sher Alam, became excited to see him drop by so early in the day. However, she didn't say anything in front of her friends. In Sher Alam's hand was a knife, shining like mercury. He was going crazy with anger, but Maimoonayi, hopelessly in love, failed to judge his mood, just as she failed to see the knife. Before she could blink, he was standing right in front of her. His eyes were red with anger and he was panting. Maimoonayi's friends began to shiver with fear like the leaves of the shame plant.

"You characterless woman. Did you feel not an ounce of shame?" Sher Alam began to shout like a madman.

Maimoonayi scoffed with a smile, and said, "What plans do you have today to indulge yourself in?"

"Indulge? I will teach you indulgence. You have been making a fool out of me for all this time. But today, I will not spare you."

"Make a fool out of you...? What even? Go and get some rest, Sher Alam. It seems to me that you have worked too hard today and the heat has gotten to your head. I've told you to be careful a hundred times," Maimoonayi kept her calm anyway and kept smiling.

"I shall not rest 'til I slaughter you. You slut. If you were going to blacken your name with Karmaye, why would you show me your cursed face?" Sher Alam screamed at the top of his lungs.

"Do...what...with...Karmaye? Karmaye is like my brother, Sher Alam. You're scaring me. One day, in all this joking, you're going to end up doing something stupid," Maimoonayi's smile was met with Sher Alam's knife.

"Maimoonayi, my child, my dear, run. I see blood in Sher Alam's eyes. My princess, protect yourself," Khala Sheikhay yelled.

Maimoonayi nearly lost her wits. "He won't kill me...he isn't just my husband, *khala*, he is also my cousin," and began to laugh in delusion.

---

274 *Lala:* Literally, "older brother"; used as a title and a term of respect when addressing a man who is older than you, a brother, a cousin, a friend's husband, or even a stranger.

"Your tricks will not spare your life, Maimoonayi," Sher Alam screamed, and grabbed Mimoonayi by her hair, shoving her on the ground. "You whore. You no longer deserve to breathe on this land in Nawagai. You shall pay with your blood for your sins."

As heartless as a serial killer, Sher Alam climbed on Maimoonayi's chest, suffocating her pure heart and, like a cruel butcher, he ran his knife over her soft and delicate throat. A fountain of young, fresh, pure, and innocent blood sprayed into the air, staining the utensils and the rotian with red. Maimoonayi's friends started to scream. Khala Sheikhay fell unconscious, and the girls cried so much that they pulled their hair out. The news spread like wildfire in all Nawagai that Sher Alam slaughtered Maimoonayi in the early afternoon. The girls left their cooking and joined the mourning procession of Maimoonayi.

With the morbid realization that Maimoonayi's blood had extinguished both the thirst of his knife and put out the fire of his anger, Sher Alam fled the village. Consumed by the horror of his own actions, he vanished into the mountains of the Swat Valley. No one from his village ever saw him or heard from him again. Although the world moved on, his memory did not fade. He spent the rest of his life shrouded in anonymity, living in guilt, and eventually, dying alone in agony.

شیر عالم، میمونئی

19

PRINCE BEHRAM AND GUL ANDAAM

ONCE UPON A TIME, in the Sultanate of Rum, there lived a king known far and wide for his wisdom and grandeur.[275] Whilst the king was blessed with boundless wealth and fortune, despite all his riches, having no heir to carry on his legacy weighed down on his heart.

This thought troubled him greatly, for he longed for a child to whom he could pass on his kingdom and wisdom. After forty long years of waiting, a son was finally born to the king. The king was overjoyed when he heard the news and named the little prince Bahram.

For six years, the prince was tutored in the palace. He learnt how to read and write, learnt his manners from the wisest of men, and was excellent at both tact and strategy. The pious and the wise both wished to work with him. As Prince Bahram reached the age of twelve, he took up practising archery and swordplay, mastering marksmanship and the lance. By the time he reached fifteen, Bahram had become well-versed in the ways of warfare. Bards sang his praises and nobles from far and wide congratulated the king on having a son so capable.

Bahram also had a kind heart; he often opened the mouth of his treasury for charity. The courtesans brought him up, teaching him the arts. He was then sent to the *Maktab-ul-Katibeen*.[276] Several scholars

---

275 *Sultanate of Rum:* A Turco-Persian Muslim empire established by the Seljuk Turks after conquering Anatolia and Byzantine territories.

276 *Maktab-ul-Katibeen:* A medieval educational institution in the Muslim world where the art of scribing was taught.

there took the responsibility to teach him science. He turned out to be the best of the best in all that he learnt.

Recognizing Bahram's valour and wisdom, the King of Rum elevated him above his most trusted advisors and entrusted Bahram with the training of sixty thousand knights. One day, the king addressed his son, saying, "Listen to me, my wise son! If you seek true wisdom, heed the counsel of others, and then act upon it the best you can. Show kindness to the weak. No city can thrive under the weight of injustice."

Bahram understood the wisdom in his father's words. He bowed, kissed his father's hands, and tried to do everything which would make his father happy. Then Bahram addressed his father, saying, "Father dear, nothing makes me happier than exploring the beauty of the countryside. I request you—please allow me to go explore my homeland. It has been my wish for many years now."

The king consented, and so, accompanied by horsemen, foot soldiers, and chamberlains, Bahram set off. After they reached the hunting grounds, Bahram encountered a fierce lion, who seemed to be frightened of nothing. As the prince was in command, it was he who dismounted to confront the lion. His companions warned him that the lion was powerful, but he paid no heed and unsheathed the sword of self-confidence.

His friends, who were with him, were shocked to hear how loudly the beast roared. Suddenly, the lion pawed Behram. He dodged and seized hold of its hind legs with a firm grip. He swung it around and the lion became dizzy. He then lifted it over his shoulders like a child and threw it to the ground. Every joint in the lion's body cracked and it died, whimpering.

Witnessing the scene, cries of "Wah!"[277] Afreen!"[278] broke out. The prince then instructed his troops to present the dead lion to the king. The monarch, too, was proud of his son. The following day, Prince Bahram set out once more for the chase. A deer caught his eye, and he raced his horse in pursuit. A few of his arrows missed their mark, but soon, he felled the deer, even though he was riding his horse.

Having completed the hunt, the prince and his men started their journey back home. Night fell, and Bahram found himself on the wrong path, separated from his retinue. By the next morning, he had given

---

277 *Wah:* An expression which would loosely translate to "Oh wow!"
278 *Afreen:* An expression used to praise finesse.

up hope of finding his hunting party. He set out to hunt all by himself on foot, though his heart was heavy with unease. For seven days and nights, he wandered through the lonely wilderness, eating the game he had hunted.

On the eighth day, he set out again, looking for game, when he heard a voice. There was a hill nearby. The landscape was dotted with Chinese-style ponds. When he trekked up a little more, he spotted a dome in the distance, lit up as if it was Eid. When he peaked inside, there was a marble throne made of four different kinds of stone. Upon it lay a figure with a face as radiant as the moon. Though it was dressed like a man, it was a statue, crafted with skill so masterful, that anyone who laid eyes on it would sacrifice their lives for it.

Bahram approached it, only to find a wise, old, white-bearded man seated nearby. Greeting him with "Walaikum As-Salam,"[279] Bahram inquired about the origin of the statue and the one who had built this: *Gul-i-Satbar*.[280]

The old man told Bahram that he was a merchant who had travelled far and wide. "Once, he went to China, the kingdom of a prosperous king, *Faghfur*.[281] His daughter, Gul Andaam, was so beautiful that even the son felt envious of her—she led many to madness and others to faint. Now that he could no longer think of anything else but her, he asked sculptors in China to carve a statue of her. Now he lives here alone, lost in thoughts of her. As for my wealth, I distributed it amongst my kin, and I have a few cattle and camels which help me get by."

The words of the greybeard pierced Bahram's heart like a dagger, setting his feelings on fire. The old man then asked Bahram his tale, who explains that he is a Prince of Rum. He recounted that he left to hunt with his men, but lost his way chasing a deer, and then fate brought him here. "I have fallen in love with Gul Andaam without even seeing her. If I am now destined to die in that city of China, I shall go meet it or return after I have stared at my *Dilruba* to my heart's content."[282]

---

279 *Walaikum As-Salam:* The response to *"Assalam-o-alaikum,"* a Muslim greeting. It translates to "and upon you be peace."

280 *Gul-i-Satbar:* A life-size statue of a flower.

281 *Faghfur:* The title of the Emperor of China.

282 *Dilruba:* A title for the beloved.

The old man cautioned Bahram, warning him that Gul Andaam is both fickle and vain. "If you are wise, forget it, and go home. Countless princes like you wait for her, and even though her eyes set others on fire, she glances back at no one." However, Bahram asked him the name of the city and tells him that nothing would dissuade him from going to China.

Bahram then set off swiftly for China, following the road pointed out to him. Tears glistened on his cheeks as he sang a lament for his self-willed beloved, praying for Allah's help in his quest. He travelled for a month until he stumbled upon a beautiful grove, where he stopped to rest.

The prince sat in a picturesque spot in the garden, and, after gazing around and admiring the garden, he rested his head on his shield. Before he knew it, he was asleep. "Wake up and be warned!" said a voice. Bahram raised his drowsy eyes to find a woman before him with a *khancha* in her hands.[283]

Curious, Bahram asked about who he owed this hospitality to. The woman explained that the garden garden belonged to Saifoor, the King of *Jinns,* who had four brothers, each of whom possessed great power and magic. She also introduces Sarasia, their sister, as the sender of the food and herself as the midwife.

Sarasia had sent the food as a kind gesture, along with a message for Bahram: he must leave quickly before her brothers return from their hunting trip. The prince responded, "I am but a weary traveller, seeking respite for a short while." The maid warned him once again, but Bahram could only muster, "When are we ever truly free from trouble and grief?"

Just as Bahram finished the food, thanked Allah, and the maid removed the tray and went back to the palace, a cloud of dust announced the arrival of a group of horsemen. Among them, one rider stood out, towering like a mountain, with another well-armed companion following closely behind. As they approached the garden, the leader called out in anger, demanding to know who dared to rest in their garden. He ordered his companion, Shamas, to capture the intruder and bring him before him, threatening to sever his head from his body without hesitation.

---

283 *Khancha:* A large, wooden tray which can be used to serve food for at least 4-6 people. It has space for salad, two plates of rice, curry, naan, and drinks.

Shamas rode forth and confronted Prince Bahram, demanding his surrender. But the prince, asserting his innocence as a mere traveller, refused to yield to the unjust accusation. In response, Shamas drew his scimitar, and Bahram rose to meet Shamas, swiftly disarming him and binding him to a nearby tree. As Shamas cried for help, he could have been heard from miles away. Kamaas followed his brother, only to meet the same fate. With Samaal and Kamaal also bound to the tree, Saifoor came swinging his spear at Bahram. "Be warned. Do not think yourself a warrior, fighting boys."

"Come at me. You shall learn the rules of combat," Bahram retorted, severing the head of Saifoor's lance, who then drew his sword, but the prince skillfully parried each blow with ease. Bahram aimed a decisive blow at Saifoor, whose sword fell out of his grip. As the fight continued, the prince called out, "The horses are not at fault. Let us dismount," and the battle continued on foot. Bahram lifted Saifoor above his head, only to hurl him forcefully to the ground and sit atop his chest, questioning the strength and might Saifoor had boasted about.

With Saifoor defeated and bound tightly to a tree, Bahram thanked Allah for his success and prepared to execute them. "Today is the last day this path shall be treacherous to travellers. The tyrant does not deserve mercy. Today is the day death is at your door."

As he poised to sever their heads, a voice rang out, reminding him of his dad's counsel: to show mercy to the weak and kindness even to one's foes, for they might become allies in return. Surprised, Bahram looked up to find a beautiful woman standing before him. For a split second, he stopped in his tracks, lost in her beauty, which then reminded him of Gul Andaama. Reciting a couplet full of longing, he turned to the woman, asking her who she was.

It was Sarasia herself, who apologised on behalf of her brothers and admitted defeat. She requested Bahram to spare their lives, to which he agreed, for she had sent him food. However, he then asked her how she knew of his father's words and his promise. Sarasia explained that she was out travelling and was present at his dad's court when he made the promise. Enraged, Bahram thought she was lying. "I travel on my way to grief, and they were looking forward to killing me too. It shall not be wrong if I end this *fitna* here and now."[284]

---

284 *Fitna:* The cause of chaos and mischief.

Unmoved by Sarasia's pleading, it was not until she promised that her brothers would never harm a traveller again that Bahram relented and freed them. She skillfully unbound her brothers. Saifoor approached Bahram with blisters on his feet and his head uncovered, and nearly fell at his feet, repenting. The prince advised him to refrain from earning the *baddua* of the traveller before he left, and Saifoor promised to be kind.[285]

Saifoor then asked Bahram one last favour. "Please do not turn down my request, my brother. Be our guest for a night. Who knows when we shall meet again or if we shall ever see one another again." Bahram happily accepts the invitation, and the palace comes alive with celebrations as if it were Eid. Saifoor and his brothers promise both warriors and wealth, should Bahram ever need it.

The prince ventured into the garden, taking in the tranquil scenery. He then reclined on Saifoor's throne. He signalled to his brother Shamas to summon all the nobles of the town so they could pay homage to Prince Bahram. The people of the city gathered at the palace, showing due respect to the prince. The commoners soon left and only the nobles were left behind. The mehfil was indeed fit for a king, with the music enchanting all who heard it. After a while, Bahram asked Saifoor to wrap up the festivities and announced his intention to depart for China. "Bring me my horse and my spear, the journey is long and arduous. I must be on my way."

"My brother, before you leave, can you join us to fight a *Deo* who goes by the name of Afrad? He troubles us and our kingdom's victory against him has eluded us," Saifoor requested.

Bahram tells Saifoor that they all needn't go after him and asks for directions to Afrad Deo's abode. Whilst Bahram promises that the jackals of the desert shall feast on his severed head and pray for Bahram after they eat their fill, Saifoor and his brothers insist on accompanying him, but agree to standing a little way off.

Bahram, followed by Saifoor, his brothers, and the nobles, rode to war. As they approached the lair of Afrad Deo, they witnessed thick smoke rising to the skies. Saifoor explained that Afrad blew smoke when he was asleep. Bahram warned his companions to stay back and ventured forth.

---

285 *Baddua:* A prayer to Allah for harm to befall someone.

Inside Afrad's lair, Bahram found the *Deo* asleep on a dais, resting his feet on another. Nearby, in a well, was a young woman held captive, with heavy chains around her ankles. "Who are you?" asked Bahram.

"I am a *peri*. Tears stain my eyes because I am held captive. I do not know what the world thinks, he only looks at me and does not touch me, but here I am, trapped, with no way out."[286] Her voice trembled. "Tell me, where have you come from? Beware, this *kafir* will crush you.[287] If he wakes up, you will wake up. If you value your life, please go back. If he awakens, he will devour you in one monstrous mouthful, sharpening his teeth on your bones."

"I have come in search of him. I have no other purpose in my heart. Either I will sever Afrad's head from his body on this plain or he will feast upon me. It is not for men to be afraid of war," Bahram responded, tightening his *kamarband* before he pulled Afrad's leg.[288] Afrad slumbered on and pulled his leg back.

With a sudden cry of "Allah Hu Akbar," Bahram leapt towards Afrad, who woke up in panic.[289] "Who goes in my house?" he bellowed.

"I, who have come after you, and your demise," Bahram barely finished his sentence as Afrad aimed for the prince with his mace raised with both hands. The strike would have shredded a mountain, but Bahram skillfully dodged it and plunged his sword straight into Afrad's chest, severing the veins in his heart. Afrad tried to strike back, but he fell to the ground and writhed in agony before turning cold. His blood flowed out in streams as Bahram freed the *peri*, Ruh Afza, and bestowed Afrad's treasure upon Saifoor. Shamasgul gifted Bahram a lock of his hair and told him to hold it over the fire, should he ever need his assistance. With that, the prince took his leave and set off for China.

After bidding farewell to his companions, reciting "Bismillah" as he mounted his trusty steed, he rode 'till he reached the riverside.[290] At first, he found no other soul in sight. However, his eyes soon caught sight of a caravan boarding a ship bound for China. Bahram eagerly joined the

---

286 *Peri:* A winged creature, exclusively feminine, known for being gentle, kind and beautiful.

287 *Kafir:* Non-believer; Godless.

288 *Kamarband:* A cloth tied around the waist in traditional Pakhtun male attire.

289 *Allah Hu Akbar:* Arabic for "God is Great!"

290 *Bismillah:* "In the name of Allah"—Muslims say it before they begin a task.

caravan, still yearning for the sight of his beloved Gul Andaama's rosy cheeks. After crossing the river, the prince asked his companions about how far China was. They told him he must ride for four days and nights and shall reach China on the fifth day.

Bahram bid them farewell and continued on his journey. His heart longed to see Gul Andaam; the closer he got to China, the faster he rode. When a city in China came into sight, he rested in an apple orchard and fell asleep with a grin on his face.

He woke up to two armies lying poised on either side of the city. He witnessed troopers falling wounded from their steeds amidst the fading light of evening. As darkness descended, the intensity of the conflict began to wane and each commander withdrew their forces from the field. The gates of the city were swiftly barred shut, guarded by vigilant sentries. Uncertain of what to do next, Bahram approached the citadel, only to find all its gates firmly closed. Perplexed and unsure of his next move, he stood at the gates, weighing his options.

Bahram called out to them but received no response. He then made his way to another bastion's gateway, where he encountered a warrior named Aorang, known for his bravery and hospitality. "Who are you, young traveller?" Aorang inquired loudly, "and what brings you here at this hour?"

"I am but a weary traveller," Bahram replied, "with no ill intent towards anyone. Please, open the gate and let me pass." Impressed by Bahram's demeanour, Aorang promptly opened the gate and welcomed him inside with warmth and kindness. Curious about Bahram's solitary arrival, Aorang questioned him further. Bahram explained that his caravan lagged due to the day's arduous journey but would arrive safely by morning.

Bahram asked Aorang about the reason for the war, who then recounted that the Prince of Balaghar, Behzad, came with about ten hundred thousand troops and tons of treasure in pursuit of Gul Andaam. She did not return his affections, and the *Faghfur* of China did not have the might to fight, so the princess would be taken by force sooner or later. Upon hearing this, Bahram's jealousy flared.

Determined to gather more information, he handed over his horse and clothes to the sentry and borrowed a tattered felt from Aorang. Disguised as a *faqir*, he infiltrated Behzad's camp.[291] He returned home,

---

291 *Faqir:* A wandering Muslim ascetic who lives solely on alms.

aggrieved, until he remembered Shamas's hair. He quickly set some of it alight and Shamas appeared before Bahram before he could even blink.

The prince explained the situation to Shamas, sent his greetings to Saifoor, and sent a plea for help. Saifoor and his *Jinns* descended upon Behzad's camp. Some slept through the mayhem, many died with their gear on, and several met their fate at swords just as they were waking up. Prince Bahram slayed Behzad of Balghar himself. After killing him in combat, Bahram beheaded him and fixed his severed head upon a lance. Then he announced, "It is I, Bahram, who has slayed Behzad. Let it be known to all."

He then gave over his warhorse to Saifoor, "Tend to him personally, my brother. He has been a very loyal friend and is a most precious companion." Saifoor smiled, and the *Jinns* bade farewell to the prince.

Bahram assumed his disguise of a *faqir* once again and continued to stay in the city. The following morning dawned with a chaotic yet cheerful clamour. The *Faghfur* and his retinue rode forth to inspect the aftermath, and upon finding the inscribed lance, which the *Qazi* deciphered: "It is I, Bahram, the slayer of Behzad."[292] The emperor announced a search for Bahram.

One of his viziers said, "It seems Bahram rules the clouds. There is no doubt that an army of angels came to his aid." Acknowledging his wisdom, the *Faghfur* wasted no time in gifting him a large part of Behzad's treasures. The wounded were taken to be treated. The drums were beaten in celebration, and the note and spear were entrusted to the Bursa to bear, whilst the *Faghfur* returned to his throne amidst the jubilant cheers of his subjects.

Meanwhile, Bahram, still in disguise, yearned for a glimpse of his beloved, Gul Andaama. His eyes bloodshot and his cloak tattered, he was but a *faqir* for love. He had not yet set eyes on her...a beggar in her court, a glimpse of her would have been antimony for his sore eyes. Even though he had heard the princess praising Bahram, the braveheart who had slayed Baghdad, in his heart, Prince Bahram thought how he had stained his royal snowy white robes for her sake, and yet, she was oblivious to his existence.

A few days later, word spread that Gul Andaam would reveal her face to the public. Prince Bahram, already infatuated with her, eagerly joins

---

292 *Qazi:* Local magistrate or judge.

the crowds to catch a glimpse. When he sees her, her beauty captivates him even more, fueling his longing. Unable to forget her, he sneaks into the palace at night, finding a stairway to climb up the palace walls, made with bricks of gold. From atop the wall, he finds Gul Andaam surrounded by her maidens asleep in the garden. He watched her sleep until dawn, consumed by his desire.

Another month passed by and it was time for Gul Andaam to make her public appearance once more. However, this time, Prince Bahram too caught her eye and, at that moment, love struck her heart like a dagger, igniting a flame of longing within her. Restless, she flung herself on her couch, neither sleep nor food could comfort her. She sat, eagerly awaiting Bahram's love, but heard nothing.

Now, Gul Andaam would send one of her maids, Daolatai, to collect tokens from the crowd. When she asked Bahram for a token, he tossed one of his rings to her. When Gul Andaam went over what people had sent her, she instantly recognised the ring as extremely precious and had her suspicions that it may be Bahram. "I don't think this is a *faqir*, I think it is a prince. Go meet him and find out what he wants," Gul Andaam told him.

Dolatai went to him. "If it is wealth which you crave, oh *faqir*, I shall load you with gold. If you have a foe in your homeland, let me know, and I shall lend you my forces, but who are you, and what business do you have here?" asked Daolatai as she approached Bahram.

He acts surprised and questions why she asks a stranger such questions. She introduces herself as Gul Andaam's maid and asks him for the truth. Finally getting a chance to write to his beloved, he penned his tale on paper, each letter a priceless pearl of thought, in which he declares his love, to which the princess replied with a stern warning: "Beware, most foolish Qalandar, lest you taste the vengeful blade. How dare you speak of a union with me, without a claim to a royal throne and crown? Do you not know the fate that befell Prince Behzad of Balkh? He dared to stray into the ocean of my love, and Bahram, my lover, who is indeed worthy of me, descended upon him with his forces and destroyed him. Is it best you leave China quickly?"

The prince wrote back to her once more, writing to her of the tale of Shireen Farhad, and writing that Farhad lost his life, but did not give up on his love. She wrote back to him again, narrating the tale of *King*

Nausherwan's daughter.[293] A *faqir* glanced upon her face by accident and resigned to sitting outside her palace. She advised him to leave, but he did not pay heed to her words. When Nausherwan found out, he beheaded him. Bahram sent back yet another letter narrating to her the tale of Layla and how Majnun waited at her door, and then at her grave 'til he became one with her.[294] He also revealed his identity as a prince. When Gul Andaam wrote back this time, she addressed Bahram as *"Ya Makhfi!"* before confessing that his love pierced her heart like an arrow.[295] She promises him loyalty and asks him to be patient. Gul Andaam also tells him to keep his disguise. He thanks Allah and is more than happy to stay at her door, however she wishes.

Back when Prince Bahram lost his way chasing the deer at the hunt, his retinue awaited him 'til nightfall and then reported his disappearance to the king. He commanded his men to look for the prince and announced half his capital as a prize to whoever brought news of his son. He also called upon Shabrang, the most experienced of his riders from amongst his personal guard and ordered him to either bring back Bahram or lose his head.

Shabrang sets off to find Bahram and comes across the same hill where Bahram met the grey-haired man who told him about Gul Andaam. He sees the dome, enters it, and asks the old man if a handsome young lad who went by the name of Bahram, heir to the throne of Rum, has passed by. The old merchant points to the statue and recounts to Shabrang his encounter with Bahram and tells him that he tried his best to dissuade him from the idea to pursue the princess, but he raced off to China. Shabrang breathed a sigh of relief and implored the old man to accompany him back to court and narrate the incident to the king himself, with the promise of a hefty award.

The old man agrees to accompany Shabrang and travels to court. The king is overjoyed to hear news of his son and rewards the old merchant with plenty. He also orders his men to prepare to march to China. Now

---

293 A Legendary king of the Persian Empire; featured in many notable epics, including the Tilism-e-Hoshruba.

294 This is a reference to the tale of Layla Majnun, and the madness as a result of unrequited love.

295 *Ya Makhfi:* "Oh hidden one!"—a common phrase used by many poets in several languages across the Persianate world.

a vizier of the king, Salih, known for being wise, suggested that the king not only send an army, but also write a letter to the *Faghfur*. The king appreciates the suggestion and pens a beautiful letter explaining to the Emperor of China that his son, the Prince of Rum, Bahram Khan, was in his sultanate, hit by the arrow of love.

The army set off for China after distributing alms amongst the poor and the *faqirs*, as was the custom, so that their prayers may aid their safe journey. They reached China and set up camp outside the same city. Alarmed at seeing such a large military surrounding the citadel, the *Faghfur* sent his vizier, Ganjaur, as a missive. Shabrang handed over the letter for the *Faghfur* to Ganjaur, who was astonished to hear of the matter. "Had Bahram been here, we would have known! We only know of one Bahram, and we call him Bahram *Falak*—he is a nobleman indeed, who saved our princess, and our city from the evil Prince Behzad. We are sure that the angels help him, for no mortal has ever decimated an enemy the way he did, but that is all we know about him," he exclaimed.[296] Ganjaur also recounted the letter Bahram had left, which they had struggled to understand, and Shabrang asked him to bring it to them immediately.

When Shabrang saw the letter, he recognised Bahram's handwriting. The news was delivered to the *Faghfur*, and his happiness knew no bounds upon receiving the glad tidings. He announced that anyone who brings Bahram to the palace shall be rewarded with his weight in gold. The *Faghfur* wished to ask Bahram why he fought Behzad, how he fought Behzad, were his comrade's mortal or *Jinn*, and, most importantly, he wished to see the braveheart for himself. Shabrang smiled when he heard this. "These fools are searching for Bahram everywhere other than where they should. When a man is imprisoned by a woman's locks, where else shall he be other than in her street..." he thought to himself.

Shabrang asked for directions to Gul Andaam's garden. He saw Bahram sitting nearby, disguised as a *faqir*. He was surprised to see him, for the prince's complexion had darkened, and he was covered in dust from head to toe. After observing Bahram discreetly for a while and after confirming his identity, he went and announced to Faghfur that Bahram had been found.

---

296 *Falak:* "Sky"; in context: Bahram of the Sky.

The *Faghfur* called for the *naqqara* to be beaten, ordered a robe, worked with zari for the prince to be prepared, and gifted it to Shabrang, asking him to take it to the prince.[297] Shabrang and his men rode towards Gul Andaam's garden. The vizier jumped off his horse, greeted Bahram, and accompanied him to the royal hammam. The princess was surprised to see an army heading to the palace. When she asked around, she was told that a *faqir* around there had been identified as Prince Bahram. She whispered to Dolatai, "I told you so."

Bahram was back to his glowing old self, now that he had cleaned up and was dressed like a prince. The moment Gul Andaam set eyes on him, the flame of love in her heart increased manifold. The next morning, after Fajar prayer, the *Faghfur* rode outside the city to meet Prince Bahram at their encampment. The *Faghfur* asked Bahram, and after exchanging greetings and pleasantries, he asked the prince about Behzad, how he vanquished his forces, if he was alone, and who his comrades were.

Behram told him that his comrades were not mortal, but not known to the people of China either, and promised to reveal them in due course. He then held a few strands of Shamas's hair over the fire, which caused him to appear once again. When Shamas appeared, he sent a message to Saifoor and *Faghfur*'s rather peculiar request. King Saifoor agreed to show themselves to the people of China and, after a moment's pause, a thunderous roar and billowing smoke of cannons filled the air. The ground trembled and onlookers looked up in fear. The *Faghfur* expressed his concern that Bahram's army was unsettling the people. The prince immediately asked Shabrang to restore calm, and Saifoor's retinue fell silent.

Shabrang then asked for Gul Andaam's hand in marriage and expressed his wish on behalf of his king for an alliance with China. The *Faghfur* welcomed him respectfully and, whilst he voiced his consent for the match, he told the vizeir that he needed to ask his daughter first, for it was not his decision. The princess alone would have the final say in who she weds.

Shabrang then asked Bahram to send a messenger to the princess with a proposal, to inquire about if she wishes to accept the proposal. The prince sent Sarasia and Ruh Afza as his missives. "I trust your wisdom,

---

297 *Naqqara:* Kettledrum.

شہزادہ بہرام اور گل اندام

Sarasia, and beyond that, I consider both of you to be my sisters. Please take my proposal to the princess," he asked them.

Gul Andaam had received news that Bahram would be sending his sisters. Sarasia and Ruh Afza were given a royal welcome befitting their stature. After some chatting followed by entertainment, Sarasia asked Princess Gul Andaam to accept Bahram's proposal. Gul Andaam agreed but set a condition: that Sarasia would have to marry her father, the *Faghfur*. And so, Ruh Afza and Sarasia went back to their camp and recounted the condition of Gul Andaam's acceptance. Bahram discussed the situation with Saifoor, who reassured the prince, "Sarasia is as much my sister as she is yours. I entrust you with this decision."

After several discussions and thinking amongst themselves, it was decided that the *Faghfur* would be a suitable match for Princess Sarasia. And so, amid lively celebrations, *Faghfur* and Sarasia, as well as Saifoor and Ruh Afza, were wed.

Prince Bahram and Gul Andaam were wed, and the celebrations lasted forty days. Every strand of Gul Andaam's hair was set with pearls. She looked as beautiful as a *Hoor*. The *Faghfur* gave away forty thousand maids, and tons of gold, silver, and jewels to his daughter as part of her dowry. After that, Bahram finally set off for Rome. Both the adamzaad and the jinnaat prepared to head home. It may have been a happy time, but goodbyes are always sad. Saifoor and Bahram wept as the brothers embraced each other before parting ways, as did Gul Andaam and her father. When Bahram entered the territory of Rum again, Shabrang sent word to the king, and the prince was received amid lots of cheer.

Back at his royal capital, the king thanked Allah for seeing Bahram once more and shed tears of happiness when he greeted his son. He also announced that the wedding would now be celebrated in Rum, and so, celebrations followed for another forty days. Finally, the king decided to pass his throne to the prince and announced that he would now spend the rest of his life in relative seclusion and worship of Allah. The prince was wise, fair, and just, and under his reign, the kingdom prospered for many years to come. And so, King Bahram and Queen Gul Andaam lived happily ever after.

List of References
by Language

PASHTO

Fayyaz. *Qissa da Shehzada Behram ao Gul Andamay.* Lahore, Sagar Publishers, 2006.

Pashto Music Swabi. *Shireen Farhad.* Video. YouTube, 2019, www.youtube.com/watch?v=EIm3-c3btrU

URDU

Hamdani, R., and F. Bukhari. *Pathano ke Romaan.* 1955.

Rahman, I. U. Swat ki Lok Kahanian. 1969.

"STORY OF SAIF AL MALOOK JHEEL." YouTube, uploaded by Fateh Rahman, 25 September 2021, www.youtube.com/watch?v=XSMPA0yZa5Q

PUNJABI

Baksh, M. M. *Saif al Malook.*

ENGLISH

Ganjavi, Nizami. *Layla o Majnun.* c. 1192.

—. Shireen Khusrow. c. 1180.

Notes on the Tales

SHIREEN FARHAD

Originally a Persian folktale, the story features in the *Shahnameh*, the Book of Kings. However, the original title is "Shireen Khusrow"—it was adapted into Pashto folklore with some variations. Whilst it retained its essence as a tragic romance, the hero in the original epic is not Farhad—it is King Khusrow.

The story begins with Khusrow's birth and early childhood. One day, after an argument with his father, Anushirvan, his grandfather, visits him in a dream and tells him that he will wed a woman named Shirin, whose horse is called Shabdiz.

Shahpur, a painter at court and a friend of Khusrow, tells him about an Armenian princess, Shirin, describing how beautiful she is and that she is the niece of the Queen of Greece, Mahim Banu's niece. Shahpur's words alone are enough for Khusrow to lose his heart to the princess.

Soon after, Shahpur travels to Armenia to find Shirin and, when he finds her, he shows her a portrait of Khusrow which he had painted. When she looks at it, she too falls in love with the prince and travels to Mada'in to look for him. Meanwhile, Khusrow falls out with his father and sets off to Armenia to find Shirin.

They cross paths during their journey at a stream when Shirin is bathing and Khusrow is disguised as a peasant, so neither of them recognised the other. When he reaches Armenia, Shirin's mother, Queen Shamira, greets him and informs him that Shirin is on her way to his capital in search of him.

Khusrow had to return to Mada'in after his father passed away, so he sent Shahpur to Armenia to bring Shirin with him. The two keep travelling without meeting until Khusrow is overthrown by General Bahram and flees to Armenia.

The two finally meet in Armenia, and Shirin welcomes her beloved, but refuses to marry a runaway prince. Her condition is that he fights Bahram for his crown. To win Shirin's heart and his kingdom and Mada'in back, Khusrow pays a visit to the Caesar in Constantinople, who agrees to help him win back his throne, but only if he marries the Caesar's daughter, Mariam, and promises not to take another wife for as long as she lived.

Bahram is overthrown, and Khusrow regains his throne. Meanwhile, Farhad, a mason, falls in love with Shireen. Khusrow could not stand the thought of a rival, so he sent Farhad into exile to the Behistun mountain, asking him to carve steps out of the cliff rocks.

Farhad accepts the task, hoping Khusrow will then let him marry Shirin, but the king sends false news of Shirin's death to him. Upon hearing that Shirin is no more, Farhad is heartbroken and commits suicide by throwing himself off the mountain. Afterwards, Khusrow feigns condolences to Shirin in a letter. Soon after Mariam dies, Ferdowsi writes that Shirin secretly poisoned her. Now that Khusrow was free to marry Shirin, instead, he has a tryst with a woman from Isfahan. When he gets bored of her, he travels to meet Shirin, but she refused him entry into her palace.

Disappointed and dejected, Khusrow returns to Madai'n. In a turn of events, after several heroic deeds, Shirin agrees to marry him. Only that Shiroy, Khusrow's son, falls for Shirin and murders his father, Khusrow, for her. He then sends Shirin a messenger telling her that she will wed him after a week. Heartbroken and unwilling to marry the boy who would have been her stepson, Shirin also decides to kill herself. After their deaths, Kushrow and Shirin finally become one and are buried together in a single grave.

The story was also adapted in Balochi and Brahui folklore—once again adopting the name Shireen Farhad.

As legend has it, once upon a time, Sassanid prince Khusrow II, a charming and handsome young man, had a friend, Shahpur, who was a painter of outstanding skill.

Shahpur told Kusrau about a princess he had encountered on his travels—Mahin Bano, the widowed Queen of the Kingdom, and Shireen, the Princess and Heiress to the Armenian throne.

Shireen, a well-educated noblewoman, was famed for her intelligence as well as her beauty. As fate would have it, Khusrow fell in love with a woman he had not met, only heard of. He asked Shahpur to travel back to Armenia, take Shireen in confidence, and make her fall in love with him as he had made Khusrow fall in love with her.

Shireen used to visit the lake within the palace compound every day with her friends. She watched as Shahpur gazed at them and turned her mundane daily routine into a masterpiece on canvas. Shahpur had caught Shireen's eye, and she was very curious about him. A few days later, he went to Shireen and told her everything. He gifted her a portrait of Khusrow.

In her excitement, with her heart full of happiness, Shireen could not get a wink of sleep at night. She told her aunt that she was going out for a hunt, mounted her black mare Shabdez, and left the palace.

Back at the Sassanid Court, Khusrow had fallen out of favour with his father, the Shah. Court intrigues lead to the house imprisonment of the young prince at a faraway fort.

Shireen and Khusrow crossed ways with one another as Shireen bathed near a canal that the prince passed by. However, neither recognised the other, for neither Shirin nor the prince were dressed as royals.

When Khusrow reached Armenia, he was given a warm welcome at the Armenian Court. However, soon after he got there, he received the news that his father had passed away. With the Shah now deceased, the throne was Khusrow's to claim.

When Khusrow learned that Bahran, a conspirator, had usurped the throne, he decided to stay in Armenia. In a turn of events, Shireen and Khusrow crossed paths once again in a forest. After journeying to Armenia together and consulting Mahin Bano, Shireen and Khusrow decided to tie the knot.

However, the marriage would have to wait, as Khusrow had more important matters to attend to: the matter of the Sassanian throne. He made his way to Rome, imploring King Caesar for a military alliance.

Caesar agreed on two conditions, the first of which was that Khusrow ties the knot with his daughter, Mary. The second condition was that Khusro does not remarry, for Christian tradition forbids it. Khusrow married Mary and secured the alliance. He marched against Bahran and successfully took back his crown. Whilst Khusrow and Shirin remembered one another, they decided not to meet.

Mahin Bano, too, passed away soon after Khusrow had regained his position as the Sassanid Shah, and Shireen was crowned the Queen of Armenia. Deprived of her love and having lost her mother, Shireen craved companionship, which she found in Farhad. A stone carver, architect, and sculptor, Farhad had once helped Shireen across the lake on horseback when her horse had suddenly become agitated and was refusing to step into the water. Ever since the incident, Farhad had fallen in love with her.

The word of the love affair between Shireen and Khusrow soon found its way to Mary's ears, making her furious. Shireen, on the other hand, passionately hated Mary. As fate would have it, Mary did not have long to dwell on her anger, for Shireen soon outmanoeuvred her. An Armenian spy at the Sassanid Court poisoned Mary, killing her. Khusrow could have now married Shireen, but he did not deem himself worthy of her after betraying her. He had also caught a whiff of Farhad.

He invited Farhad to his court and gave him happy tidings. Khusrow told Farhad that he would allow and bless his union with Shireen. However, the condition was that Farhad would have to construct a canal over the mountain. On the foot of the mountain, on the other side, was a pasture, at Ispahar. Shireen wanted to build a palace there, with a pond nearby.

After that, Farhad worked day-in and night-out to construct the canal some twenty kilometres long, all by himself. Little did Shireen know that Farhad was whispering her name countless times in a state of semi-consciousness, exhausted and burnt out.

Khusrow was irked when he learnt that Farhad had not died due to the exhaustion of sheer labour, and he may succeed. He put in place another scheme. Along with some of his viziers and companions, he found an old woman. He prepared her to pass on a message to Farhad.

The hag replied that she would do so. She demanded that when she journeys to give the message, in the areas nearby, the young must be kept away from their mothers, including children, as well as goats, camels, and cows.

Khusrow agreed, and the hag went to see Farhad. Farhad asked her, "I have heard strange voices. It has been happening since early morning. It sounds like sobbing. What is going on?"

"Don't you know what happened, child?" the hag asked.

"No, I do not," he replied.

"Shireen met an accident and is no longer with us. Our Queen is dead."

Farhad felt as if the ground had been snatched away from his feet. He struck himself on his head with one of his tools, and his bleeding, lifeless body rolled down the hill.

As soon as Khusrow found out that Farhad was dead, he travelled to Armenia and asked Shireen for her hand. Whilst he was travelling, news of the incident with Farhad also travelled to Shireen. She declined Khusrow's offer of marriage.

Meanwhile, Khusrow's son, Shervi, found out about Shireen, the incident with Farhad, and that his father was travelling to bring home a new bride. He plotted a coup and overthrew his father. News of the coup demanded Khusrow return to court immediately, but Shervi ordered his arrest as soon as he entered Persian territory. Shervi then travelled to the Armenian court to mark Shireen as his queen out of spite for his father.

News of Khusrow's arrest cast a dark shadow on Shireen's world. She had lost her mother, the man who truly loved her, Farhad, as well as the man she had loved for so many years, Khusrow.

Shireen mulled over the consequences of Khusrow's selfishness, and the karma he had created for himself. Perhaps, he was no better than Caesar, the villain of Shirin and Khusrow's romance, for he had done the same, if not worse, to what Shirin and Farhad may have potentially shared.

She suddenly realised that she no longer loved Khusrow. It was Farhad she wished to be reunited with. She rode to the mountain where Farhad had been working and hiked to the exact spot where he had killed himself. From there, she threw herself to her death. The people, well aware of what had ensued, dug up Farhad's grave and buried Shireen with him. In death, the lovers were united for eternity.

SAIF AL MALOOK

This tale has multiple variations in several regional languages besides Pashto: Punjabi, Hindko, and Balochi. However, it is said to have originally been told in Hindko, also a language spoken in the Khyber Pakhtunkhwa province, and retold as a Sufi melody in Punjabi by the mystic poet Mian Muhammad Bakhsh.

The lake mentioned in the tale is Saif-al-Malook, named after the very prince in the story. It gets its name from the name of the prince himself, "Saif" — "Malook" is derived from the word *mulaqat*, which means "to meet" in Urdu as well as other regional languages spoken in the area (Hindko and Pashto). The Queen of the Peris is sometimes referred to as *Badi-ul-Jamal* (of rare beauty).

Naran is a town and popular tourist destination in the upper Kaghan Valley in the Mansehra District of Khyber Pakhtunkhwa. The Lake Saif al Malook is a one-hour drive (Jeep ride, to be specific) from the town.

In another variation of the tale, it is not Deo Safed, but Toraban Deo, which is mentioned. It follows a slightly different storyline and is related to another lake in close proximity of Saif-al-Malook: Ansoo Jheel (*Ansoo:* "teardrop"; *Jheel:* "lake").

Once upon a time, there lived an Egyptian prince, his name was Saif-al-Malook. Hunting was one of his favourite sports, so he often travelled far and wide to find game. One day he was hunting in the midst of beautiful mountains in a faraway land when he saw a deer unlike any other. The antelope had magnificent antlers, which curled up like a snake. Mesmerised by the animal, he left his companions behind and gave the deer a good long chase.

The deer led him to a lake surrounded by beautiful flowers. Saif-al-Malook was convinced that there was something magical about this place. He had seen reflections of the sky in lakes earlier, but this lake was different. The full moon in the sky seemed to set the entire surface of the lake aglow. His suspicions turned out to be correct when he saw the most stunning of fairies sitting among the flowers.

The graceful and gazelle-eyed creature, with skin as pale as the moon, with thick, dark locks of hair falling over her shoulders introduced herself as Badri Jamala Khaperai. The prince was mesmerised by her, and a little dumbfounded. He had come to catch a deer and had found a fairy!

The prince got over his initial feelings of shock and fear and the two began to talk. Eventually, they became friends and then became lovers. They met at the lakeside every single night. The tale of their romance spread far and wide, and rightly so, for it was a love story between a fairy and a prince!

One day, Jamala did not show up at the lake. Saif-al-Malook waited by the lakeside all night for her, but she did not arrive. Dejected, he went back to his tent. The following night, the same happened. The prince became very worried. He wondered if misfortune had fallen upon his beloved fairy, so he set out to search for her.

Six years passed by with no luck, but the prince refused to go back to Egypt until he had found his fairy, his Jamala, 'til one day, he chanced upon a group of fairies bathing in the lake.

They told him that Badri Jamala had been kidnapped by Toraban Deo and he had taken her away to his fortress in Koh-e-Kaaf and locked her up. Swearing to free her from prison, Saif-al-Malook ventured into the world of the *Jinns* and rescued her from the *Deo's* fort. When Toraban discovered that Jamala was gone, he flew into a rage. In his anger, he flooded the entire valley and commanded the water to destroy everything in its path.

The flood pushed the fugitives to run over to the mountains. There, Saif-al-Malook and Badri Jamala sought refuge in an enchanted cave near the lake. Toraban kept searching for Jamala, but his efforts were in vain. He even shed tears of grief, for he had fallen in love with her, but she did not agree to become his wife. Aware of the fact that she hated him for keeping her locked away in his castle, it broke his heart because this was the only way to keep her close to him.

It is said that Toraban wept so profusely that his tears formed another lake, Ansoo Jheel, the Lake of Tears. It is also said that the couple lived the rest of their lives in the safety of the cave, terrified of being parted from each other ever again. Glimpses of the string of colourful glowing orbs floating across the lake as they dance can be seen by a lucky few when the couple comes out of the cave and dances across the lake on the fourteenth of every lunar month when the moon is full.

In Las Bela, Balochistan, the storyline is followed at a different location: the Caves of Gondrani. Whilst the cave city itself is associated with a lot of folklore, including tales which mention that it may have been built by the *Jinns* on the command of the Prophet Suleman (A), a particular legend speaks of Saif-al-Malook, a wealthy Persian or Arab merchant, and his wife Badi-ul-Jamal, whom a local Hindu ruler fell in love with and tried to win by force. However, she was a loyal wife and guarded her honour whilst her husband fought fiercely to keep her safe. A shrine was erected near the caves in their honour.

LAYLA MAJNUN

Layla Majnun is originally an Arab folktale absorbed into Pashto folklore. It was one of the first tales to have been translated into Pashto. Known as "Qissa Leila aw Majnu," it was adapted from the retelling of the great Persian poet Nizami. It is his retelling which has been adapted for this book. Having been a part of local storytelling traditions for so long, the story made inroads into the language, inspiring many proverbs and similies in Pashto.

DILBACHAK AND THE PRINCE

This folktale was captured expressly for the purpose of this publication. It was recorded in Kohat. An aged woman from the Mian Khel tribe narrated it to us.

The Mian Khel are one of the tribes of the Daman Plains, as are the Gandapur, Babar, Kundi, Storyani, and the Daulat Khel. Although the tribespeople are ethnically Pakhtun, they speak Hindko as a first language. This tale was specifically narrated in the Kohati dialect.[298]

Other dialects include Peshawari, which is spoken in the old city of Peshawar, and some adjacent rural areas. Additionally, there is also the Hazara Wali dialect, spoken in Azad Kashmir, Abbottabad, Mansehra, Kaghan and adjoining areas, and Dera Wali, is spoken in Dera Ismail Khan and is greatly influenced by the variety of Saraiki spoken in the area.[299]

---

298 Elphinstone, M. An account of the kingdom of Caubul, and its dependencies in Persia, Tartary, and India. Published by Longman, Hurst, Rees, Orme, and Brown, 1815.

299 Parekh, R. "Literary notes: Hindko language and two-volume Hindko-Urdu dictionary." *Dawn, 6 Feb.* 2023, https://www.dawn.com/news/1735620

THE DEO AND THE PRINCESS

This folktale was documented specifically for inclusion in this book. It has been narrated to us by a Yousafzai resident of Zakhi Chaar Bagh, Nowshera.

ADAM KHAN DURKHANAYI

The couple is laid to rest halfway between their villages. It is believed that when Durkhanayi was being buried, people felt that there were not one but two corpses in the grave. When they peeked into the shroud, it was Adam Khan's body. Their gravestones are now a popular tourist attraction and a mausoleum of sorts.

The wood from the tree of Adam Khan's grave is believed to be enchanted—any musician who plays with a *mizrab* from the wood of that tree will have magic in his fingers and begin playing beautifully.

Baaz Dara is a cluster of villages in Batkhela, Malakand. Each of them is differentiated with a second name, as is common with many villages in Khyber Pakhtunkhwa. It includes Baaz Dara Bala (Adam Khan's village), Baaz Dara Payan (Durkhanayi's in-laws), Bara Baaz Dara (Durkhanyi's village), along with Palai Dara.

BEHRAM KHAN AND PERI GULAB BANO

The first accessible source for the story is the Folkloristan website. It was submitted to us in writing by a regular reader hailing from Mardan.

KHADI BEBO

The story is set in what we now know as three countries: Afghanistan, Iran, and Pakistan.

MUSA KHAN GUL MAKAI

Swabi is located on the banks of the Indus River, 132 kilometers west of Islamabad, and 100 kilometers east of Peshawar.

Kohistan is a sparsely populated district with a mountainous topography, also in Pakistan, just west of Chilas. It is split into East and

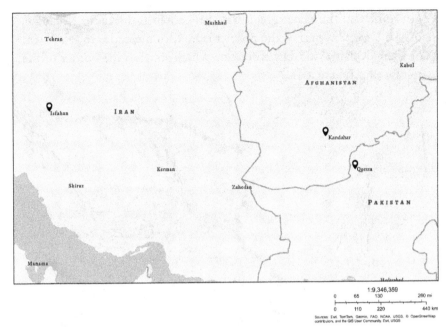

Map of Iran, Afghanistan, and Pakistan Borders. Source: Mapped using ArcGIS

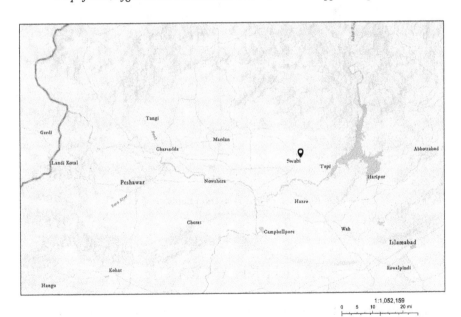

Map of Swabi. Source: Made with ArcGIS

West Kohistan. The eastern region is also known as the Indus Kohistan, whilst the western part of the district is in-turn divided into two: Swat Kohistan (Kalam), and Dir Kohistan, which touches the border of the Emirate of Afghanistan.

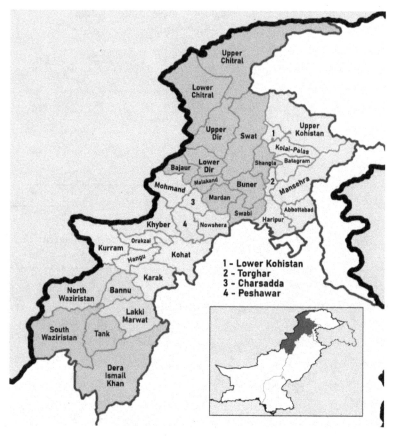

Map of Kohistan. Source: Wikipedia Commons Library

FATEH KHAN RABIA

The young boys, Karmaye and his friends, aim for women carrying pitchers full of water. It is quite a popular motif also found in other tales in the region, including the Raja Rasalu story cycle from Punjab.

DUR BIBI DUR

The first accessible source for this story is the Folkloristan website. It was narrated to us by a resident of Peshawar who is ethnically Pakhtun and tribally Khattak.

YOUSAF KHAN SHERBANO

The story is sometimes alternatively titled "Yousaf Karah Mar." However, it is far more commonly known as "Yousaf Khan Sherbano."

The Karah Mar hilltop is a living memory of the couple: it is the final resting place of the Princess of Shera Ghund, Sherbano, and the Prince of Turlandi, Yousaf. It is believed that the treasure of love is hidden within them. The hill is in fact even known by the name "Sher Ghunda"—commemorating Sherbano. All three locations in the story are within District Swabi, Khyber Pakhtunkhwa, Pakistan.

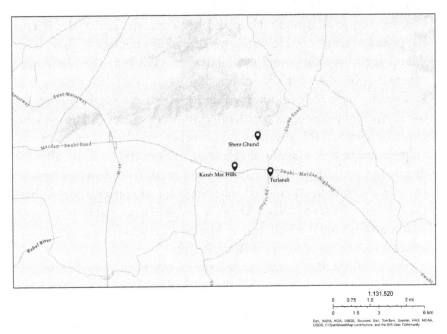

Local Map. Source: Made with ArcGIS

SHER ALAM MAIMOONAYI

In another variation of the tale, we learn Sher Alam's fate. It goes as follows:

In the village of Nawagayi, there were two close friends. They made a promise to betroth their future children—a boy and a girl—to strengthen their bond. One friend had a son named Sher Alam, and the other had a daughter named Maimoonayi. Both the children grew up to be incredibly good-looking. Just as their fathers had agreed, they were married.

Sher Alam was a jolly young fellow who loved hosting extravagant feasts for his friends and guests. After he married Maimoonayi, she tried to help him spend less and focus more on their time together. But Sher Alam's best friend, who relied on his generosity, felt threatened by Maimoonayi's influence. He would often keep Sher Alam away from home with various excuses. Maimoonayi was troubled by her husband's obliviousness to his friend's manipulation. She tried talking to Sher Alam, but he just laughed it off.

One day, as Maimoonayi voiced her concerns again, the friend happened to overhear. He was angered by her attempts to limit Sher Alam's spending. He vowed to find a way to kill her, even if it meant convincing Sher Alam to do it himself.

One night, Sher Alam returned home late from a nearby village. As usual, his *Hujra* was open to all, offering hearty meals to anyone who came by. Among the guests was a traveller who had stopped at the village mosque before nightfall. Hearing of Sher Alam's hospitality, he decided to join the gathering and enjoy a meal. As the night wore on, the friends and guests enjoyed tobacco, tea, and conversation. When they ran out of tobacco, Sher Alam's friend sent a servant to fetch Sher Alam's pouch from the main house. Maimoonayi sent out a pouch which she had embroidered for Sher Alam herself.

In the *Hujra*, the friend handed the pouch to the traveller, telling him to keep it. Unaware, the traveller tucked it away. Later, when Sher Alam returned and joined his friends, the friend asked the traveller to pass Sher Alam some tobacco. The traveller pulled out the pouch, which Sher Alam instantly recognised.

Sher Alam was furious to see the pouch in a stranger's hand. He moved to confront the traveller, but his friend quickly pulled him aside, claiming an urgent matter to discuss. The friend whispered that he had spotted Maimoonayi talking intimately with the stranger, and seeing the pouch confirmed his suspicions. He added that he didn't want to cause a scene but felt Sher Alam shouldn't be deceived like this.

The friend pretended to calm Sher Alam and suggested he talk to Maimoonayi first. But Sher Alam, consumed by anger, rushed home and abruptly woke Maimoonayi, accusing her of betrayal. She greeted him with a smile, thinking he was joking, but he was serious. Demanding answers about the pouch, she explained how the servant had asked for it on his behalf. Doubting her, Sher Alam drew his knife. She swore her innocence and cried that she would never forgive him for his lack of trust.

In a fit of rage, Sher Alam fatally struck Maimoonayi with his knife. As news of the tragic incident spread, the traveller came forward, swearing he never knew Maimoonayi. The servant also confirmed he had fetched the pouch without Maimoonayi's involvement. Consumed by guilt, Sher Alam vanished into the hills, but tales lingered of a tormented soul calling out for his lost love, Maimoonayi.